It was not

It was bound to happen to Alex eventually, considering the monklike existence he'd been living. But of all people, why did the chemistry have to happen with Lizzie Hamill?

He couldn't explain it. She wasn't his type. He'd never been attracted to unsophisticated women, or innocent smiles or uncontrollable red hair. Yet, the more he was around Lizzie, the stronger the attraction became. It had only been twelve hours since she'd burst into his life—how powerful would the attraction get if she stayed around longer?

Good God, he didn't want to risk finding out.

Dear Reader,

May is the perfect month to stop and smell the roses, and while you're at it, take some time for yourself and indulge your romantic fantasies! Here at Harlequin American Romance, we've got four brand-new stories, picked specially for *your* reading pleasure.

Sparks fly once more as Charlotte Maclay continues her wild and wonderful CAUGHT WITH A COWBOY! duo this month with *In a Cowboy's Embrace*. Join the fun as Tasha Reynolds falls asleep in the wrong bed and wakes with Cliff Swain, the very *right* cowboy!

This May, flowers aren't the only things blossoming— we've got two very special mothers-to-be! When estranged lovers share one last night of passion, they soon learn they'll never forget *That Night We Made Baby*, Mary Anne Wilson's heartwarming addition to our WITH CHILD... promotion. And as Emily Kingston discovers in Elizabeth Sinclair's charming tale, *The Pregnancy Clause*, where there's a will, there's a baby on the way!

There's something fascinating about a sexy, charismatic man who seems to have it all, and Ingrid Weaver's hero in *Big-City Bachelor* is no exception. Alexander Whitmore has two wonderful children, money, a successful company.... What could he possibly be missing...?

With Harlequin American Romance, you'll always know the exhilarating feeling of falling in love.

Happy reading!

Melissa Jeglinski
Associate Senior Editor

Big-City Bachelor

INGRID WEAVER

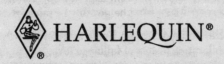

HARLEQUIN®

TORONTO • NEW YORK • LONDON
AMSTERDAM • PARIS • SYDNEY • HAMBURG
STOCKHOLM • ATHENS • TOKYO • MILAN • MADRID
PRAGUE • WARSAW • BUDAPEST • AUCKLAND

ISBN 0-373-16828-4

BIG-CITY BACHELOR

Copyright © 2000 by Ingrid Caris.

Visit us at www.eHarlequin.com

Printed in U.S.A.

ABOUT THE AUTHOR

Ingrid Weaver admits to being a compulsive reader who loves a book that can make her cry. A former teacher, now a homemaker and mother, she delights in creating stories that reflect the wonder and adventure of falling in love. When she isn't writing or reading, she enjoys old *Star Trek* reruns, going on sweater-knitting binges, taking long walks with her husband and waking up early to canoe after camera-shy loons.

Ingrid recently received the Romance Writers of America's RITA Award for Best Romantic Suspense Novel.

Books by Ingrid Weaver

HARLEQUIN AMERICAN ROMANCE
828—BIG-CITY BACHELOR

WHITMORE AND HAMMIL

Alex's cooking tips—

1. *Put spaghetti in pot and bring to boil. (Don't forget the water!)*

2. *When smoke alarm sounds, dinner is ready.*

WHITMORE AND HAMMIL

Lizzie's management tips—

1. *Give bonus to staff members who share and play nicely together.*

2. *Ignore client tantrums, but offer oxygen if client turns blue.*

Prologue

"We may have a slight problem, Alex."

Leather groaned as Alexander Whitmore pushed away from his desk and leaned back in his swivel chair. The day couldn't get any worse, could it? The presentation for the Starcourt account had bombed this morning. By noon the housekeeper had called with yet another threat to quit— this time the twins had painted her cat purple. Blood was throbbing at his temples in a prelude to one of his little-men-with-big-sledgehammers headaches, but somehow he forced himself to remain calm. Taking a deep breath, he regarded his lawyer warily. "How slight a problem?" he asked.

Jeremy Ebbet touched a hand to the knot of his tie and cleared his throat. "I'm afraid that Roland didn't sign the papers before he...departed. It was so sudden, you see. No one could have foreseen this...occurrence."

Roland. No. It wasn't possible. The man was haunting him. "We had reached an agreement more than a week before the accident," Alex said. "That was over a month ago."

"Well, there was a letter of intent." Jeremy repositioned his briefcase across his bony knees, pressing his feet together tightly at the ankles. His steel-rimmed glasses flashed opaque in the light from the window, giving the gaunt lawyer a distinctly insectoid appearance. ''Unfortunately, when I met with Roland's attorneys this morning I discovered that Roland didn't sign the letter, either. He did initial the changes, so I'm sure he wanted to go through with the sale. The terms we had worked out were exceedingly generous.''

Generous? Alex ground his teeth. He would have been forced to liquidate more than forty percent of his assets in order to meet Roland's exorbitant demands. But it would have been worth it to finally have complete control of Whitmore and Hamill, the company they had founded thirteen years ago.

Alex Whitmore and Roland Hamill. They were as different as two men could be. At first, the tension their conflicting management styles had created had been good, providing a stimulating, electric environment that contributed to their rapid success. With Roland's flamboyance and Alex's solid dependability, Whitmore and Hamill had become one of the busiest advertising agencies in Manhattan.

Yet as their success had grown, so had Roland's restlessness. He'd gradually withdrawn from the day-to-day running of the business, leaving the tedious responsibility of making money to Alex. Aside from swooping in every now and then to pick up his half of the profits and exercising his fifty percent control by hiring an assortment of loose cannons and prima donnas, Roland hadn't been part of Whitmore and Hamill for more than two years. The buyout had been inevitable.

But then Roland Hamill had tried to race a freight train to a crossing and had lost.

Alex raised a hand to pinch the bridge of his nose, trying to ignore the confused emotions that arose whenever he thought of Roland. Analyzing his feelings was something Alex had never had the time nor the inclination to do, yet he knew that he felt the loss of his partner on more than a business level. Sure, he'd wanted to be rid of him, but not like this.

It was a senseless death. Reckless, irresponsible and completely avoidable. And spectacular. Like most things about Roland.

"That fifty percent is mine," Alex said, clenching his jaw.

"I'm sorry," Jeremy said, holding up a copy of the agreement. "Without a signature on this paper, we would have a difficult time proving our case in court."

"In court? It won't come to that, will it?"

"For the sake of the business, we should try to avoid a legal challenge at all costs."

Alex stretched forward and picked up the paper by one corner. If only he'd insisted that Roland sign the paper before he'd left that day. If only it hadn't been foggy and the road hadn't been slick. If only the freight train had reached that crossing ten seconds later.

If only Alex had followed his instincts and had said no to Roland Hamill thirteen years ago.

But Alex rarely allowed himself to follow his instincts. He didn't act impulsively or let spontaneity interfere with logic. All that was better left to the Rolands of the world.

So even though he wanted to crush the useless paper in his fist and pitch it across the room, even though he wanted to kick something, hard, instead he controlled his frustration and scanned the printed lines once more, hoping he would find some way to salvage this mess. "What about our original partnership agreement?" Alex asked. "Can't I get control through that?"

"I checked the contract very carefully before I came here today."

"And?"

"Since all the original loans have been paid off, Roland owned his shares outright. They are considered part of his estate."

"And?"

"And what?"

"What happened to his estate?"

"He bequeathed the entire thing to his last surviving blood relative."

"I thought he didn't have any family. No one came to the funeral."

"Evidently there had been a falling out three decades ago."

"Knowing Roland, that doesn't really surprise me," Alex muttered.

"It took the entire three weeks since his accident to track down and verify his beneficiary. Clarke, Parker and Stein, who are acting as Roland's executors, notified her only yesterday."

"Her?"

"A niece." Jeremy shuffled his papers again and traced the name that was printed on the top one. "A Miss Elizabeth Hamill of Packenham Junction, Wisconsin. As I understand it, she is the only child of his deceased older brother."

The hammering in Alex's temples spread to the back of his head. Had he really thought the day couldn't get any worse? "Do you mean to tell me that half my company, fifty percent of this business, is now owned by some stranger in Hicksville?"

"Uh, Packenham Junction. It's a dairy farming area. Evidently they're famous for their cheese."

"Cheese. *Cheese?*"

"And dairy products."

"If he wasn't already dead, I might kill him myself," Alex muttered.

"Excuse me?"

"Roland. I think he did this deliberately."

"As a matter of fact, he did. There was no question of his competence at the time he made his will. Once it is out of probate and all the appropriate papers are signed, Miss Hamill will be...uh..."

"My new partner."

"Correct."

Alex tossed the useless agreement onto his desk and tightened his hand into a fist. "I don't suppose she knows the advertising industry? Has a degree in business? Experience in marketing?"

"I'm sorry, Alex. I haven't had the opportunity to investigate her background. We only became aware of her existence this morning."

Alex rose slowly, moving with the unnerving grace and the deceptive patience of a big cat. With a sound disconcertingly close to a growl, he paced across the room. He looked at the framed awards that decorated the wall, testimony to the life he'd built. He'd come a long way since he'd scrawled his plans on a grimy basement windowpane.

Success bought wealth, and wealth bought security. Not just for him, but for his sons. The twins would never have to go through what he did. They'd never have a moment's worry about the food they ate or the clothes they wore. Their playroom alone was larger than the place he'd lived in as a child. There was nothing they didn't have. And once complete control of Whitmore and Hamill was in his grasp, their future would be assured.

"I don't care if she's a Nobel laureate in economics,"

he said finally. "I won't share my company with another Hamill."

Jeremy cleared his throat. "But according to the law—"

"We'll make her an offer."

"Excuse me?"

"For Roland's shares. Make her an offer as soon as possible."

"And if she won't sell?"

"We'll soften her up first. Woo her. Dazzle her. Do whatever it takes. But we need to move quickly before she has a chance to consider alternatives." He strode to the window and clasped his hands behind his back. "I'll approach this like one of our campaigns."

"That would solve our problem, wouldn't it?"

"And it would also make Miss Elizabeth Hamill a very wealthy woman."

Jeremy snapped his briefcase shut. "I'll get started on this right away."

"Fine. Keep me informed."

"I certainly shall. But in the event that we aren't successful…"

Alex twisted around, fixing the lawyer with a steady glare. "She'll sell."

"Well, if she's anything like her uncle…"

Alex pressed his fingertips against his temples. "God, let's hope not. There couldn't be two of them in the world, could there?"

Chapter One

Curling her fingers around the ends of the armrests, Lizzie Hamill counted backward from ten, willing herself to turn her head when she reached zero. Statistics showed that this was the safest form of travel possible. People did it all the time. The laws of aerodynamics weren't about to be repealed. It was downright cowardly not to look out the window at least once.

"Two," she whispered. "One." She took a deep breath. "Zero." Nothing happened. "Zero," she repeated, lifting her hands to her cheeks and forcing her head to move.

Air rushed from her lungs in a high-pitched squeak. There was so much sky. Bluer than a morning in January, wider than the horizon from Hanson's Bluff, brighter than a sunrise on the ripples at the bend of the creek. It was so vast, so...awesome. How could anything be so beautiful and so terrifying at the same time?

Heart beating in a hard lump in her throat, Lizzie stared, fascinated despite herself. She was thirty years old and this was her first time in an airplane. She had expected to be nervous, had every right to be nervous, and yet...

And yet, it was the same sky she had seen every day of her life, the same one that arched over the house on Myrtle

Street. Why should she be afraid of it just because she was seeing it from a different viewpoint?

Gradually, her pulse began to steady. There was a confusing mix of emotions churning inside her. Along with the fear was something else, something unfamiliar. It was a stretching, restless kind of itch that she couldn't identify, as if she were responding to...what? Challenge? Adventure?

Hardly. She was the least adventurous person she knew. She was Auntie Liz, good old Lizzie, always available to baby-sit the kids or whip up ten pies for the church bake sale. Until now, the most adventuresome thing she'd done had been to sneak nine items through the eight-items-or-less line.

Yet here she was on a plane. Not just any plane, but one that was taking her to New York City. Could this really be happening?

She dropped her hands, slowly leaning forward until the tip of her nose touched the glass. The land spread out beneath her like a quilt that had been washed too many times, its colors mellowed, its stitching puckered into hills and valleys. In stately slow motion, it rolled past, indifferent and unaware.

And so very, very far away.

Lizzie felt her stomach roll. She hadn't been able to eat breakfast this morning. Bad move. Considering what she was going to be facing when the plane finally landed, she should have girded herself with a five-course meal. Lord knew she could have afforded it.

She was an honest-to-goodness heiress.

Well, as much of an heiress as Packenham Junction had ever produced. It was still difficult to believe, but the lawyers assured her there'd been no mistake. Her Uncle Roland Hamill, the black sheep of the family, the man whose name hadn't been spoken above a whisper in all her growing years, had left his entire estate to the niece he had never met.

Poor Uncle Roland. She'd been saddened to learn of his death, but it was a distant sadness, not the heart-wrenching grief she'd felt when her parents had died. She knew almost nothing about him. There hadn't been any photographs of him in the family album, although there had been some boyhood pictures of her father that had obviously had sections torn off. What had driven him away from his home? Why had her father hated him so much?

And what on earth was she going to do with all the money?

Well, not all that much money. His lawyers had already handled the sale of Uncle Roland's condominium and his furniture, but most of the proceeds had gone toward paying his debts.

And that was a shame. Lizzie's stepsister, Jolene, was pregnant again, and with the sporadic nature of Tim's work, they could use some money. Zack, her youngest stepbrother, was due to start college next fall and Benjamin, the oldest, had confessed that business at the cheese factory had been steadily declining. Despite their circumstances, though, her adoptive siblings, true to the stubborn nature of the entire Pedley clan, had been adamant about not taking any of her inheritance.

"It's yours, Lizzie," Jolene had said on the drive to the airport this morning. As usual, the task of family spokesperson had fallen to her. "For once in your life, you have something that's just for you."

"But I couldn't possibly—"

"Yes, you can. Your uncle wanted you to have it."

"I feel weird about it, though. I mean, why should he

pass everything on to me when we didn't even know each other?''

"Well, who else was there? He never married, never had children of his own, right?"

"Right."

"So why are you still so hesitant? It's a wonderful opportunity."

"I know, but it's all been so sudden."

"It's just like a fairy tale, Auntie Liz," Marylou said breathlessly, leaning forward to grasp the top of Lizzie's seat. She blew a pink bubble and popped it noisily against the roof of her mouth. "The good princess, struggling to make ends meet, is suddenly transformed by the wave of a magic wand and is whisked away to an enchanted kingdom."

"I'm going to New York, not Never-Never-Land," Lizzie said, shaking her head at the irrepressibly whimsical seven-year-old. "And working at the day care center isn't exactly sweeping up cinders."

"But Mom's your stepsister," Marylou continued, her eyes sparkling as she expanded the fantasy.

"Mmm. That's true. Do you think we could call her evil, though?"

"She makes everyone eat broccoli."

"That's true, too." She glanced at Jolene. "You evil thing, you."

"I knew all those bedtime stories you read my kids would warp their minds," Jolene muttered under her breath as she fought to steer the old station wagon around a bend in the road. "But getting back to our topic, we were talking about your inheritance."

Lizzie sighed. "I still don't know what I'll do with it if I don't share it with the rest of you."

"We'll survive just fine. It's you we're concerned

about,'' Jolene said. "After all the years you've devoted to taking care of other people, it's about time you had a chance to focus on yourself.''

"Maybe you could go shopping,'' Marylou said helpfully. "There's this really cool green dress with sparkles on it that's in the window of McBride's.''

Lizzie smiled wryly. "I know the one. Thanks for the suggestion, but I'm not sure how well sequins would stand up to a roomful of three-year-olds with finger paints.''

"There won't be any three-year-olds or finger paints where you're going,'' Jolene said. "And I think it would be a great idea to do some shopping while you're away.''

"This is a business trip, remember?''

"Sure, but it's *your* business you're going to visit.''

"I don't think that part has quite sunk in yet, either. What on earth am I going to do with fifty percent of Whitmore and Hamill?''

"Run the company, of course.''

At Jolene's deadpan comment, Lizzie burst into laughter. "Oh, now that's almost as good as working at the day care in sequins,'' she said when she caught her breath. "Me? A business tycoon?''

Jolene didn't join in her laughter. "Why not? You're smart enough to do whatever you put your mind to.''

"That's sweet of you to say, but—''

"You know it's true. You started up your own business already, didn't you?''

"That's different. The day care is just organized babysitting.''

"It's a business,'' Jolene insisted. "And who has been helping Ben with his books for the past six years?''

"I always helped him with his math homework. It's just a hobby.''

"Hah. You managed to run Dad's farm when you were

only nineteen. Why, if you hadn't turned down that scholarship so you could stay and take care of us—"

"That's ancient history, Jolene. The family needed me, and I don't have any regrets. I'm perfectly happy just as I am."

There was a pregnant pause. "Are you?"

"Of course," she said quickly. Automatically. Because she already knew from experience how useless regrets could be. One of the most painful phrases ever spoken was *if only*. So she didn't speak it.

"Do you really own a company, Auntie Liz?"

"Well, part of it."

"Hey, cool."

"I'll bring you some of their stationery for a souvenir, okay?"

As the engines droned on and the miles slipped past beneath her, Lizzie thought about her promise to her niece. She didn't know much about the advertising business, but she was pretty sure that owning half the company involved more than lending her name to the letterhead. If all that was expected of her was her name, Mr. Whitmore wouldn't have arranged this trip in the first place, would he?

That lawyer, Jeremy Ebbet, had been so kind over the phone, expressing his sympathy over the loss of her uncle and offering to help her sort out all those bothersome legal technicalities of inheriting the partnership, as he'd put it. He'd said that Mr. Whitmore had personally asked him to invite her to visit their office, insisting the entire staff was eager to meet Roland's niece. It must be true, since Mr. Whitmore was paying for her plane ticket and even her hotel room.

And as if that weren't enough, yesterday an extravagant

bouquet of flowers had been delivered to the house on Myrtle Street, compliments of that nice Mr. Whitmore.

Relaxing back into her seat, Lizzie speculated about the owner of the other name on the Whitmore and Hamill letterhead. Uncle Roland would have turned fifty this fall, so his partner was probably around the same age. Not for the first time, she tried to imagine a face to go with the name, but the image that popped into her head was a cross between a white-bearded fairy godmother and Santa Claus in a three-piece suit.

He'd sent her flowers. Flowers. That was another first. She wasn't the kind of woman to whom men sent flowers. A flower pot, maybe. Once while she'd still been seeing Bobby, he'd shown up at her doorstep with a foot-high cedar tree, its roots dripping clods of fresh earth on her welcome mat. She'd smiled and thanked him, of course. It had been a sensible gift, since she'd been looking for something to plant beside the fence in the side yard. But still, there was something so wonderfully impractical about flowers. And sequins.

She shifted, tugging down the hem of her short navy-blue skirt. What did she need with sequins? This suit was her best outfit, one she'd managed to keep in good condition for several years by saving it for special occasions. Like the weddings of her friends, and the christenings of her friends' children, and all the other events that marked the milestones of life. Of *other* people's lives.

Not that she minded, she thought hurriedly. She loved her job, her friends and her family. She loved seeing them happy, and hearing their children call her "Auntie Liz." She had finally come to terms with the fact that no one was going to call her "Mom."

She really was perfectly happy, no matter what Jolene said, right?

But if that was the case, why had she jumped at the chance to make this trip? Why had she spent the past week training not one but two women to take her place at the day care? Why did she get this heart-pounding, palm-sweating feeling each time she thought about her uncle's…no, *her* company?

The plane banked in a wide, slow turn and the window tipped toward the ground. Lizzie braced her hand against the side of the fuselage and craned her neck to see the new view that unfolded. Her stomach didn't roll quite as badly this time.

Just like any new experience, once you got the hang of it, flying wasn't so bad after all.

The flight was forty minutes late by the time it landed at La Guardia. Tinged with gray, bleak as a closed barn door, the airport spread in drab determination across the patched asphalt. Inside the terminal, the air was thick with humidity and laced with the babble of strangers. Everyone appeared to know exactly where they were going and were in a heck of a hurry to get there, so Lizzie hitched the strap of her carry-on over her shoulder and let the stream carry her along to the baggage claim.

"Oh, Lord love a duck," she whispered when she caught sight of the uniformed man standing beside the glass doors. Even though they didn't have anything like this in Packenham Junction, she'd watched enough TV to recognize an honest-to-goodness limousine chauffeur when she saw one. And he was holding up a neatly lettered sign with her name on it.

That nice Mr. Whitmore had said that he'd arrange to have someone meet her flight, but she hadn't expected anything quite so fancy. Dragging her suitcase behind her, she hurried to claim her ride before the limousine turned into a pumpkin.

The hotel room that had been reserved for her turned out to be a suite with a carpet that was thick enough to swallow small animals. There was a dazzling bouquet of flowers on the desk in the sitting room and another on the long, low dresser in the bedroom. And as if that weren't enough to make her head spin, on the round coffee table in front of the couch there was a huge basket loaded with fresh fruit and a bottle of wine with a glittering gold bow, all compliments of Alexander Whitmore.

What an exceptionally generous man that Mr. Whitmore must be. He was being so kind to the partner he didn't even know, what a wonderful relationship he must have had with her uncle.

One hour later, after a hair-raising trip in a taxi and an elevator ride that made her ears pop, Lizzie finally arrived at the thirty-sixth floor of the glass-and-steel tower that housed the offices of Whitmore and Hamill. Taking a deep, fortifying breath, pleased that she didn't have to resort to counting backward this time, she moved across the reception area and stopped in front of a semicircular desk.

A slim, ruthlessly blond woman who looked as if she could have just stepped from the pages of *Cosmopolitan* smiled politely. "Good afternoon."

Lizzie clasped the worn handle of her best purse and smiled back. "Hi."

"May I help you?"

"I'm here to see Mr. Whitmore."

The woman traced a lethal-looking red fingernail down the list in front of her. "And your name?"

How long had it been since she'd been someplace where people didn't know her? She wouldn't have needed to identify herself to Mabel at the Packenham Clinic, and her dentist's wife always greeted her by name on the rare occasions she nerved herself up to go for a checkup. But this was a different place. A different world, according to Marylou.

"Miss?"

"I'm Lizzie Hamill."

There was a strangled gasp. "Miss Elizabeth Hamill?" She nodded.

The woman pressed a button on the blinking array in front of her, lifted a telephone receiver to her ear and spoke quickly before hurrying around the desk to Lizzie's side. "Please, come with me. I'll show you directly to the conference room. Mr. Whitmore's been expecting you."

Treating her with all the deference due visiting royalty, the receptionist, who said her name was Pamela, ushered Lizzie toward a pair of doors at the other end of a wide hall. Assuring her that Mr. Whitmore was on his way, Pamela waited until Lizzie stepped inside, then closed the doors discreetly, leaving her alone.

Lizzie glanced around. Conference room? The place was long enough to double as a bowling alley if they got rid of the table. There were enough chairs here to accommodate a Pedley family reunion, although she doubted whether the place would look quite as pristine once they were through with it. She leaned over the table, checking her reflection in the mirror-polished surface, then gave one of the swivel chairs a spin.

Framed posters decorated the walls, many of them scenes from familiar commercials. She recognized the neon colors of a soft-drink ad and the desert landscape that provided the background for a line of luxury cars. Dominating it all, though, was the elegant sign at the other end of the room. There, on the wall, engraved on a huge brass plaque in letters as long as her forearm, was...

"My name," she breathed.

Well, her uncle's name.

Pursing her lips into a soundless whistle, she walked the length of the gleaming table and touched her fingertips to the scrolling letters. Even though she wasn't the Hamill the sign had been made for, seeing it still gave her a thrill. No, it was more complicated than a thrill. It was a restless, stretching kind of tickle, like the one she'd felt on the plane. It was as if that unacknowledged part of her was still responding to challenge and adventure.

Run the company.

Her mouth quirked as Jolene's outrageous comment came back to her. Ridiculous. Tracing the outline of her name was as close as she was going to come to the kind of person her Uncle Roland must have been.

The doors at the other end of the room clicked open. Lizzie used her sleeve to rub her fingerprints off the sign and turned around. At her first sight of the man whose tall frame filled the doorway, she splayed her hand over the letters once more, only this time it was for balance.

With the purposeful, controlled tread of a prowling animal, he moved closer. No, he was too civilized to be compared to an animal, wasn't he? His shoes gleamed with a polish as glossy as the table, and his charcoal suit and snow-white shirt were as crisp as a new dollar bill.

Lord, he was too good to be true, she thought, trying not to stare. No man really could have hair that thick and black, or eyes that seductively brown, or cheekbones that strong or a jaw that square. His nose was perfect, straight, strong and regal. He smiled, and masculine lines in the shape of twin brackets framed his perfect mouth. His teeth were perfect, too. And as if to ensure that all that perfection wouldn't get monotonous, there was a dimple in his chin.

He stopped in front of her and held out his hand. "Welcome to New York, Miss Hamill."

His voice was as impressive as his appearance. It was
deep and rich, with the polish of aged mahogany and the
power of distant thunder. It was a voice that would be
equally at ease commanding a legion of knights on horse-
back or murmuring incantations over a love potion.

She cleared her throat, certain there was a frog in it
somewhere. "Hello," she croaked. She dropped her hand
from the sign and extended it tentatively, uncertain
whether she wanted to risk destroying this hallucination by
trying to touch it.

"I'm Alexander Whitmore," he said, enclosing her fingers in a warm, firm and indisputably real grip.

Alexander Whitmore? No. He couldn't be. This man
was at least one and a half decades away from fifty, no
more than a few years older than she was. He didn't look
old, or kindly. Or anything as bland as *nice*. "Mr. Whitmore?"

"Please, call me Alex," he said in that love-potion
voice.

"Alex," she repeated like a tongue-tied idiot, although
her tongue was feeling too thick and clumsy to do anything
as agile as tying itself in a knot.

This was her partner? This man with the bedroom-brown
eyes and toothpaste-ad smile was the man behind the name
that was linked to hers? The man who had sent her flowers? Twice? And wine?

Of all the things that had happened in the past few
hours—heck, in the past few weeks—this topped them all.
Maybe she was dreaming. Maybe in another second she
would wake up to the sound of her alarm clock and her
neighbor's yappy poodle. Yes, it had to be a dream. What
other explanation could there be? No living, breathing man
could actually look like…that.

Or maybe it was more than a dream. Maybe, as Marylou had said, Lizzie really had managed to fall into a fairy tale.

She must have. Of course. It was the only reasonable explanation.

Because if this was a fairy tale, then she had just come face-to-face with an honest-to-goodness Prince Charming.

IT WAS ALL working like a charm, Alex thought, holding on to his smile as he extricated his hand from Miss Hamill's grip. So far she had been cooperating beautifully. The campaign that he and Jeremy had planned was off to a flying start. And from the starry-eyed look on her face, his new partner was well on her way to being thoroughly softened up. Good God, it was going to be almost too easy. Like taking candy from a baby.

He sidestepped the burst of conscience that followed that thought by reminding himself he would be doing her a favor. Candy wasn't good for babies. Besides, why should he feel sorry for her? She was a Hamill, wasn't she?

Yes, she was a Hamill. Of that there was no doubt. She had the same uncontrollable red hair as her uncle, although she'd made a valiant effort to confine it into a knot at the back of her head. She had the same devilish arch to her eyebrows, although naturally hers were a narrower, feminine version. There were echoes of Roland in her broad forehead and her pointed chin, too, but the rest of her face was uniquely hers.

She poked at a strand of hair that had corkscrewed loose from its knot. "Mr. Whitmore?"

"Alex," he corrected gently. "May I call you Elizabeth?"

"Well, sure. If you want." She pressed her lips together

and appeared to be wrestling with her tongue. ''But most people call me Lizzie,'' she burst out.

He watched as a blush spread over her cheeks. It gave her a wholesome, fresh-from-the-farm appearance. Damn, she wouldn't last a day in the ruthless environment of the business world. He definitely would be doing her a favor by making sure she returned to Hicksville as soon as possible. ''Lizzie,'' he said.

''Yes?''

''You wanted to ask me something?''

''Oh.'' She chewed briefly on her lower lip. She had full lips and a generous mouth that looked as if it were perpetually on the verge of a smile. ''Oh, not really ask you, I guess.''

He waited, watching with interest while her deepening blush spread to the roots of her hair. When was the last time he'd seen a woman blush, or known one who was even capable of blushing?

''I wanted to thank you for the flowers,'' she said finally. ''And the fruit and the wine. I didn't try the wine yet, but I'm sure it's really good.''

''It was the least I could do, considering how you've traveled all the way here to visit us. I want you to feel welcome.''

''Oh, I do. You've been so kind.''

Kind? If she was impressed by those throwaway gestures, persuading her out of her shares was going to be even easier than he'd hoped. ''Please accept my condolences over the loss of your uncle.''

''Thank you.''

''His death was so unexpected, it must have come as quite a shock.''

''I'd never met my uncle,'' she said, glancing toward the wall behind him. ''It's a shame, but you would have known him much better than I did, being his partner and everything.''

''Roland was a memorable character.''

''Did he think up those ads?''

Alex didn't need to look at the posters to give her an answer. ''No, unfortunately your uncle didn't take an active role in the company for the last few years. Jeremy will be able to explain all of that to you later.''

''Jeremy Ebbet, your lawyer?''

He nodded. ''But we have some time before we have to wade through all the legal business, Lizzie. Would you be interested in seeing the rest of the office?''

She hesitated for only a moment before her mouth gave in to the smile that had been hovering. ''Thanks, I'd like that.''

The smile took him off guard. It dimpled her cheeks and made her eyes sparkle. And it was so warm and innocent and genuine, it zinged right past his brain to stir an unexpected, unwelcome and unmistakably masculine response.

The reaction jarred him. He shouldn't be feeling anything at all for Lizzie Hamill. He never let emotions interfere with business, and this was purely a business relationship, one that he hoped to terminate as soon as possible.

She turned away, and despite his best intentions, his gaze dropped. The loose-fitting blue suit didn't reveal much about the rest of her body, but from what he could see as she walked toward the door, his new partner had an astoundingly shapely pair of legs.

He knew he shouldn't even be noticing, but he nevertheless found himself taking in the view, from her trim ankles to the beginnings of her luscious thighs. His gaze paused on the vulnerable, pale skin at the backs of her knees and he stared, oddly transfixed.

For a crazy instant, he wondered what it would be like to touch her there, to stroke his fingertips along those tender hollows. How would she react if he did? Would she freeze him with a look, the way Tiffany used to? Would she slap him with a harassment suit?

Or would another blush spread across her cheeks? Would those devilish green eyes sparkle with interest? Would her incredibly expressive mouth move into another smile?

What was the matter with him? It must be stress. The future of the company, the security he'd planned for his children, it all depended on his ability to persuade Lizzie out of her shares. Whether she knew it or not, she was his adversary.

So he simply wouldn't allow himself to be affected by her smile or her legs or her wholesome attractiveness. Right. Discipline and control, that's what was necessary to keep the company running smoothly. That's what kept his life running smoothly.

The only aspect of Miss Lizzie Hamill that he could consider attractive was the fifty percent of his company that she owned.

And the only part of her body that he was concerned about was the hand that would sign over her shares.

Chapter Two

"And this is my office," Alex said, holding open a door.

Lizzie stepped inside eagerly, knowing this was the culmination of her guided tour of Whitmore and Hamill. Maybe now they would get down to business and she'd learn what her responsibilities in this company would be. Besides lending her name to the letterhead, that is.

For the past hour or so Alex had ushered her around the entire complex layout of the thirty-sixth floor. They had progressed from meeting rooms to the tape editing rooms and the layout studio and then on to an array of individual offices ranging from windowless cubbyholes to spacious corner rooms.

As Alex had introduced her to the rest of the staff, she'd been astounded by the number and the variety of the people who worked here. She met a few fashion plates who could have been clones of Pamela the receptionist, and she also met some genuinely friendly people who had claimed to have been very fond of her uncle. It had been a pleasant experience, since overall the staff had treated her with the same polite hospitality that Alex had been displaying.

Their last stop had been the office her uncle had used, but there had been little to see there—Alex had already explained that Roland hadn't been involved with the company for a few years. Lizzie had lingered, hoping to find some clue to the character of the man she'd never known, but the shelves and the desk were bare, giving away nothing that could begin to satisfy her growing curiosity.

Walking into Alex's office now, Lizzie admitted to herself that her uncle wasn't the only partner of Whitmore and Hamill that she was curious about.

"Why don't you relax for a while?" Alex suggested, pausing beside the door. "I'll ask Rita to make us some coffee while we wait for Jeremy."

Lizzie smiled and agreed, pleased that her tongue seemed to have recovered fully from its initial paralysis.

Alex slipped out of the office with the same animal grace that characterized all his movements. His voice drifted back through the doorway as he spoke quietly with the dour, middle-aged woman he'd introduced as his secretary. Even though Lizzie couldn't make out the words, she tilted her head, simply enjoying the sound. No matter how often she heard him speak, his words still evoked thoughts of spells and fairy tales.

She might never get used to his appearance, either. What normal woman would? Especially one whose last suitor had considered a ripped-out cedar tree to be romantic.

Hold on there, girl, she cautioned herself. This was her business partner. Their association had happened literally by accident. Just because she had trouble keeping her imagination in check didn't mean that she had to let him know about it. Prince Charming. Lordy, he'd think she was a complete fool if he ever knew the thoughts she'd been entertaining about him.

Lizzie turned from the door and walked slowly around the room, pausing to read the framed certificates that attested to awards of excellence that the company had won. *Her* company. Whether it was deserved or not, she felt a surge of the same kind of pride she'd felt on seeing the plaque with her name.

It's yours. For once in your life, you have something that's just for you.

Well, it wasn't all hers. Fifty percent of it was Alex's. Clasping her hands behind her back, she moved toward the massive L-shaped oak desk that dominated the spacious office. There was a computer set up on one side and an area for paperwork on the other. No clutter marred the polished surface, though. Everything was neatly aligned, from the gold pen set and the leather-trimmed blotter to the telephone that wouldn't have looked out of place on a space shuttle. Even the picture frame was angled so that it was parallel to the pen set.

Picture? After a quick glance at the empty office doorway, Lizzie moved closer and picked up the frame to get a better look. To her surprise, it was a photograph of a pair of boys. Brothers, perhaps even twins, judging by the smiles that were reflections of each other. They both had black hair and dimples and were completely captivating. Almost as captivating as...

Who? Their uncle? Their father? What relation were these children to Alex? They had to be related somehow. There was a strong resemblance to him, not only in their coloring but in their expressions. Even though the boys appeared to be no more than five years old, there was a definite twinkle in their eyes that would probably develop into full-blown charm by the time they grew up.

Lizzie felt herself smile in response.

"Rita reminded me it's getting late," Alex said, striding into the office with two steaming cups of coffee in his hands. "We'll try to wrap up our business with Jeremy as quickly as possible."

"That's fine with me." She glanced up. "Who are these adorable kids?"

He hesitated when he saw what she was holding. "They're my sons."

"I can see the resemblance. What are their names?"

"Jason and Daniel. Jason's the one on the left."

"They really are adorable. How old are they?"

"They'll be five in a few months."

Her smile grew. "Twins. I figured that. We have a pair of twin girls in the day care center where I work. They're always full of mischief, but they're only three so the mischief isn't that hard to contain."

"You sound as if you enjoy your work."

"I love it. I'm a sucker for kids, always have been." She replaced the photograph on his desk and reached to take the cup he was holding out to her.

He moved the photo she had replaced, realigning it so that it was parallel to the pen set, then guided Lizzie to the sitting area in front of the corner window. He waited until she had settled comfortably into one of the deep burgundy armchairs before taking the matching one across from her. "So, how long have you worked in the day care business, Lizzie?"

"Almost four years now."

"And before that?"

"Oh, I worked at the Packenham Dairy and then helped my stepbrother Benjamin at the cheese factory."

He sipped his coffee slowly, watching her over the rim of his cup. "Cheese," he repeated.

She nodded. "Pedley Cheese. He couldn't afford to keep me on, so that's why I started up the day care center."

"That's an interesting switch. What made you decide on day care?"

"It seemed to come naturally. Like I said, I'm a sucker for kids. Probably because of my family."

"Oh? I thought you were your uncle's only surviving relative."

"I mean my stepfamily. When my father died, my mother remarried, and her new husband was a widower with three young children of his own. I was fourteen, and as the oldest kid in the household, I ended up helping raise the little ones."

"Do your mother and stepfather still live in Packenham Corners?"

"Junction," she corrected. "Packenham Corners is on the other side of the county line."

"Sorry."

"That's okay," she said generously. "Lots of folks get them mixed up. Anyhow, my stepfather, Warren Pedley, still lives on the family farm about ten miles from town, but my mother died the year after she married Warren."

He sat forward, bracing his forearms on his thighs as he cradled his cup between his hands. "That must have been very difficult for you."

She shook her head, not wanting to remember those dark years of her adolescence. "The Pedleys were wonderful. They always made me feel like one of the family."

"And in return, you tried to pay them back by being helpful," he said.

The accuracy of his insight startled her. They had met less than two hours ago, yet he had zeroed in on one of the major reasons her life had taken the direction it had. She studied him over the rim of her cup. Maybe there was more to him than a pretty face.

Of course he was more than a pretty face, she thought, exasperated with herself for dwelling on his appearance. The success exhibited by the luxury of the Whitmore and

Hamill offices, as well as the famous ads and slew of awards that were displayed on the walls, made it obvious that there had to be plenty of intelligence behind those brown bedroom eyes.

"I suppose you're right," she continued. "I still like to help them out, but instead of baby-sitting them, I baby-sit their children. Except for my youngest stepbrother. He's a long way from settling down and raising a family of his own." She heard the wistful note in her voice and shifted uncomfortably. "Of course, with so many nieces and nephews to love, he could be happy just the way he is."

"You sound as if you're still very close to your family."

"Oh, yes. We're not blood relatives, but we're still close." Her gaze strayed back to the photo of the twins. "You're very fortunate to have two sons. They look like fine children."

"Thank you."

Suddenly she realized what should have been obvious at her first glance of Alex's children. It had taken two people to produce those boys. That meant they had a mother, too.

She glanced at the large, capable-looking hands that clasped his coffee cup. There was no sign of a gold band on any of those long fingers, but that was no guarantee these days.

Was Alex married?

Not that it should make one whit of difference to her, of course. So it was simply polite curiosity, from one business partner to another, that prompted her to ask the next question. "Does your wife take care of the children while you work?"

"Excuse me?"

"As a day care provider myself, I was simply wondering who's taking care of Jason and Daniel."

"My housekeeper, Mrs. Gray. She's been with us for the past few months."

Simple curiosity, she told herself again. "I know several working couples who would prefer to have someone in their home like that."

"Mrs. Gray certainly keeps things running smoothly."

"What kind of work does your wife do?" she asked, abandoning her attempts at subtlety.

"I'm not exactly sure what Tiffany does these days. Right now she's in Europe."

Well, that answered her question. Sort of. "I see."

"We divorced three years ago, Lizzie. She's on her honeymoon with her new husband."

She felt a blush warm her cheeks. Darn. He'd probably known what she was angling to find out all along. "I'm sorry."

He lifted his shoulders in a shrug that would appear casual if it weren't for the way his knuckles whitened on his coffee cup. "These things happen. One learns from one's mistakes."

She felt a stirring of sympathy for him, coupled with a strange urge to reach out and cover his hands with hers. Instead, she placed her empty cup on the table beside her and laced her fingers in her lap. "So," she said in a blatant attempt to change the subject, "how did you get into the advertising business, Alex?"

The flash of white knuckles disappeared as if it had never been. His charming smile was firmly back in place. "The art of persuasion has interested me from the time I finished college. After my first position with an advertising firm evaporated when the company failed, I decided to establish my own agency."

"Is that when you met my uncle?"

"Yes, we met through a mutual acquaintance. Roland

and I formed a partnership and the rest, as they say, is history.''

She suspected there was probably a lot more to the story, but before she could form her next question, there was a quiet knock on the open door.

Alex glanced over his shoulder, then rose to his feet. ''Hello, Jeremy.''

The man who walked into the room looked exactly as Lizzie would have expected from hearing his voice on the phone. At least this wasn't a surprise, she thought wryly.

Jeremy Ebbet was a few inches short of six feet and a few pounds shy of filling out the shoulders of his pin-striped suit. His hair was dark blond and thinning and his face bore the long-suffering worry lines of a farmer in a drought. After shaking hands with Lizzie and exchanging a few stilted pleasantries, he sat on the edge of the chair beside Alex, set his briefcase on his knees like a grasshopper with a wheat husk and clicked open the lid.

''We appreciate your willingness to clear up this situation so promptly, Miss Hamill,'' he said, adjusting his steel-rimmed glasses with a poke of his index finger.

Alex crossed his arms over his chest and leaned back in his chair while he listened to Jeremy set the second phase of their plan into motion.

As Alex had advised him, Jeremy emphasized how Roland hadn't been involved with Whitmore and Hamill for years, and how the company had been running profitably under Alex's sole control. Lizzie nodded, already prepared for this by the carefully chosen comments Alex had made during their tour.

''Your uncle was in the process of negotiating the sale of his shares when he met with his tragic accident,'' Jeremy said, withdrawing a sheaf of papers from his briefcase and passing them to Lizzie. ''Here's a copy of our offer.''

She nibbled on her lower lip as she concentrated on reading, drawing Alex's attention to her mouth yet again. Her generous, ready-to-break-into-a-smile mouth. Alex had been distracted by it unexpectedly throughout the course of the afternoon. Especially when it had curved with a touch of wistful sweetness while she'd been looking at the picture of his sons.

Damn. She might be going about it in a completely different manner, but if he didn't maintain control of his thoughts, in her own way Lizzie might prove to be as disruptive to the smooth course of his life as her uncle had been.

Yet another reason to close this deal and get her on a plane back to Packenham Corners. No, Junction. Whatever.

"As you can see," Jeremy continued, "we have substituted your name for Roland's, since you are now the sole owner of his fifty percent."

She stopped nibbling and pursed her lips in a whispered whistle.

The pucker made Alex think about kissing. He shifted in his chair and focused on her hand, the one that would hold a pen.

"Is that what my shares are worth?" she asked in a voice that approached a squeak.

"It's an excellent offer," Jeremy said.

"Lord love a duck."

"Excuse me?"

"I had no idea." She looked up, turning toward Alex. "This is so fast. I just found out I own half the company, and now you want to buy me out?"

Alex wrenched his gaze from her mouth and met her eyes. "It must be overwhelming for you, but I'm sure you see that it would be the best solution for everyone." He paused a moment before adding the final nail. "It's what Roland would have wanted."

"But I had thought that... I mean, when you arranged for me to come all the way out here..." She trailed off, shaking her head as she looked at the paper in her hand. "Do you mind if I take this back to the hotel with me?"

"Go ahead," Alex said. "Take all the time you want to consider it, Lizzie. I don't want you to feel pressured."

"Thanks. I need to think about this."

Alex pushed back his sleeve and checked his watch. "Let's continue this discussion tomorrow. In the meantime, why don't we grab dinner and then catch a Broadway show? I understand this is your first visit to New York?"

She folded the offer and slipped it into her purse, then smiled and nodded her head.

Like taking candy from—

Rising to his feet, Alex refused to listen to the nagging little voice. He also refused to acknowledge the tug at his pulse as he noted the way his partner's plain navy blue skirt molded delectably curved thighs as she shifted to stand up.

And the way her lips softened with her smile.

And her eyes sparkled with earthy sensuality.

And the touch of her fingers on his skin when she took his hand sent a shock of heat through his nerves...

But apart from that, everything was progressing according to plan.

THE SCENTS of smoldering candles and expensive perfume were as subtly pervasive as the background hush that permeated the restaurant. The black-suited waiters didn't bustle, they glided. Polished silverware winked from the white linen tablecloths and tiny lights twinkled in the crystal wineglass Lizzie held. Clutching the stem securely, she lifted it in response to Alex's toast.

"To New York," she repeated, taking a healthy sip of the wine Alex had ordered. It was as smooth and sweet as spring water with honey.

"What would you like to see tomorrow?" he asked. "The Statue of Liberty? Times Square? The museum?"

"The Statue of Liberty, I think."

"Wonderful. It's been years since I went there."

She took another sip of wine as she listened to the sound of his voice. She was vaguely aware that he was detailing the tour he planned to take her on tomorrow, but as had happened before, she paid more attention to his voice than to his words. And why not? She might as well enjoy it while she could. His devastating handsomeness, the dazzling restaurant, the wine…come midnight, it would probably all disappear.

That would be a fitting end to this fairy tale, wouldn't it?

She should have seen it coming. Lord, she must be pathetic to confuse, even for a minute, the attention Alex had been showering on her. He wasn't being kind. This was purely business. What other possible reason could there have been for someone like him to whisk her to New York and give her flowers and treat her to dinner at a restaurant with no prices on the menu?

Considering what he was willing to pay her for her uncle's shares, what would the cost of a few roses and a filet mignon matter?

She put down her glass and toyed with her fork, annoyed with herself for the disappointment that was totally misplaced. Her imagination had really gotten the better of her again, that's all. Of course, he wouldn't want someone he didn't know for a partner. Of course, he'd think she would be anxious to sell her half of the company and scuttle back to her stable, safe, secure, *happy* life in Packenham Junction.

She should have seen it coming, she thought again, poking at a morsel of meat that had already gone cold. She was Auntie Liz. Good old Lizzie. The perpetual baby-sitter and bridesmaid, destined to exist forever on the periphery of other people's lives.

In a way, there was a fitting irony to the situation. This entire trip, what she'd seen as her one chance at adventure, had the sole purpose of ensuring that she would return home and stay right where she'd always been.

"Is there something wrong with your meal?"

She put down her fork carefully so it wouldn't clang and disturb the hush. "No, it's delicious."

"I could have the waiter bring you something else."

"Please, don't bother," she said, reaching for her wine once more. She knew she shouldn't be drinking it, considering the fact that she still hadn't eaten anything today, but swishing dollar-a-mouthful wine through her teeth was another one of those things she might as well enjoy while she could.

Alex had made her a generous offer. Heck, it had more zeros than she'd seen in one place since she'd sneezed while she'd been typing out the day care center's financial statement. With that much money, she could build a new barn for her stepfather, pay off Jolene and Tim's mortgage, even pay Zack's way through Harvard.

That is, if they would accept the money.

What a stubborn bunch her family was. It must hark back to their pioneer roots, when money in the bank was a foreign concept and people bartered for what they needed. Too bad Whitmore and Hamill didn't make milking machines or something else useful.

Her lips curved at the thought of the immaculately groomed Alex Whitmore being involved with anything as mundane as a milking machine. He probably wouldn't know which end of a cow to install it on. With his long fingers and firm grip, though, he likely wouldn't have too much trouble coaxing out the milk by hand.

She glanced across the table, and a slow flush rose to her cheeks at the mental image of Alex with his long, strong fingers turning his attention to such an earthy task. If the way he moved was any indication, there was plenty of physical strength beneath his sophisticated appearance. Plenty of determination behind his good manners, too. He'd have a gentle, purposeful touch, the kind that would soothe and stimulate at the same time. And he'd be murmuring soft words in that deep, love-potion voice of his, and his brown eyes would grow smoky, and...

Lordy, he was one impressive specimen. Maybe it was the excitement of this whole situation, but never in her life had a man made such an immediate impact on her. She wasn't so naive as to confuse physical attraction for something deeper, yet knowing what it was didn't do anything to eliminate it.

It had never been that way with Bobby. Even when he'd been stripped to the waist on those hot summer days on her stepfather's farm, and his shoulders had flexed with the effort of slinging those hay bales around, and his jeans had clung damply to his hips and thighs, she had never felt more than a comfortable kind of interest.

If she ever had the chance to see Alex Whitmore flex his muscles while he was half-naked and gleaming with sweat, she doubted if she would feel anything close to comfortable.

With a sickening clunk, her wineglass tipped over, spill-

ing the remainder of its contents across the tablecloth in a
sudden flood.

Alex whipped the linen napkin from his lap and
stemmed the flow. "Sorry, I must have jarred the table,"
he said.

She knew that he knew that her own fidgeting had been
responsible for the mishap, yet he was willing to take the
blame in order to spare her embarrassment. He was a regular...prince. A bubble of laughter hiccuped past her lips.

"Would you care for some dessert, Lizzie?" he asked,
righting her glass and moving the wine bottle out of her
reach.

"No, thank you, Alex."

"Some coffee? We still have some time before the show
starts."

Oh, Lord, he must think she was on the downhill side
of tipsy. She wasn't even close to the edge, empty stomach
or not. Compared to Bobby's homemade cordial that could
clear sinuses and blister paint, this stuff was cream soda.
If her faculties were impaired at all, it was from the effects
of Alex's presence, not the wine—the man was too appealing to be legal.

"Is there anything else you'd like, Lizzie?"

*Sure, you can strip to the waist and sling some hay
bales.* "Do you ever do any modeling?" she asked impulsively.

"Excuse me?"

"You know, posing for any of the advertisements the
company does."

He looked startled. "No, we use an outside agency.
Why?"

"Oh, I was just wondering. Considering the way
you..." She stopped herself before she could blurt some-

thing out about the way he looked. "Um, I thought it might cut costs."

"That particular cost-cutting method hasn't been necessary so far."

"Oh. That's good. I mean, I'm glad Whitmore and Hamill is doing all right."

"With each campaign we try to find individuals who would match our needs and the client's expectations. My job consists of coordinating the people who work for me, making sure things run smoothly—"

"Us," she interrupted.

He lifted an eyebrow.

"Who work for us," she said, blushing at her own audacity. "I haven't sold out yet."

A muscle twitched in his cheek. He pressed the napkin more firmly against the puddle of wine. "Running a company doesn't suit everyone, Lizzie. Your uncle found it much too restricting. That's likely why he gradually withdrew from the day-to-day business over the past few years."

She restrained herself from rolling her eyes. She'd lost count of the number of times Alex had stressed how her uncle had been eager to sell. As an angle of persuasion, it was starting to wear thin.

Besides, the more she heard Alex talk about Roland, the more she suspected there were other reasons behind the imminent end of their partnership. Although Alex hadn't openly criticized her uncle, obviously they hadn't gotten along.

But that didn't mean *she* couldn't get along with him, did it? She got along with everyone. After all, as Packenham Junction's perpetual bridesmaid and baby-sitter, she had plenty of experience keeping other people happy. Sure, these New York types were different from the people back

home, but under their three-piece suits they were still people, right?

And she could readily imagine what was under Alex's
three-piece suit...

"What's going to happen to the company name if I sell
you my shares?" she asked quickly.

"The company name?"

"Whitmore and Hamill. I'm the last Hamill, so if I'm
gone, would you change the name?"

He hesitated. "What would you like me to do?"

"I'd like the name to stay the way it is."

"Well, it could prove confusing for our clients."

"As a tribute to my uncle."

"I see."

"Uncle Roland never married and he didn't have any
children to remember him. Maybe he wanted me to make
sure there would at least be the company name for him to
leave behind for posterity."

"All right. If that's what you really want."

*No, what I really want is to see you naked and sweaty
and flexing—*

She bit her lip. She really had to stop dwelling on that
fantasy. Or at least get herself a different one. "Why are
you so anxious to buy me out, Alex?"

A flash of emotion briefly hardened the planes of his
face. It was no more than a subtle tightening of his jaw, a
twitch of his eyelids, and if she hadn't been so conscious
of his every nuance, she would have missed it. Yet it
wasn't the first time she'd seen a crack in the smooth image he projected. This had happened before, when he'd
mentioned his divorce.

"Alex?"

He blinked, and the moment of emotion was gone. "I

believe that the company would have a much more stable, secure future with one person controlling its direction.''

"Didn't you get along with my uncle?''

"It's no secret that we had our differences with respect to management decisions, but I'm thinking on more practical terms than that. During the past few years, the necessity of having to go through the motions of contacting Roland each time we needed to make a major decision caused delays and confusion. That will all be eliminated once you sell your shares to me.''

"If I agree.''

"Lizzie, you'd be so much more comfortable without the headache of this responsibility. You said you enjoy your work at the day care center, and you're so close to your family. Think of all that you could do with the proceeds of the sale.''

"I have been thinking about it.''

"It's really the best solution.''

She toyed with her wineglass, tipping it forward to roll the base in arcs along the tablecloth. Was it really the best solution?

Giving up her college scholarship in order to keep the farm running while her stepfather recovered from that tractor accident had been the best solution. So had opening up a day care center in the house on Myrtle Street when Bobby had destroyed her dreams. Twenty years from now, when the children she was caring for brought their own children to her, would she look back on this adventure and say, "If only?''

Frowning, she set her glass beside the puddle of wine and looked at Alex. "I admit I don't know all that much about the advertising business, and I might not have a fancy degree in economics, but like most people from the country, I know about horse trading. Or to be more exact, cow trading.''

His eyebrows went up. Balling the napkin in his fist, he watched her in silence, his jaw tightening.

She hesitated. ''What is it?''

''For a minute there you sounded just like your uncle.''

Whatever he meant by that, she took it as a compliment. Encouraged, she pushed her plate away and leaned her forearms on the edge of the table. ''The way I see it, inheriting my uncle's shares is like being given a cow that I'm not sure how to deal with.''

''I see. Please, go on.''

''Well, apart from the drastic and permanent option of fixing beef stew, there are always other choices when it comes to getting rid of livestock.''

''Such as?''

''Okay, first of all, it's important to have a good idea of what the cow is actually worth so you can get a fair price. No offense, Alex, but I'm going to have my own lawyer look over the offer Jeremy drew up.''

''Naturally.''

''And there's another point to consider,'' she continued. ''When a cow is healthy and producing milk, it might be better to keep it.''

He pushed his plate aside and leaned forward in a movement that mirrored her earlier one. ''What exactly are you saying?''

What was she saying? She wasn't too sure herself, but the more she thought about this, the better it seemed. ''I could make quick money by selling the cow, but in the long run I might be better off keeping the cow and selling the milk.''

''So you'd expect me to…milk your cow for you?''

Long, strong fingers squeezing warm flesh… Lizzie

moistened her lips. "Well, you said my uncle didn't involve himself in the business for a few years. It might have been inconvenient for you at times, but you said you managed to stay profitable, so what difference would it make if I did the same thing? If I hung on to my half, I could be a silent partner."

He looked at her mouth, his jaw tightening. After a breathless minute, he raised his gaze to hers.

Lizzie felt another one of those crazy tickles whisper through her stomach. There was yet another option here. She didn't have to be merely a silent partner. What if they both…milked the cow? "Alex?"

A muscle twitched in his cheek. "Yes, Lizzie?"

"What kind of qualifications did my uncle have?"

"I'm not sure I understand."

"To work in advertising. Did he go to the same college you did, or take a course or something?"

He remained silent for so long, she was about to repeat the question before he finally answered. "No."

"Really?"

"Your uncle learned through experience. He relied on instinct and inspiration rather than formal education."

The tickle turned into a tingle as the seed Jolene had planted began to take root. "Even though I enjoy my day care business, it can get along without me, so there's nothing stopping me from staying in New York for a while." She cleared her throat. "This is something you might not have thought of, Alex, but if I learn all I can about the company, I could help you out."

"Help me out?"

"Sort of give the company another perspective."

"Another perspective?" His voice was growing quieter with each phrase he repeated. Rather than sounding soft, though, he sounded as ominous as rumbling thunder.

She smiled. "You know, just like Uncle Roland."

Alex didn't return her smile. Silence stretched out between them as he continued to stare at her. Something gleamed in the mesmerizing brown depths of his eyes. Challenge. More than challenge. Awareness.

Lizzie shivered at the thrill that went through her body. She felt herself respond, and she wasn't even sure what she was responding to. All those tickles and tingles that made her palms sweat…how much was due to her interest in her company…and how much was due to her interest in her partner?

Alex fought to keep his expression impassive. How could her mouth look so appealing when she was talking about exerting control of the company, *his* company?

This wasn't progressing at all according to plan.

Then again, how could he expect any woman who used barnyard analogies to explain the concepts of a market economy to behave predictably?

Just like Uncle Roland.

He hadn't believed that there could be two people like that in the world. And there weren't. Despite her innocent charm, Elizabeth Hamill was far more dangerous than her uncle. Because she was threatening far more than his business. She was threatening his self-control.

He wasn't a man who acted impulsively. He relied on logic to guide his actions. And there was nothing logical about the sudden urge he had to lean across the table and taste Lizzie's lips.

First thing tomorrow, he'd tell Jeremy to increase the offer for her shares. And if that didn't work—

The silence between them was broken abruptly by a purring ring from Alex's jacket. He jerked, yanking his attention away from his new partner's lips to reach into his pocket and pull out his phone.

"Mr. Whitmore? Are you there?"

At his housekeeper's panic-stricken tone, he reflexively stiffened. Great. Now what?

It took less than a minute for Alex to find out what had put the panic in Mrs. Gray's voice. All thoughts of his business and his partner were swept away by a wave of anxiety. Flipping the phone shut, he crammed it back inside his jacket and surged to his feet. "I'm sorry, Lizzie," he said, already moving away. "I'll have to meet you at the theater later. Something's come up at home."

She hesitated for less than a second before she wiped her palms on her skirt, grabbed her purse and rounded the table to follow him. "Hold on, partner. I'm coming with you."

Chapter Three

Alex saw the trail of destruction the moment he turned past the stone gateposts and started up the driveway. Twin ruts carved a crooked path across the lush lawn, leading to a tangle of crushed rosebushes. Mrs. Gray's brown sedan sat in the center of the flower bed, its front wheels sunk to the axles in the damp loam, its right fender crumpled against a tilted marble birdbath.

The damage wasn't anywhere near as bad as his housekeeper had made out in that frantic phone call, but still, it was enough to make Alex's blood run cold. If the car had turned the other way, if it had rolled toward the street instead of the garden, if it had been going faster—

He screeched to a stop in front of the house and ran for the door. Distantly, he was aware of Lizzie getting out of the car to follow him. She had refused to be left behind—like her uncle, she appeared to have a stubborn streak. He should have insisted that she go back to her hotel, but he hadn't wanted to spare the time to argue. Right now, all he cared about was seeing his sons.

"Jason! Daniel!" he called, striding into the foyer.

"They're in here, Mr. Whitmore," Mrs. Gray said.

Alex veered toward the front room. The twins were sitting on the sofa. Mrs. Gray had insisted that they were unhurt, but Alex couldn't breathe until he crossed the floor and was able to see them for himself.

"Hi, Dad! Are you mad at us?"

"Yeah, are you mad at us?"

Smears of dirt the same color as the dark loam of the flower bed clung to the cuffs of the twins' pyjamas. Faint traces of the same dirt streaked their hands and cheeks, yet there was no sign of scrapes or bruises.

Dropping to his knees in front of them, Alex ran his hands over their arms and legs, reassuring himself that they were all right, then wrapped his arms around their shoulders and pulled them against his chest. His lungs heaved. "Thank God," he said roughly.

"He's not mad," Jason mumbled into Alex's jacket.

"Told ya," Daniel said, squirming in his father's embrace.

"Mrs. Gray said we had to wait for you. She said you'd be mad. She said we were gonna get it."

"She made us sit here *forever*."

"What are we gonna get, Dad?"

Alex closed his eyes, allowing the nightmare images that had tormented him on the drive home to fade. Jason and Daniel really were all right.

"I wasn't going to let them out of my sight," Mrs. Gray said. "I wanted you to see for yourself what these two hooligans did."

He swallowed hard. "I saw the car, Mrs. Gray."

"I'm giving you my notice, Mr. Whitmore. I'll be leaving as soon as I pack my suitcase."

That made it three times in the past week she'd threatened to quit. A new record. Alex took a deep breath and turned his head to look at his housekeeper.

Mrs. Gray was perched on the antique settee, the least comfortable piece of furniture in the room. She lived up to her name. The starched dress that she wore was a sober gray, as was her tightly curled hair. Even the long-haired cat that curled on her lap was gray, except for the spots where its fur still bore traces of the twins' purple paint.

The housekeeper had come highly recommended by the agency Alex had always dealt with. And she'd lasted almost four months, which was longer than any of her predecessors. But one look at her closed expression and he suspected that she might actually follow through with her threat.

"I'll have the damage to your car repaired, Mrs. Gray," he said. "And we can discuss your salary—"

"Don't think you can buy me off this time, Mr. Whitmore. Your money doesn't solve everything. Never in all my years have I worked with such—" She broke off, extending her arm to point a shaking finger at his sons. "Mark my words, they're on the path to a life of crime. You don't need a housekeeper, you need a warden."

He rose to his feet, keeping his hands on the twins' shoulders. "We'll talk about this later."

"They're bad seeds. They're demon children. They—"

"Mrs. Gray," Alex said. "That's enough."

At his harsh tone, she pressed her lips into a bloodless line and stood up, cradling her purple-tinged cat to her chest. She glared at the twins, then sniffed and stalked out of the room.

"She's a goner," Jason said happily.

"Yeah," Daniel said, bouncing on the sofa cushion.

Alex heard a door slam in the depths of the house.

He had never particularly liked Mrs. Gray, but her loss was going to throw a major wrench into the smooth-running machinery of his life. He wanted to kick something. He wanted to tip back his head and vent his frustration in a blistering string of curses. But as always, he did neither.

He breathed in deeply, striving for control, feeling a familiar throbbing start at his temples. The men with the hammers were already warming up.

"Hey, who's that? Is she gonna be our new sitter?"

Alex followed the direction of his son's gaze. Lizzie was standing just inside the doorway, her lips parted as she took in the scene.

Wonderful, he thought. This was a hell of a way to impress a new partner. How much farther off track could his plan to dazzle her get? "Boys, this is Miss Hamill. And, no, she's not your new baby-sitter." He turned to Lizzie. "I'm sorry I dragged you out here," he began.

"No, it's understandable. You were worried." Lizzie crossed her arms and rubbed her palms over her sleeves, glancing toward the bay window that overlooked the garden. Even from within the lighted room, the glint of Mrs. Gray's car was clearly visible in the moonlight. "You're better off without her."

"What?"

"If that was your housekeeper, you're better off without her. Losing control of her car is one thing, but blaming it on innocent children..." A blush rose in her cheeks. "Sorry, it's none of my business."

Her defense of his sons, as misplaced as it was, brought an unexpected rush of warmth. It was a different warmth from the kind caused by her smile. But it was just as unwelcome. He frowned, trying to remember what he'd told her about the accident on the way over here. "Mrs. Gray wasn't driving."

"That's even worse. If she let someone else—"

"We were only borrowing it," Daniel interrupted.

"We were *sharing*," Jason said. "Barney says it's good to share."

"It was just like our cars," Daniel added.

"Except it went *fast*."

"Yeah, real fast."

Alex shuddered as he pictured his children treating the ton and a half of metal like another one of their toys. He'd given them battery-powered cars a month ago. He'd thought the boys had enjoyed puttering around in them, but evidently they hadn't been satisfied. They'd only been training for the real thing.

Lizzie looked from one twin to the other, her eyes widening with dawning comprehension. "You mean that..." Her gaze settled on Alex. "Are you telling me that these children were driving?"

He nodded stiffly.

"But..." She looked at the boys again. "How?"

"Jason stood on the seat to steer and I pushed on the pedals," Daniel said, twisting on the sofa to face Lizzie. "Smart, huh?"

She lifted her hand to her mouth, her eyes sparkling. "Oh, Lord love a duck."

"We took the keys when Mrs. Gray went to the bathroom," Jason said. He wrinkled his nose. "She stays in the bathroom forever."

"Forever," Daniel echoed.

"It was easy. Just like our cars. 'Cept the key made a weird noise until I let go of it. Like this. *Kshckkk,*" he said, doing a fair imitation of the sound of grinding starter gears.

Alex tried to keep his tone even, despite the anxiety that pulsed along his nerves whenever he let himself think about what could have happened. "What you did was wrong, boys. It was dangerous. You could have been badly hurt."

"We only wanted to borrow it. We were going to give it back," Daniel said, pushing out his lower lip.

"See?" Jason mumbled to his brother. "He *is* mad. Told ya."

"Don't be stupid."

"I'm not stupid. You're the one—"

The budding squabble was halted by a muffled shriek from the back of the house.

Alex grimaced. Now what?

"Uh—oh," Daniel said, climbing over the back of the sofa and dropping to the floor.

Jason scrambled after him. "Uh—oh."

There was the sound of a door opening, followed by Mrs. Gray's indignant shout. "Mr. Whitmore, there are worms in my suitcase!"

Without a backward glance, the boys ran out of the room and headed for the stairs.

LIZZIE SIGHED as she sank into the luxurious cushions of the ivory-colored couch. She looked around, marveling once more at the beautiful room. Like the Whitmore and Hamill office, Alex's home practically oozed wealth and sophistication. It was like something out of a decorating magazine, from the lustrous wood of the delicate side tables to the pale upholstery and the antique settee.

Except magazine photos didn't usually include muddy footprints.

Her gaze dropped to the cushion beside her. Against the elegant ivory brocade, dark smears of dirt marked the place where Alex's sons had been sitting. The twins had also tracked part of the flower bed across the carpet. Evidently, they had been barefoot and in their pyjamas when they had decided to take their housekeeper's car for a spin.

It must have terrified Alex when he'd heard about the accident. It could have turned out so much worse. As it was, the damage wasn't serious—the tow truck that he'd

called had already extracted the car from the flower bed
and had hauled it away to the body shop. The lawn and
the rosebushes could be patched up easily enough. But it
didn't look as if Alex's housekeeper was going to retract
her threat to quit. From the sound of things, Mrs. Gray
was still intent on leaving…as soon as she cleaned the
worms out of her suitcase.

Despite the gravity of the situation, Lizzie couldn't prevent the grin that tugged at the corners of her mouth.
Worms. Had they been squiggly little earthworms or the
big slimy nightcrawlers? Well, that was one advantage of
living in the city. At least the twins didn't have ready
access to snakes and frogs.

Those boys were something else. A real pair of charm-
ers, just like their father. Neither of them was big enough
to see over the steering wheel of Mrs. Gray's brown sedan,
but they hadn't let that stop them. They weren't even five
years old, but they'd had the ingenuity and resourcefulness
to figure out how to drive a car. Obviously, when they set
their minds to doing something, they didn't let anything
stand in their way. Did they get that determination from
their father, too?

Probably. When it came to his business, he could be
pretty single-minded about what he wanted. Was he the
same way when it came to…other things? What was he
like when he wanted a woman? How would it feel to be
the object of such unwavering purpose?

Lizzie's smile faded. Couldn't she stop dwelling on that
for more than a minute? She should be ashamed of herself
for continuing to lust after Alex under circumstances like
these.

He wasn't any prince out of a fairy tale. He was worse.
He was a real man with real children. And the emotion

she'd seen on his face when he'd held his sons was so real it brought a lump to her throat even now.

What other emotions did he keep locked away behind his charming image? What would it be like to have the power of those emotions directed at her?

Was he as passionate a lover as he was a father?

Muffling a groan, she put her head in her hands. Coming home with him had been a mistake. She'd been finding Alex irresistible enough already, but now that she'd seen him with his children, she was, as the twins so nicely put it, a goner.

Chimes echoed from the hall. Lizzie lifted her head and twisted around just as Mrs. Gray marched past the doorway, a bulging flight bag in one hand, her cat cradled to her chest with the other. Voices rose from the direction of the foyer.

Lizzie hesitated for only a moment before pushing to her feet and moving toward the commotion. The front door stood ajar. Light spilled past the pillars that flanked the entrance onto the curving driveway where an old Chevy idled just to one side of Alex's dark green sports car. A woman with hair the color of mouse fur helped Mrs. Gray put her bag in the trunk of the Chevy, then got behind the wheel. Without looking back, Mrs. Gray slid into the passenger seat and closed the door with an indignant thump. Seconds later, the car pulled away.

"Well, that's it then."

At the deep voice, Lizzie jumped. She hadn't heard Alex approach—for a large man, he could move surprisingly quietly. She glanced over her shoulder. "What?"

He walked over to close the door. "Mrs. Gray went to stay with her sister."

"I guess that means she actually did quit?"

"Yes. I'll have the rest of her things sent to her. She didn't want to use her suitcase."

The suitcase. Lizzie pressed her lips together to keep her smile to herself. She was sure Mrs. Gray hadn't seen much humor in those worms. And it didn't seem as if Alex had, either.

Sympathy coursed through her as she took in his appearance. Poor Alex. He looked more like a harried father than a suave businessman. He'd discarded his jacket and loosened his tie. The top button of his shirt was undone and his hair was rumpled into uneven furrows, as if he'd been raking his fingers through it.

Yet to Lizzie's eyes, he didn't look disheveled, he looked adorable. And he also looked more…approachable than he ever had before.

"I'm sorry to have left you on your own for so long like this, Lizzie," he said, coming over to stand in front of her.

"That's okay. Are the boys in bed?"

"As far as I know. They appeared to be asleep when I left them."

"I'm sure they've had enough excitement for one day."

"I hope so," he muttered.

"They're all right now, aren't they?"

"They weren't hurt. Thank God the car wasn't going fast."

She tilted her head, noticing the fine lines that radiated from the corners of his eyes and the tension that tightened his jaw. "What about you?" she asked.

"Me?"

She dropped her gaze. Beneath the fine cotton of his white shirt, his shoulders were stiff with the same tension she saw in his face. "I've been through my share of accidents with the children at my day care," she said. "Mishaps like swallowed buttons or bumps from swings, and it's been my experience that kids are a lot more resilient than their parents.''

"I'm fine," he said. "It's Jason and Daniel I'm concerned about."

"Of course, you're concerned."

"They had no idea how dangerous their latest stunt could have been."

"I'm sure they didn't."

"I still don't understand how Mrs. Gray could have been so negligent as to let this happen."

"It isn't easy to keep track of two active boys, especially a pair who are as resourceful as your twins," she said, although she didn't know why she would be trying to make excuses for his housekeeper. The woman had looked like a humorless disciplinarian.

"The job should be simple enough," Alex said. "I'll have to make sure the next person I hire is more capable."

Lizzie ignored the twinge of irritation she felt at his dismissive tone. He didn't really think that taking care of children was simple, did he? He seemed too intelligent to make a dumb statement like that—it must be his lingering anxiety over the twins' close call. "They seem like great kids," she said.

"They're the reason for everything I do," he said softly, seeming to talk more to himself than to her. As if realizing his lapse, he cleared his throat and attempted a smile. "I'm afraid we missed the curtain."

"What curtain?"

"The play I promised you."

She couldn't very well tell him that she'd found this glimpse into his home and his emotions much more fascinating than any Broadway play. "It's okay. But I guess

I'd better get back to the hotel,'' she said, taking a step backward.

"I'd drive you myself, but now that Mrs. Gray isn't here, I can't leave the boys.''

"No, of course not. I'll call a taxi,'' she said, taking another step.

Afterward, she was never sure exactly how it happened. Undoubtedly, the chain of events was triggered by the chunks of dirt from the flower bed that had been trailed inside by Alex's sons. Lizzie's heel came down on a pebble, causing her shoe to slide across the floor unexpectedly. Normally, it wouldn't have been difficult to regain her balance, but because her attention was still focused on Alex, she was slow to react. By the time she did, Alex had already caught hold of her arms to steady her.

Her hands flattened against his chest. "Oh!'' she gasped. "Sorry.''

"No, it's my fault. I should have warned you about the dirt on the floor.''

She shook her head. This was just like what he'd done when she'd spilled her wine at dinner. They both knew that it was her own clumsiness that was responsible for her stumble. He was still trying to be a…prince. Her lips twitched.

His clasp on her arms loosened, but he didn't let her go. "Are you all right?''

She nodded, splaying her fingers over the front of his shirt, feeling a jolt of pleasure from the warmth that rose from his body. And she had a sudden greedy urge to discover what his skin would feel like under her palms…and to see how his chest would look all naked and sweaty…

"It's been a long day. You must be exhausted.''

Oh, did he have to use that love-potion voice? How was she supposed to get a grip on her imagination when he merely had to open his mouth to make her start fantasizing again? She lifted her gaze to his lips. And speaking of mouths, she doubted whether the dollar-a-mouthful wine she'd been enjoying at dinner would be able to compare to a taste of Alex—

"Lizzie?"

And his kiss would probably be a lot more potent than Bobby's cordial. Then again, she suspected that just about anything of Alex's would be more potent than something of Bobby's. "Mmm?"

"I may have to delay our tour of the city tomorrow until I arrange a replacement for Mrs. Gray. And then there are a few things I need to take care of at the office before I pick you up."

"I don't mind waiting," she said. "And if you can't find a baby-sitter, you could always bring the boys with you. It wouldn't be so bad, as long as you check their pockets for worms, and keep them away from the car keys, and don't let them near any purple paint."

"What?"

She glanced up at him and smiled. "I couldn't help noticing what they did to your housekeeper's cat. I hope you took a picture."

It began at the corners of his eyes, as the lines that had been etched with tension started to crinkle with amusement. It spread to the narrow dimples that appeared in his lean cheeks, then finally to his lips as they stretched into an answering smile that wasn't perfect or controlled or charming. Instead, it was real.

And just as Lizzie was trying to absorb the impact of the first genuine smile she'd seen Alex give, he did something that stole her breath altogether. He laughed.

It was brief, and it seemed to surprise him as much as it surprised her, yet it surrounded her with the sudden warmth of sunshine breaking through a cloud. It made her think of hazy August afternoons and skinny-dipping in the pond, of dust motes in the hayloft and sweet kisses trailing down her neck....

"Lizzie," he said, lifting his hand to her cheek. "You have such a refreshing way of looking at things."

Her skin warmed as a blush tingled its way up her neck. His fingertips were smooth, unmarred by the rough calluses of a farmer, and she couldn't help imagining those long, strong fingers squeezing heated flesh... There was a lot to be said for a man without calluses.

She moistened her lips. "You have a wonderful laugh," she murmured.

Alex leaned closer, stroking his thumb over the rise of her cheekbone. "I don't remember the last time I felt like laughing."

"Well, I'm a big believer in doing what comes naturally."

"That's just what Roland used to say."

"He did?"

"Uh-huh. Usually just before he tried to talk me into some offbeat scheme."

That was the second time tonight he'd compared her to Uncle Roland. Maybe she was more like her uncle than she'd thought. The idea pleased her. More than that, it gave her a sudden inspiration. "You know, Alex," she said. "Seeing as how we're partners and all, I might be able to help you out tomorrow."

"How's that?"

"Um, you said you needed time to find a replacement for Mrs. Gray."

"Yes, but..." His thumb stilled. His expression sharpened. "You want to help? What did you have in mind?"

Standing this close to him, with his warmth and his scent

filling her senses, she wasn't about to tell him what she really had in mind, since it involved getting naked and sweaty and—

"I do have some skills that would be useful here," she said quickly. "Especially since you're in a bind with your child care situation."

"I couldn't possibly impose on you that way, Lizzie."

"No, really. It wouldn't be an imposition at all. That's what partners are for, isn't it?"

"That's very generous, but—"

"Alex, it makes sense. And I do want to help. We can go on that tour anytime."

He moved his hand to her shoulder, his fingers curling in a gentle caress. "It's a tempting offer."

And that wasn't the only thing that was tempting, she thought, swaying toward him. "Then how about it? Everyone says I'm a quick study. As long as you tell me what to expect, I'll be able to follow your schedule. Besides, there's nothing like on-the-job training."

"I doubt if you'd need much training, Lizzie."

"Thanks for the vote of confidence, Alex. I have to start someplace, and if Uncle Roland could do it, so can I."

His forehead wrinkled. "Your uncle never baby-sat my boys."

"What does that have to do with it?"

"While I know you must miss the children at your day care center, in all good conscience I couldn't take advantage of you like that, Lizzie. I'm sure you didn't come all the way to New York just to baby-sit. You'll get plenty of that when you go home, so even though I appreciate your offer—"

"Wait a minute, Alex," she interrupted. "Did you think I was offering to baby-sit?"

He paused. "You weren't?"

She shook her head. "Heck, no. Like you said, I get plenty of that back home. I'm talking about helping out at Whitmore and Hamill. I can fill in for you there while you try to find a new housekeeper."

"But—"

"Sometimes the best way to learn to swim is to jump in. You said that my uncle learned from experience, so the way I see it, this would be a great opportunity for me to start learning the business. It's what we talked about at dinner, remember? After all, I am your partner."

For a minute he stared at her in silence. All traces of the humor that had softened his face only moments ago disappeared. So did the warmth. Dropping his hands, he stepped back. "I remember our conversation vividly, but what you're proposing is out of the question."

"You need my help."

"Lizzie, anyone can learn to baby-sit, but a business requires certain skills that—"

"Hold on there. Taking care of children can be just as challenging as running a company. And if you combine child care with housekeeping duties, it's even more difficult. It requires its own special skills."

"I'm sure it does," he said soothingly.

"Have you ever done it?"

"What?"

"Have you ever tried to do the laundry and cook a meal while you took care of a houseful of children?"

"No, but you can't seriously compare that kind of job with the responsibilities of running my company."

"*Our* company," she reminded him. "I still own half."

A muscle jumped in his cheek. "I'm fully aware of that, Lizzie."

"Dealing with children and keeping a household running smoothly are very much like dealing with an office staff and keeping a business going. It involves a lot of the same basic managerial skills and quick thinking, it's just a difference in the scale of the operation.''

He shook his head. ''Lizzie, I'm sorry, but you're over-simplifying things. No offense meant, but any responsible adult can do my housekeeper's job or work in a day care center. Running Whitmore and Hamill is something else entirely.''

Until today, she likely would have agreed with him. She'd spent most of her life downplaying her capabilities, but there was something about the way Alex was looking at her, his gaze gleaming with that combination of challenge and awareness, that made her want to prove to both of them that he was wrong. Maybe it was the lingering effect of the dollar-a-mouthful wine, or the thrill of the plane ride, or the sight of her name engraved on that brass plaque…

What would Uncle Roland have done?

Without having met him, there was no way for her to know for certain, but somehow Lizzie was positive that her uncle would have been willing to take a chance. So why shouldn't she? After all, what did she have to lose? If she let this opportunity slip by, she might as well pack her bags right now and catch the next flight back to Pack-enham Junction.

Her pulse pounding with anticipation, Lizzie took a deep breath and drew herself up. ''Let me get this straight,'' she said carefully. ''Do you honestly believe that someone with your skills and experience could do your house-keeper's job more easily than someone with my skills could manage Whitmore and Hamill?''

''Yes, I do.''

Her lips stretched into a reckless grin. ''Want to bet?''

Chapter Four

Alex frowned, certain he must have misunderstood her again. She couldn't possibly be suggesting... "A bet?"

"Let's call it a friendly wager," Lizzie said. "You manage your household tomorrow and I'll manage the office, and whoever can keep things running the most smoothly wins."

He stared at her. "You can't be serious."

"Don't you think you'd be able to handle a housekeeper's duties?"

"Of course, I could handle that. Anyone could."

Her eyebrows lifted in a devilish arch. "You think so? How many trained, professional housekeepers have you gone through in the past year?"

"That's irrelevant."

"A lot, huh? That proves my point. It's not as easy as you think."

"Lizzie, I'm sure your intentions are good, but you have to admit you're not qualified to take on a job as involved as this."

"That didn't stop Uncle Roland," she said, smiling tentatively.

Roland. Alex gritted his teeth. He couldn't forget she was a Hamill. And the family resemblance went deeper than her appearance. Beneath her wholesome, fresh-from-the-farm innocence there was a mind that was as sharp and ambitious as her uncle's. And like Roland, she had a special talent for coming up with off-the-wall ideas whose sole purpose seemed to be to shake up his nice, orderly existence.

It was his worst nightmare. It was precisely what he'd feared would happen when he'd heard what Roland had done in his will. Only a month ago, the dream of complete control of the company had been within Alex's grasp, but now...

Where had it started to go wrong? At what point had the situation spun out of control?

Probably from the moment Alex got his first good look at Lizzie Hamill's legs.

Raking his hands through his hair, he turned around and strode across the foyer. He had to deal with this carefully. He couldn't afford a confrontation over their partnership because if Lizzie took it into her head that she was going to claim her uncle's place, Alex wouldn't have the right to stop her. His only recourse would be a long, drawn out legal battle that would probably be even more harmful to his company than Lizzie's ineptness.

He pressed his fingertips to his temples, trying to drive away the dull throbbing. For a while there, when Lizzie had stumbled into his arms, he had forgotten about his headache. He'd been so caught up in her smile and her scent and the sensation of her hands against his chest that he'd forgotten just about everything else, too.

It was nothing but chemistry. As inexplicable and senseless as it was, it was only a natural reaction. It was bound to happen to him eventually, considering the monklike existence he'd been living since his divorce. After the lesson Tiffany had taught him, he hadn't wanted to risk letting any woman get close to him again. But of all people, why did the chemistry have to happen with Lizzie Hamill?

He couldn't explain it. She wasn't his type. He'd never been attracted to unsophisticated women, or innocent smiles, or uncontrollable red hair. Yet the more he was around Lizzie, the stronger the attraction became. It had only been twelve hours since she'd burst into his life— how powerful would the attraction get if she stayed around longer?

Good God, he didn't want to risk finding out. He had to think. He had to approach this rationally.

Her heels clicked on the marble tile as she followed him across the floor. "I don't see why you're so opposed to the idea, Alex," she continued. "I wanted to get a feel for what the company does, and this is as good a time as any, right?"

Wrong. He didn't want her anywhere near his company. If he went along with this crazy bet, she would undoubtedly bring about the most disastrous day in the history of Whitmore and Hamill....

He inhaled sharply. That was it! If she was so determined to get a taste of the advertising business, maybe he should give her what she asked. It wouldn't take more than a few hours for her to realize how ill-suited she was. After a full day, she'd probably be more than ready to give up her crazy idea about being an active partner. The havoc she would undoubtedly wreak would be a small price to pay if it convinced her to relinquish her shares.

Damn, he couldn't believe he was even considering this. It would be totally unfair to take her up on her bet, since there was no way he could lose. He'd run a profitable business for more than a decade. Stepping into a house-keeper's role would be child's play. Lizzie, on the other hand, would be completely out of her depth.

But if that's what she wanted…

Squaring his shoulders, he turned to face her. "Just for tomorrow?"

Her lips curved into one of her teasing, maddeningly kissable smiles. "Are you worried about the damage you'll do at home?"

"That's not what worries me."

"Good. It'll be fun, you'll see. Now, what about the stakes?"

"Stakes?"

"What do you want if you win?"

A kiss, he thought immediately. He wanted to pull her back into his arms and lower his head and meld his mouth to hers and revel in her freshness and innocence. He wanted to forget who she was and who he was and simply be a man who was feeling an illogical, irrational attraction to a woman…

He frowned, pulling back. No, that's not what he should want. He wanted her gone, the sooner the better. "You decide."

"Whoever wins buys dinner?" she suggested.

Alex clasped Lizzie's hand to seal the bet. It wasn't exactly the approach he'd planned, but for the cost of a meal and a day with his sons, what did he have to lose?

LIZZIE STEPPED OUT of the elevator and pressed a hand over her stomach, trying to quiet the butterflies. The hall was dim and the semicircular reception desk where Pamela usually sat was still deserted. In her determination not to be late, she'd ended up getting here too early.

Well, that was good. She was going to need some time to figure out what the heck she was supposed to do today.

Taking a deep breath, Lizzie smoothed her skirt and started toward the office at the end of the corridor. She hadn't been able to sleep last night. It hadn't only been the strange bed and the strange city, it was the excitement. This was even better than that plane trip. She couldn't remember the last time she'd felt this eager to start the day.

The first thing she needed to do was to check Alex's calendar and then go over his schedule with Rita—it had been her experience that secretaries tended to know what was going on better than their bosses. And Lizzie was sure that the rest of the staff would be able to answer any questions that came up—they'd seemed cooperative enough when she'd met them yesterday.

Alex had said that his job consisted of coordinating the people who worked for Whitmore and Hamill, so Lizzie was pretty sure she could do that, at least for one day. She had plenty of experience in delegating work. Considering the juggling acts she'd done while she'd managed the farm, taken care of the younger kids and her bedridden stepfather, enrolled in those correspondence courses in accounting and helped Ben start up the cheese factory, concentrating on one business at a time couldn't be all that far beyond her capabilities.

But Alex's capabilities were another matter. Poor Alex. It wasn't his fault that he obviously had no idea what he was in for. Plenty of men didn't appreciate just how demanding the role of a housekeeper could be. Judging by what she'd seen of those twins, they'd probably keep Alex hopping for most of the day. Maybe it hadn't been entirely fair of her to goad him into this bet, since there was no way he could win. She'd just have to be extra gracious when she bought him dinner.

If his day at home was even half as bad as she expected, he'd be needing a decent meal.

Talk about a win-win situation. Not only was she going

to have the chance to prove she could be part of Whitmore and Hamill, she was going to spend another evening with her partner.

And then, who knew? If they spent enough time together, maybe their partnership could expand to a more...personal level.

Her steps slowed as she neared the door to Alex's office. He was way out of her league. He was rich and sophisticated and had an ex-wife named Tiffany. She grimaced, imagining the elegant woman who probably went with that name. Probably a model-thin blonde who called everybody "dahling" and who had long nails that clacked when she took out her platinum credit cards.

Still, Lizzie had definitely seen a flash of *something* in Alex's gaze when they'd stood so close together. Was it really too much to hope that she wasn't the only one who felt the tug of awareness, that growing connection between them? Maybe the next time she stumbled into his arms, he'd stroke more than her cheek. Maybe he'd release those emotions he tried so hard to keep under control and she'd discover whether his lips really did taste as good as they looked and...

She paused beside Rita's desk, raising her hands to her cheeks as she felt the spreading blush. Just the thought of Alex was enough to get her pulse thudding. Who cared if he was light-years out of her league? There were some signals between the sexes that were universal. Since Bobby, she hadn't been willing to take a chance with another man. Maybe it was time she did.

Whitmore and Hamill. Their names were already linked on the company letterhead. She'd come this far, so why not go for broke? This trip might turn out to be more than a chance for adventure, it might be a chance to resurrect her dreams of love and children of her own and—

"Don't argue with me, Jeremy. I want it ready by the end of the day."

The muffled voice jarred her back to reality. She'd been so wrapped up in her imaginings that she hadn't realized that someone else had arrived. She dropped her hands and glanced around.

"Are you sure, Alex? A twenty percent increase would leave you in a difficult position."

"In the long run, it'll be worth it."

Lizzie frowned when she realized that the voices were coming from Alex's office. From the sound of it, Alex was in there with his lawyer.

Why wasn't he at home with the boys? Unless he'd brought them with him. But if that were the case, why hadn't she heard them? Those twins hadn't struck her as the type of children who would be content to sit quietly while their father discussed business.

"I take it that your campaign to, uh, soften her up is going well?" Jeremy asked.

Curious, Lizzie moved closer to the office. The door wasn't exactly ajar, but it hadn't been completely closed, either. A narrow strip of light seeped past the edge, along with the conversation that was going on inside.

She probably shouldn't interrupt—it was obviously a private meeting. But if this campaign they were talking about was important enough for Alex to arrange a meeting at this hour, then it was her duty to learn about it, wasn't it? she reasoned, reaching for the doorknob.

"It took a few unexpected turns," Alex said. "But I'm confident I'll get a satisfactory outcome. After today, she'll be ready to sell."

"To tell you the truth, I'm not surprised," Jeremy said. "From what I saw during our meeting yesterday, she was completely dazzled, just as you planned. Actually, she appeared to be quite taken with you.''

Yesterday? Lizzie hesitated. She hadn't known that Alex had met with a client yesterday. He'd been busy with her right up until that meeting in his office with Jeremy…

She bit her lip on a wave of embarrassment as the realization struck. Dazzled…a campaign to soften her up… They were talking about *her*. Oh, Lord. She'd known that Alex was being nice to her because he wanted to buy her out, but she hadn't realized she'd been that transparent about her feelings. How on earth was she going to face Alex after this?

''That's irrelevant,'' Alex muttered.

''Not really,'' Jeremy said, clearing his throat. ''If you, um, encourage her, she'd probably be more cooperative.''

Encourage? Lizzie thought. Like taking her home with him, and letting her meet his children, and catching her when she stumbled and stroking her cheek…

There was a brief silence before Alex spoke again. ''Any personal relationship between the two of us is out of the question,'' he said firmly. ''The sooner I can send Elizabeth Hamill back home, the better. She doesn't belong here. And after today, she'll see that for herself.''

''What do you mean?''

''Why do you think I agreed to this absurd bet?''

''To tell you the truth, I had been wondering about that.''

''Her expertise is limited to children and cheese, so she's bound to fail today. And once she does, she'll get rid of her misguided notion about becoming my partner. Damn that Roland,'' he said, his voice growing closer. ''This is all his doing. If Lizzie wasn't a Hamill, I could almost pity her.''

Absurd bet? Misguided notion? *Pity?*

Alex's words struck her like a pail of water that had been left on the porch in December. He had stated flat out that there was no chance of a relationship between them. He hadn't even taken her idea about contributing to the company seriously. He wasn't going to let her prove herself. He didn't have any faith in her abilities at all. While she'd been dreaming of a genuine partnership, he'd only been humoring her. He wanted to send her back home.

God, she'd been an idiot. A pathetic, softened-up, bedazzled fool. Alex didn't want her. He would never want her. He only wanted to use her.

It was Bobby all over again.

Before she could move away, the doorknob was wrenched out of her hand and Alex walked into her.

She staggered backward with the force of the collision. Alex muttered an oath and dropped his briefcase to grasp her shoulders. "Lizzie! Are you all right?"

The pain she felt in her chest wasn't only physical, but she wasn't ever going to admit that he'd hurt her. It was her own fault, her own stupidity, just another example of good old Lizzie's pathetic imagination.

Clenching her jaw, she met his gaze. "Hello, Alex," she said tightly.

"I'm sorry," he said. "I didn't know you were already here."

Hurt and humiliation continued to churn inside her, but now something else joined them. It was anger. Good, clean, straightforward fury. At Alex. At herself. At life for teasing her with hope, yet again, only to snatch it away. "Yeah, I figured that out."

He released her shoulders and stepped back, straightening his tie. "The staff won't be in for another hour or so. Is there anything I can help you with?"

She stared at him, wishing that she had the ability to

control her emotions as well as he did. Despite what she'd heard, despite what she told herself, she still felt a lingering warmth from the place where he'd touched her. And somehow, that only made her anger grow. "Where are the boys, Alex?"

"Excuse me?"

"Daniel and Jason, remember? Your sons?"

"They're at home," he said, leaning over to retrieve his briefcase. "I had a meeting—"

"Who's watching them?"

He straightened up. "I arranged for a baby-sitter."

"A baby-sitter? You mean you already found a replacement for Mrs. Gray?"

"Not yet. This is just a college girl who comes in on occasion. Luckily, she was free this morning."

She glared at him. Lifting her hand, she poked her finger into his chest. "That's cheating."

"Now, Lizzie," he began.

"You were supposed to do your housekeeper's duties. That includes staying with your boys, right? Or are you conceding our wager already?"

"There were some details I needed to take care of here first—"

"So I heard." Brushing past him, she walked into his office. "Hello, Jeremy," she said.

The lawyer glanced from her to Alex, his Adam's apple bobbing jerkily as he swallowed. "Uh, good morning, Miss Hamill."

"You might as well call me Lizzie," she said, stopping when she reached Alex's desk. "We'll probably be working together. Unless you share Alex's nasty habit of dishonesty."

Jeremy's eyes widened behind his glasses. "Uh…"

"There's no reason to overreact, Lizzie," Alex said, following her across the office.

She moved behind his desk before he could reach her and turned to face him, more secure now that there was a barrier of wood between them. "Gee, Alex. Maybe I've been working with children and cheese too long, but back where I come from, people are expected to keep their word when they agree to a bet, even if it's absurd, even if they figure they'll win."

He stiffened. "How long were you listening?"

"Long enough. You have no intention of working with me as a partner, do you? You figure I'm going to fail."

To his credit, he didn't try to deny what she'd overheard. Keeping his movements carefully controlled, he set his briefcase on a corner of the desk and held out his palms. "I'm sorry, Lizzie. But maybe it's best to be honest about this."

"Honest?" She snorted. "Why did you come here today, Alex?"

"I had a meeting with Jeremy."

"To ask him to increase the offer on my shares? You could have done that on the phone." Her gaze sharpened. "What's in the briefcase, Alex?"

Jeremy gave a strangled cough and retreated to the armchairs in front of the window.

"Well?" she persisted.

"Just some papers," Alex answered. "Nothing you should be concerned about."

She stepped around the chair, slid the briefcase in front of her and snapped open the lid. It was crammed full of files and glossy reports. On top of the pile was an embossed leather notebook. She snatched it up and flipped it open.

It took her a moment to realize what she was looking

at. When she did, a fresh surge of anger stabbed through her. She'd been so gullible, so trusting. Good old Lizzie. Always trying to please everyone else, always putting her own wants last.

And always trying to see princes where there were nothing but toads.

"This is your calendar," she said. "Tell me, Alex. How was I supposed to do your job without this?"

"As I said yesterday, I'm sure your intentions are good, but you're not qualified—"

"I'm a Hamill," she said. "That's all the qualification I need to be a partner in this company." She waved the leather notebook in his face. "But you weren't even willing to give me a fair chance, were you? That's why you wanted to get here before me and remove everything I'd need if I wanted to succeed, right?"

"No, I wanted to be able to reschedule my appointments personally to ensure our clients didn't become concerned. I was merely being prudent."

"Prudent?" She slammed the book on the desktop. "You were trying to rig the bet!"

He didn't flinch. "I wouldn't put it like that. No one could blame me for trying to minimize the possible damage of a day of amateur management. I don't want to risk the welfare of my company on some whim."

"*Our* company," she said through her teeth.

"Perhaps on paper, but realistically—"

"Hey, I might be straight off the farm, Alex, but I know when someone's trying to keep me away from my cow. As long as I own fifty percent of Whitmore and Hamill, I don't need your permission or your approval for anything. Right, Jeremy?"

Jeremy squirmed and tried to sink farther into the armchair. "Uh, that's correct."

Alex breathed in hard, his nostrils flaring. "Stay out of this, Jeremy."

"I'm sorry, Alex, but since I'm acting as the firm's sole attorney at the moment, technically I do work for Miss Hamill as well."

Lizzie nodded. "I'm glad you see it my way."

Alex braced his fingertips on the desktop and leaned toward her. "What's it going to take for you to sell, Lizzie? You want more money? Fine. I'll double my original offer."

"Maybe I don't want your money, Alex. Maybe I want—" She broke off, aghast at the words that she'd almost said. What did she want? Not Alex. No, she wasn't going to be that much of a fool. "I want what's mine," she said.

"So do I."

"You want more than that. You want me gone."

He stared at her in silence, his gaze snapping with intensity. But she wasn't fool enough to mistake his emotion again. No, that confusing mix of challenge and awareness wasn't for her, it was for the business.

With disbelief, she felt her eyes fill. Blinking the tears away, she pushed back her sleeve and checked her watch. "Don't let me keep you, Alex. The twins are probably expecting their breakfast."

"Lizzie, there's no point continuing this farce of a bet."

"Not as it stands, no. But what if we raised the stakes?"

"What do you mean?"

"You want me gone," she repeated. "Fine. If I lose, I'll leave."

He jerked. "What?"

"You heard me. I'll sell you my shares and go home to Packenham Junction."

"Why would you agree to that?"

Why? Her hopes of a partnership, any kind of partnership, with Alex were shattered. Yet she still had something to prove. All the years of helping everyone else, all the times she'd been sensible and self-sacrificing, everything she'd told herself she was happy with suddenly came into merciless focus. For her pride, for herself, she wasn't going to let her uncle's legacy slip away without a fight. She propped her fists on the edge of the desk. "What good is owning half the cow if you never let me milk it?"

"Why do you keep mentioning cows?" Jeremy asked. "Alex, are you investing in livestock?"

Alex ignored him, his gaze never wavering from Lizzie's. "Are you sure you want to do this?"

"You don't believe in me, but my family does, and I think my uncle did. I'm betting that I can run this business profitably, and I'm fully willing to gamble my half of it to find out. At this point, I have nothing to lose."

"One day isn't long enough to determine a profit."

"Then we'll make it a month. I run the business and you run your house." She paused. "But if you lose, you sell me one percent of Whitmore and Hamill."

His jaw tightened. "That would put you in control."

"Yes, it would. If that's what it takes to give me a choice, then that's what I want. Think of it as the New York version of betting the farm." Her heart pounding, she lifted her chin. "Everything or nothing, Alex. Winner takes all."

"Agreed."

His quick acceptance surprised her. But it shouldn't have. He'd already been convinced she was going to lose. She gestured toward the calendar she'd found in his briefcase. "After the way you tried to fix our original bet, how do I know you won't try to cheat me again?" she asked.

Anger flashed in his gaze. "I wasn't cheating, I was being practical."

She narrowed her eyes. "Benjamin's brother-in-law thought he was being practical when he played poker with a marked deck, but he ended up with a black eye and a dent in his pickup just the same. But maybe people who work in a cheese factory and don't wear suits on their day off have a different definition of honor."

"Jeremy," Alex growled. "I want you to be a witness."

"Better put it in writing, Jeremy," Lizzie said. "Pack it full of lawyer words like *whereas* and *notwithstanding* just so there's no weaseling out."

Moving reluctantly, Jeremy reached for the pad of paper on the table in front of him and uncapped his pen. "Perhaps you both should take some time to reconsider."

"No need," Alex said. "Effective immediately, I am taking a one month leave of absence from Whitmore and Hamill and will act as housekeeper and sole caregiver for my children. Elizabeth Hamill will take over my duties at the company. If Whitmore and Hamill shows a profit after thirty days, then I agree to sell her one percent of the shares in the company." He leaned farther across the desk until his face was mere inches away from Lizzie's. "And if at the end of thirty days the company shows a loss, Miss Hamill agrees to sell me her fifty percent."

Jeremy scribbled furiously. "Alex, I can't condone this. It's very irregular."

"And," Lizzie said, her pulse racing as she returned Alex's gaze. "Any evidence of cheating, no matter how minor, will mean forfeiting the bet. That includes hiring any form of household help."

Alex narrowed his eyes. "Fine. Furthermore," he said, his voice growing ominously quiet. "In the interest of the company, I reserve the right to monitor Miss Hamill's performance. To do that, I'll need full access to this office at any time.''

''All right,'' Lizzie said. ''But let's keep this even. I have a right to monitor Mr. Whitmore's competence in his household duties, so I'll need full access to his house at any time, too.''

''Go ahead. Better yet, why don't you move in?'' Alex said through his teeth. ''The housekeeper's suite happens to be vacant.''

''Fine. Just so long as the bill I've racked up at that fancy hotel you put me in comes off the books *before* we start keeping track of the profit.''

''Fine.''

''Great.''

Alex's teeth were clenched so tightly, a muscle ticked in his jaw. His nostrils flared. ''There's one last condition.''

''Name it.''

''If either party reneges on this agreement before the end of the full month, they forfeit the bet.''

Lizzie nodded sharply. ''Agreed.''

''We'll start as soon as I can inform the staff about the temporary change in management.''

''Go ahead and tell whoever you want, Alex, but the bet doesn't start until Jeremy gets everything drawn up in legalese and I see you sign it,'' Lizzie said. ''I'm not gullible enough to rely on a handshake to seal the deal this time.''

If she'd expected to prick his temper with the insult, she was mistaken. He didn't reply. Instead, his gaze dropped to her lips. And despite herself, Lizzie immediately thought of another means they could use to seal their agreement. The way they were both leaning across the desk, it wouldn't take much for either one of them to lean a bit farther, to close the gap between them until their lips melded....

It was completely crazy to think about kissing him. After what he'd said about her, and what he'd done, kissing him should be the last thing on her mind. She was angry, she was hurt and she'd been a fool. Yet with her emotions running high and her blood pumping and her breath coming in quick, sharp pants, her body was too stimulated to care.

"You're not going to get what you want, Lizzie," Alex murmured.

Maybe not. Then again, that all depended on what it was that she wanted.

Chapter Five

Alex scanned the document carefully, pleased to see that Jeremy had done a thorough job in spite of the rush. Alex's copy of the countersigned agreement had been delivered to the house by courier first thing this morning, with every *t* crossed and *i* dotted and even a few *whereas*es and *notwithstanding*s thrown in for good measure. So as soon as Lizzie checked out of her hotel—and settled the bill—the bet would officially be on.

And thirty days from now, Whitmore and Hamill would be all his.

And Lizzie would be gone.

Determinedly, he tamped down the stab of regret at the thought of her leaving. He *did* want her gone. He didn't want her in his company or in his life. And despite the unorthodox way it would come about, he would be giving her more than a fair price for her shares. In the long run, he hoped she'd see that it was the best solution. For both of them.

Now all he had to worry about was whether or not there would be a company left at the end of the month after Lizzie got through with it.

He slipped the agreement into the top drawer of the antique desk, then leaned back in the chair and rubbed his jaw, feeling the unfamiliar rasp of unshaved whiskers. If it wasn't for the concern about what was happening to his company in his absence, he might have enjoyed this time at home. How long had it been since he'd had a vacation? It must have been years, probably since before the twins were born, back when Roland had still pulled his weight in the business.

Now he remembered. He and Tiffany had spent a week in Paris. Paris had been Tiffany's choice, but she'd been more interested in the fashion houses than the culture. No, actually they hadn't spent the entire week there. His wife had grown bored and had wanted to return home early. It hadn't been what he would call a relaxing vacation.

But he'd done his best, hadn't he? He'd bought Tiffany whatever she wanted, no matter how expensive or frivolous. And after the twins had come along, he'd let her choose this house and hire the decorator, and he'd never complained about the spindly antiques that looked as if they'd crack beneath his weight. He hadn't objected to her parties or her trips to Aspen or her demands for a new car practically every time the ashtray got full in the old one. He'd given her everything he was capable of, yet it hadn't been enough. He would have been better off not marrying in the first place....

He shook his head, not wanting to reopen all the old wounds. Tiffany had said she loved him, but *love* was just a word, a tool that women used in order to get their way. He'd learned from his mistake. He would never set himself up to be vulnerable to that kind of failure again. He was in control of his life now, and a permanent relationship with a woman wasn't something that fit into his plans. Still, while he no longer believed in marriage, he could never regret the fact that marriage had given him Daniel and Jason.

Lacing his fingers together, he stretched his arms over his head and glanced at the clock. It had been a long time since he'd spent a full day with his sons. They'd still been asleep when he'd looked in on them before he'd come downstairs this morning. Just as he had expected, it was shaping up to be a quiet day.

He doubted whether things were going this smoothly for Lizzie. The revised campaign for Starcourt was scheduled to be presented to John Fletcher this afternoon. It was an exercise in futility, since even the impossible-to-please Fletcher knew that nothing short of a miracle would salvage that account. Alex would wait until the dust had settled before he called Lizzie for a progress report—she was bound to feel bad about a failure on the first day of the bet, and it wouldn't be sporting if he gloated. In the meantime, he might as well take advantage of this unaccustomed leisure time and have another cup of coffee, he decided, pushing away from his desk and tucking the morning paper under his arm as he left the study.

Something gritted under his feet as he crossed the hall. Frowning, he noticed the scattered bits of dirt that dulled the floor. For a split second he wondered why Mrs. Gray hadn't already seen to it, but then he shook his head ruefully and turned toward the kitchen. It was odd how accustomed he'd grown to the type of life he lived now. He'd have to take care of that floor after breakfast. No problem there. All he'd need would be a broom.

What would Lizzie think if she knew that he already had plenty of experience wielding a broom? Sweeping the floor at Shannahan's Fruit Market had been his very first job. He'd been fourteen and big for his age, so it hadn't taken long for him to progress to box boy and then to produce manager. He'd worked every spare minute after school and on the weekends, trying to save each penny he earned. Come to think of it, he hadn't taken a vacation then, either.

An acrid smell struck Alex the moment he pushed through the swinging door to the kitchen. He wrinkled his nose and looked around, trying to determine the source. He was sure he hadn't left anything on in here except for the coffeemaker…

"Great," he muttered, setting his newspaper on the stove as he strode to the counter. A tarry black coating covered the bottom of the glass carafe that should have held his second cup of coffee. Evidently, he'd failed to put enough water in the thing and it had boiled dry.

In truth, he wasn't all that disappointed. The first cup that coffeemaker had produced this morning hadn't been anywhere near as good as the kind Mrs. Gray used to make, but he was bound to get the knack of it next time. Automatic coffeemakers weren't particularly complicated. He'd simply clean out the bottom and start again.

He eyed the stack of dishes beside the sink, reminding himself to load those into the dishwasher after he rinsed out the coffeemaker. But the moment he put the carafe under the faucet, there was a loud crack. Shards of shattered glass clunked into the sink and he was left holding nothing but a plastic handle and an empty metal collar.

Alex shut off the water and stared at the empty handle. He couldn't believe he'd done something that stupid. Whether he was accustomed to automatic coffeemakers or not, any schoolkid knew what happened when hot glass came into contact with cold water. Clenching his jaw, he looked at the line of blood that was welling up on the pad of his thumb where a piece of glass had sliced his skin. He wrapped a handkerchief around it, then picked the rest of the glass out of the sink.

He was just putting the last of it in the garbage when

he heard a low rumbling coming from outside the house. Vibrations traveled through the floor to the soles of his feet. Puzzled, he looked past the breakfast nook to the bay window just as a bright yellow bulldozer lumbered across the lawn.

"What the…" Alex pressed the handkerchief more firmly against his thumb and strode outside.

A man in coveralls stood at the edge of the drive, directing a dump truck past the gateposts as it turned in from the street. When he caught sight of Alex, he hurried toward him. "We'll get started as soon as you show me where you want it. You're lucky we had a cancellation. Our equipment's usually booked up for weeks at this time of year."

"What?" Alex asked. "What are you talking about?"

"The swimming pool." He propped a pencil behind his ear and looked at a clipboard. "This is the Whitmore place, right?"

Alex nodded, tilting his head to read the work order the man was pointing to. The name of the landscaping company he'd called yesterday was at the top of the paper, along with his address, but… "There must be some mistake," he said. "I didn't order any pool. There already is one behind the house."

"You sure?"

"Yes, I'm sure. All I ordered was a gardening crew to repair the lawn and the front flower bed." He waved at the truck driver, trying to get him to stop, but it was too late. The vehicle's oversize tires sank into the ruts where the grass had already been chewed up by the bulldozer.

"Must have been Ethel who took the order," the man said, shaking his head as he pulled a phone out of his coveralls. "Poor kid. She's been under stress lately. Boyfriend trouble," he added with a wink. "Don't worry, Mr. Whitmore, we'll get this straightened out in a minute."

The minute stretched into twenty while a tearful Ethel tracked down her boss in order to get the necessary authorization to cancel the work order. It wasn't until half an hour later that the last of the heavy equipment finally rumbled back to the street. Alex rubbed the back of his neck as he surveyed the fresh damage. Compared to this, the tracks the twins' joyride had left were barely noticeable.

"Great," he muttered, turning back toward the house. He could really use a second cup of coffee right about now. He looked at the blood-spotted handkerchief he'd wrapped around his thumb. He could also use a bandage.

The moment he neared the side door, he heard a high-pitched noise coming from inside. Concerned, he increased his pace, following the sound back to the kitchen. It wasn't until he saw the flames that he realized the noise was the smoke alarm.

The newspaper that he'd left on the stove was on fire.

Alex grabbed the fire extinguisher from its hook beside the door and depressed the trigger. A stream of foam shot down the front of his shirt and splashed to the floor. Smoke continued to billow upward as the paper crackled. Swearing under his breath, he rotated the extinguisher, adjusted his aim and moved closer. Within seconds, the flames were smothered beneath a quivering layer of white.

He coughed, waving his arm to get rid of the drifting wisps of smoke. How the hell had that happened? he wondered, reaching out to switch off the stove. He was positive he hadn't touched the controls for the elements—

"Hey, that was cool!"

"Can I have a turn?"

Over the continuing shriek of the smoke alarm and the

ticking and hissing of the cooling element, Alex heard his sons' voices. He lowered the fire extinguisher and looked around.

Jason and Daniel were perched on top of the work island in the center of the kitchen, their bare feet dangling as they swung their legs back and forth. A frying pan rested beside one twin, an open box of pancake mix was beside the other and a dusting of white powder covered them both. "Hi, Dad!" they chorused.

His hands shaking, he set the extinguisher on the floor and stared at the boys. They appeared unhurt. No burns, no soot. As a matter of fact, they were both wearing identical grins. He swallowed hard. "What happened?"

"We were gonna fix breakfast," Jason said.

"Mrs. Gray always fixes pancakes on Thursdays," Daniel added, rubbing the flour from his nose with the back of his hand.

"Yeah. Where's Monica?"

"What?" Alex shook his head, unable to concentrate over the continuous shriek of the alarm. "Hang on," he ordered. "Don't either of you move." He searched for the source of the noise, finally spotting the smoke detector on the ceiling just in front of the swinging door. Gritting his teeth against his aching eardrums, he searched in vain for a switch to turn the alarm off, then pried the cover off and yanked out the battery.

His ears ringing in the sudden silence, he went over to where the twins were sitting. "All right, what happened?" he repeated.

Jason and Daniel exchanged looks, their grins fading.

"Boys?"

"Hey, where's Monica?" Daniel asked, hopping to the floor. He skipped over to where the flame-retardant foam had spattered in front of the stove and stamped his feet.

White droplets splashed up the legs of his pyjamas. "She gave us French toast yesterday. Maybe she can fix pancakes."

"Monica had exams and won't be coming here today," Alex said. "You're not going to have a baby-sitter. I'll be staying home, so I'll fix your breakfast."

They both stared at him, their mouths dropping open.

For some reason, the shock on their faces made Alex feel guilty.

Why would they look so surprised? Because he was staying home, or because he was going to cook? Granted, he spent most of his time at work, but there was no reason to feel guilty over that. It was a fact of life for working parents everywhere. It wasn't as if he neglected his sons. And all the time he spent away was for their sake, so he could give them what he'd never had. "I've decided to take a...vacation," he continued. "So for the next few weeks, it'll be just the three of us."

"Hey, *cool*," Daniel said. "Can we go to McDonald's like last night?"

Still disturbed by the twinge of guilt, Alex was about to agree in spite of his loathing for fast food. But then he remembered the conditions Lizzie had put on the wager. Would going to a fast-food place instead of cooking dinner himself be considered cheating? He wasn't going to risk giving her grounds to claim that he forfeited because of a cheeseburger. "Not tonight," he said, his gaze going to the charred remains of his newspaper. "Who turned on the stove?"

"Don't remember," Jason mumbled as he dropped to the floor. He raced over to his brother, bracing his legs to skid through the foam.

Alex raked his fingers through his hair distractedly. He winced when he felt the cut on his thumb open up again.

"Well, regardless of who did it, you both could have been badly hurt. I don't want you to do it again."

"Okay," Daniel said, bending over to investigate the fire extinguisher.

"I'd prefer it if you don't touch that," Alex said.

Daniel grabbed the canister and squeezed the trigger. Foam squirted onto Jason's toes, eliciting a round of giggles.

"Give me a turn," Jason demanded, grabbing for the fire extinguisher.

"Daniel, put it down," Alex ordered, moving to intercept him.

Daniel danced out of reach and squirted his brother again before he whirled around and ran out of the room.

Jason whooped and raced after him.

"Jason, Daniel, you come back here!" Alex called, increasing his pace. The moment he stepped on the trail of foam, his feet shot out from under him. The next thing he knew, he was flat on his back, staring at the cloud of smoke that hung beneath the ceiling.

And at that precise moment, the telephone began to ring.

LIZZIE DRUMMED her fingers on the edge of her uncle's desk as she listened to the ringing on the other end of the line. Alex had better not be trying to put something over on her again, she thought, pressing her lips together. The terms of the bet had been laid out in black and white. And he'd signed it. So if he thought he was going to play her for a fool before she had the chance to check up on him…

The anger that had propelled her through yesterday hadn't completely worn off. Neither had the hurt. That was good, Lizzie thought. She had a feeling she was going to need to draw on both in order to get her through the next thirty days.

There was a click and a loud clunk, as if someone had dropped the receiver. A second later, a gravelly voice came on the line. "What?"

Lizzie hesitated, glancing at the high-tech telephone she'd commandeered for this office. According to the name that was displayed on the screen, she was connected to the Whitmore place, but this sure didn't sound like her partner. She lifted her eyebrows. "Alex?"

He cleared his throat. "Hello, Lizzie," he said, his voice restored to the smooth, love-potion tones that she knew. There was a wet squeak, then a squishy sound, as if he had just slid his hand through some kind of lather....

Her hand tightened on the receiver. Lather? Had she caught him in the shower? Was he even now standing there on the other end of the line with his skin beaded with water and a towel wrapped around his hips...or maybe no towel...?

She slammed the door on that particular thought. It was that love-potion voice of his, that's all. She had no interest in what he was doing or how he was dressed, as long as he was fulfilling his half of the deal.

"I wanted to be sure you received your copy of the agreement," Lizzie said, sitting up straighter.

"Yes, Jeremy couriered it a few hours ago. I assume that you received yours?"

"Jeremy had it delivered to the hotel before I came in this morning."

"I see. And how are things at the office, Lizzie?"

She eyed the stack of files that Rita had dropped on the desk half an hour ago. Lizzie had asked to see summaries of the firm's major accounts, as well as the financial statements of the past two years. It was going to take her a lot longer than she'd figured to become even moderately familiar with the business—every available surface in her uncle's once vacant office was covered with material she needed to study. "Things are going fine here," she answered. "What about you?"

There was a faint splash. "No problem," he said.

She made a wry face. She'd been expecting him to be in the middle of some kind of crisis by now, but instead, he was lounging around in the bathroom. She must have underestimated his abilities. "And how are the boys?"

"They're fine. As a matter of fact, I was just going to get them some breakfast. Is there something else you wanted to discuss?"

A knock sounded on the office door. Lizzie glanced up to see Rita standing there with another armful of files. She waved her inside. "Not at the moment, Alex. If I think of something, I'll let you know tonight."

"Tonight?"

"Yes," she said, gesturing for Rita to put the files on the leather couch beside the wall. "I've checked out of the hotel, so I'll be there by eight."

There was a pause. "You mean you're moving in here tonight?"

"It's what we agreed on, remember?"

He coughed. "Of course. Excuse me, but I have something on the stove," he said abruptly. "Goodbye, Lizzie."

The dial tone hummed in her ear. Lizzie replaced the receiver and leaned forward, propping her chin on her palm. What was that little bump in her pulse all about? It couldn't be because she was going to see Alex tonight, was it? Because she wasn't going out there to see *him*. No, she had darn good reasons for moving into his house. She had to make sure he wasn't cheating. Besides, that fancy hotel suite with the cat-swallowing carpet was costing Whitmore and Hamill more than nine hundred bucks a night, so it made sense to economize. She had the feeling that by the end of this month, every penny was going to count.

"Excuse me, Miss Hamill, but the meeting's due to start in five minutes."

Lizzie's chin slid off her hand. She jerked her head up to look at Rita. "What meeting?"

"The Starcourt presentation."

She hurriedly flipped through Alex's calendar, running her finger down the day's appointments. "It's not scheduled until this afternoon."

"Mr. Fletcher called to move it up," Rita said. She brushed some dust from the sleeve of her pale rose suit. "I'm sorry. I thought you knew."

Lizzie swallowed a sigh of frustration. When Alex had assembled the staff yesterday to announce the change in management, he had instructed them to give his partner their full cooperation during his leave of absence. No one other than the two of them and Jeremy knew exactly what was at stake, but evidently not all of the Whitmore and Hamill employees were pleased about the arrangement.

Instant loyalty would be too much to expect, especially from Alex's secretary, so Lizzie wouldn't gain anything from a direct confrontation. It was the same way when she'd taken over the Pedley farm. The hired hands had balked at following her directions until she'd proven to them that she'd known what she was doing. She'd simply have to do the same thing here.

Darn. It really would have been simpler if Whitmore and Hamill was in the business of making milking machines.

Pushing away from her desk, Lizzie swiveled her chair toward the credenza behind her. "Starcourt," she murmured, reaching for one of the files she'd scanned earlier. It was easy to find, since it was by far the thickest. Unfortunately, the surplus of paper wasn't due to the success of the account, it was due to the number of problems.

Starcourt wanted an attention-grabbing campaign to boost the sales of their fledgling direct-to-consumer computer distributorship. The last presentation had been a month ago, and it had been received so poorly by John Fletcher, the president of Starcourt, that he had demanded Whitmore and Hamill come up with an entirely new approach.

Lizzie glanced at her watch and stood up, tucking the file under her arm. There was no time to find out what the team in charge of this account had planned. Alex had said his job was to coordinate the people who worked for them, so she'd have to have faith in their talent.

Raised voices were coming through the double doors of the conference room when Lizzie reached it. Several familiar faces were already gathered around the long, polished table. Drew Endicott, one of the people who wrote ad copy, was seated near the middle of the table. Perspiration gleamed on his bald pate as he stared fixedly at the glossy paper in front of him. Mandy Brown, a graphic artist who made Lizzie think of Janis Joplin in a business suit, was positioning a stack of poster boards on an easel that had been set up at the other end of the room. Judging by Mandy's pale cheeks and unsteady hands, she was as nervous as Drew. Addison Smith from the research department was flipping a pencil between his fingers so quickly it blurred, and Oscar Radic from accounting seemed to have tightened his tie to the point that it was cutting off his air supply.

This was the team who had been working on the Starcourt account. Not exactly a confidence-inspiring group.

"If you're going to show me the same old artsy pap as the last time, don't bother." A man Lizzie didn't recognize was standing at the head of the table. Short and barrel-chested, with a square jaw and a crew cut, he looked more like a bulldog than a business executive. Crossing his arms, he scowled at the easel and then at Mandy. "I'm not selling perfume. I'm selling computers. What's the matter with you people? I told Whitmore to give me something different."

Lizzie paused on the threshold, tamping down an urge to flee. Just because Alex was having an easy day so far didn't mean she was about to give up as soon as the going got rough. She focused on the brass plaque that was engraved with her name, remembering the way the scrolling letters had felt beneath her fingertips. How would Alex handle this situation; how would her uncle? Or more to the point, how would she?

Well, she wasn't going to learn to swim by standing on the shore. Taking a deep breath, she silently counted backward from ten, then pasted on a smile and walked into the room. "Mr. Fletcher?" she asked, extending her free hand toward the bulldog. "I'm Lizzie Hamill, Alex's partner. I'll be filling in while he's on a leave of absence."

"Hamill?" the man asked, pivoting toward her.

"Yes, that's right."

He looked at her hair, then grasped her hand and peered into her face. "Any relation to Roland?"

"He was my uncle."

"Damn shame about that accident," he said gruffly. "He was a one of a kind."

"You knew my uncle?"

"It was because of him I chose this company in the first place," he said. "So you'll be taking over from Roland? I hope this means you people will come up with something worth my while this time."

So did she, Lizzie thought as she placed the file on the table in front of her and took a seat.

But fifteen minutes into the presentation, she knew they were in trouble. Although Drew and Mandy had created what to Lizzie's eyes was a slick, colorful and sophisticated approach, it definitely tended toward ''artsy.'' The more they talked, the farther John Fletcher's square chin thrust out. Finally, he shook his head and pointed at the poster currently displayed on the easel. ''It looks just like every other ad I've seen. It's just a picture of a computer and a bunch of numbers.''

The project team shifted uncomfortably for a moment before Addison spoke up. ''We believe the scarlet background will make your computer products immediately identifiable to the consumer,'' he said, tapping his pencil against the glossy cover of the report in front of him. ''Our surveys have shown that your target market is young, highly educated and very technologically sophisticated.''

''That's why we need something that will get their attention and set us apart,'' Fletcher said. ''I asked you to give me a gimmick. A hook.''

''With all due respect, Mr. Fletcher,'' Oscar said, tugging at the knot of his tie so he could swallow, ''launching a high-tech product like a computer is very different from the office machines your company has been producing until now.''

''Don't give me that. A tool is a tool. I didn't stay in business for twenty years by letting my products intimidate me. Sure, I don't know how to put them together, but I know how to sell them.'' He turned suddenly to Lizzie. ''Do you know anything about computers?''

She hesitated. ''I'm no expert, but I have several nieces and nephews who are. So is Zack, my youngest stepbrother.''

"And what would get their attention?"

"Food," she said immediately. "They're teenagers," she explained when Addison tossed his pencil down in exasperation.

"Food," Fletcher repeated slowly. "How would you tie that in to our computers?"

Drew shifted in his chair. "You could always promise a supply of junk food with a computer purchase," he suggested. "Potato chips, Twinkies."

"The chip-munching computer geek is a negative stereotype," Addison said immediately. "It would alienate the very market you're after."

"He's right," Fletcher said. "That won't do."

Lizzie chewed her lip in thought. Alex had said that her expertise was limited to children and cheese, so why not go with what she knew? "What about cheese?" she asked suddenly.

Drew shook his head. "There's no connection."

"Sure there is," she said. "Every computer has a mouse, doesn't it?"

Addison snickered while Oscar coughed to cover his laugh. But John Fletcher wasn't smiling. He stared at Lizzie. "Cheese for the mouse?"

"Cheese for the mouse," Lizzie repeated, nodding her head. "It's just the kind of silly joke that would appeal to the kids who use computers."

The smothered laughter faded into silence. For a full minute, no one spoke. Gradually the atmosphere started to change as the tension in the room turned to possibility.

Mandy took the posters off the easel and tilted her head, a smile working across her face. "I like it."

Drew sighed. "Mandy, it's crazy."

"No, think about it. It's so visual. It could be worked into every kind of ad we do. Even into the logo. And it's so low-tech, it would have a lot of appeal for the novice computer user.''

Lizzie looked around the table. ''We could still use Drew's suggestion. What if we included a sample of cheese with every product?''

''I'd have to work out the numbers,'' Oscar murmured. ''There would be an additional cost.''

''I'm on good terms with the manager at Pedley Cheese,'' Lizzie said, already thinking about the business she could send her stepbrother's way. ''I'm sure he'd give us a good deal.''

''There are all kinds of regulations concerning the sale of agricultural products,'' Oscar continued. ''We would have to check the state and federal—''

''That's a minor detail,'' Addison interrupted. ''I'm starting to think this isn't such a bad idea. It's so off the wall, we'd get news coverage. We could send publicity tapes to all the major networks to coordinate with the launch.''

''And we'd have tie-ins to the packaging,'' Mandy added, her hands moving quickly as she sketched her ideas in the air. ''Other companies are already using apples or Holstein markings, so why not cheese?''

Another silence fell as everyone looked at John Fletcher expectantly. For a full minute, he continued to stare at Lizzie. Then he slapped his palms on the table and stood up. ''Okay, I like it. Work out the details and send me the first mock-ups by Monday.''

Stunned with how quickly everything had turned around, Lizzie rose to her feet and accepted his congratulations. She barely heard what he said as she walked him to the elevator. By the time she returned to the conference room, the celebration was spreading into the corridor and Lizzie was smiling so widely her cheeks ached.

One day down and twenty-nine to go. Just like flying, running the company wasn't going to be so bad once she got used to it.

Chapter Six

The taxi pulled away, its red taillights fading into the darkness as it moved down the curving driveway. Looping the strap of her carry-on over her arm, Lizzie nudged her suitcase forward with her toe and shifted the cardboard box of files so that she could ring the doorbell. After two minutes with no response, she grasped the brass knocker and gave it three sharp raps. When there was still no reply, she frowned and looked around her.

There was no mistake. This was Alex's place, all right. Even if she hadn't double-checked the address when she'd arrived, she recognized those stone gateposts at the end of the driveway. Yes, and there were the ruts across the lawn, the crushed rosebushes and the tilting birdbath. She paused. She hadn't realized the ruts were so deep or the grass was so torn up—that brown sedan of Mrs. Gray's must have been heavier than it looked.

Obviously, Alex hadn't gotten around to calling his landscaping company. Probably because he'd spent too much time lazing around in the bathtub, she decided.

Heaving a sigh, she balanced the file box on her knee and reached for the doorknob. It was late. She was exhausted, and in no mood to see him gloat. After her initial success with Starcourt, the day had turned into a blur of meetings to attend and reports to study. Right now, she didn't really feel like checking up on Alex's progress. All she wanted was to kick off her shoes and crawl into bed, but before she could do that, she had this entire box of files to go through.

The door swung open suddenly, pulling her off balance before she could let go of the doorknob. The box of files fell to the doorstep and she lurched forward, colliding with a broad, solid and very familiar chest. Strong hands grasped her arms to steady her. That felt familiar, too. So did the tingles that automatically skittered across her skin and the quick thump of her pulse.

Oh, heck. This just wasn't fair. All he had to do was touch her, and she was dazzled and charmed and everything else she'd vowed not to be. Pressing her lips together, she stepped back quickly.

Alex dropped his hands at the same time, as if he regretted the contact as much as she did.

Well, of course he'd regret it. Now that everything was out in the open, he no longer had to keep up the pretense of being a prince. And it wasn't even midnight yet.

"Hello, Lizzie," Alex said, coolly polite. "Won't you come in?"

She brushed at the wrinkles in her suit and moved inside. "I hadn't intended to barge in, Alex. I rang the bell, but…" Her words trailed off as she focused on his shirt. He was wearing a pale blue polo shirt instead of his usual tailored white button-down, but that's not what caught her attention. Dried blobs of some flaky pale substance streaked the front. One shoulder was smeared with a sooty gray stuff and at the edge of his collar there was a long, limp strand of something that almost looked like…

"Is that spaghetti?" Lizzie asked, staring in disbelief.

Alex lifted his hand to brush off his collar and ignored her question. "I wasn't sure I heard the doorbell."

She raised her gaze. A day's growth of heavy black whiskers bristled along his jaw. There were more smears of the sooty gray stuff on his forehead and the tip of his nose. "What on earth happened?"

"I was in the kitchen cleaning up after dinner," he explained. "It's difficult to hear anything over the running water."

"No, that's not what I meant," she said. "I mean what happened to you? Is that soot on your nose?"

"Possibly." He rubbed it with the back of his hand. A soggy bandage was wrapped around his thumb. "We had a small fire."

"What happened to your thumb...did you say a *fire?*"

"It was nothing."

"Did you burn yourself?" she asked. Without stopping to think, she reached for his hand.

Before she could touch him, he stepped past her to pick up her suitcase. "It's nothing. Just a scratch." He brought her things inside, then set the box of files on a nearby table and closed the door.

"Oh, Lord," she murmured, glancing behind her. "Those ruts on the lawn, they're new, aren't they? Are they from a fire truck?"

"No, the fire was minor, just some paper that ignited in the kitchen. The damage to the lawn is from the dump truck and the bulldozer."

"Did you say bulldozer? What was it doing here?"

"It was a minor mix-up with the landscaper," he said smoothly. "No problem."

"No problem? Don't give me that, Alex. You look as if you've been dragged backward through a baler."

"A what?"

"It's a machine that rolls hay into bales." She shook her head, then looked around the entrance hall. A cluster of miniature toy cars, a baseball glove and a stray sneaker littered the floor. Trails of crusty white flecks similar to the kind on the front of his shirt spattered the wall. The decorator-magazine neatness that she'd seen the last time she'd been here must have gone through the same hay baler as Alex.

Obviously, his first day at his new "job" hadn't gone as well as she'd thought, despite the way he'd lazed around in the morning. The evidence was all around her.

Well, this was what she'd wanted, wasn't it? When she'd first come up with the idea for their bet, she'd expected that things wouldn't go smoothly for him. And now that there was much more at stake than merely a dinner, she should be pleased that he was having problems. Because the more problems he had, the easier it would be for her to win.

So why had she wanted to take his hand and fuss over whatever injury was hidden beneath that bandage? Why did she have this crazy, overwhelming urge to move closer and put her arms around him? Why did she want to wipe the soot from his forehead and smooth her fingers through his hair and ease the tension from his face with a kiss…?

She tamped down her urges and took another quick step back. She seemed to be doing that a lot around him lately. "It looks as if you had a rough day, Alex."

He shrugged stiffly. Beneath the stubble and the soot, his face maintained a distant coolness. "As you can see, I've had a few minor mishaps, but nothing I couldn't handle."

She shouldn't be feeling sorry for him. His posture and his expression clearly showed he wouldn't accept any sympathy even if she chose to offer it. And that was fine with her. She didn't need any more rejections. Despite the way his "mishaps" were documented all over his shirt, she had to remember that this was the same man who wanted to take the shares that her uncle had entrusted to her and send her back to Packenham Junction.

Deliberately, she searched for the anger that had helped propel her through her day. And tucked way down behind her concern and all those pesky tingles and pulse thumps, she found it. "Ah, yes. You mentioned that any competent adult could handle a housekeeper's job. Have you changed your mind?"

"Today was exceptional. I expect things to return to normal tomorrow."

"I'll look forward to seeing that."

"I'll show you to your rooms," he said, picking up her suitcase once more. "The housekeeper's suite is at the back of the house, on the first floor. It consists of a private sitting room, a bedroom and bath, but of course you're free to go anywhere in the house. Were you planning on an inspection tour tonight?"

"What?"

"That's why you're here, isn't it? To monitor my progress?"

"That's the general idea. Mostly I want to make sure you're not cheating, but from the looks of things—" she waved her hand "—I doubt whether you needed any outside help to create this mess."

His jaw tightened. "Thank you for the vote of confidence."

"I'm just returning the favor," she said. "I'd say I have the same amount of confidence in your ability to manage this household as you do in my ability to manage our company."

He brushed another piece of limp spaghetti off his shirt

with his free hand, then fixed her with a hard look. "Speaking of *our* company, how was your day, Lizzie?"

She gave him a smug smile. "Better than yours, I'd say."

"That's all right. You don't need to go into detail."

"Why? Did you get a progress report from Rita?"

"I didn't have time to talk to anyone today, but I already know the Starcourt presentation was scheduled for this afternoon."

"It was moved up to the morning."

"That sounds like something Fletcher would do. The account was on shaky ground to begin with, so don't take the failure personally."

"I didn't—"

"One loss like that won't ruin the company irreparably."

"But—"

"Still, you might want to reconsider the idea of prolonging this arrangement for the full thirty days. Neither of us wants Whitmore and Hamill to go bankrupt."

She snapped her mouth closed on the protest she was going to make. He thought she'd failed. Worse, he'd automatically *assumed* she'd failed. At least she'd waited until she'd seen the evidence of his disaster before she gloated. "I'm not giving up, Alex," she said finally. "But anytime you want to throw in the towel, go ahead." She looked pointedly at his shirt. "No, on second thought, maybe you'd better hang on to that towel. You could use some cleaning up."

A muscle twitched in his cheek. "Thanks for the housekeeping tip."

"Oh, think nothing of it. That's what partners are for."

LIZZIE SMILED sleepily and snuggled her face against the pillow. The room was filled with flowers. Huge, extravagant bouquets of them. They were on the floor, on the dresser, the window seat, everywhere. And the plain single bed had transformed to a high, velvet-canopied feather mattress fantasy that was fit for a princess. The clip-clop of hooves sounded from the corridor, then the door burst open and a tall, dark-haired prince strode toward her, a satin-lined cloak swirling around his long legs, his arms full of more flowers and a large green bottle of wine. No, not wine, it was a love potion.

Mmm. She knew this had to be a dream. Her prince was smiling at her, and she was smiling at him instead of wanting to dump the flowers on his head—

"Shh. Hurry up."

"I can't. It's too squishy."

At the furtive whispers, Lizzie's dream retreated into the recesses of her subconscious mind. One by one, the bouquets disappeared. The mattress hardened. The cloaked man gradually faded until all that was left was a teasing memory of warmth and the familiar scent of his lime aftershave.

Her nose twitched. The smell was growing stronger.

"But Dad said she wasn't our sitter. He said she's his partner."

"She's in the bed. She has to be our sitter."

"Yeah, I guess so. Wish we still had the worms."

"Shh!"

There was a long hissing noise, followed by more whispers and a spate of giggles.

Lizzie came awake slowly. Long years of experience with nephews, nieces, cousins and stray animals had taught her to be cautious. Even before she'd finished her teens, she'd acquired the talent of remaining perfectly still while her mind climbed the rest of the way back to consciousness.

This wasn't the blossom-strewn bower of her dream. She was in the housekeeper's suite in Alex's house. And judging by the light on the other side of her eyelids, it was already morning.

"Right there, Jase."

Another brief hiss.

"Hey, cool."

Lizzie cracked one eye open a slit. The first thing she saw was a looming white mass. It must be the spare pillow. Beyond that, Jason and Daniel were leaning over the edge of the bed, their faces wearing identical expressions of intense concentration.

She recognized that look. Whether kids lived on a dairy farm or in a fancy million-dollar house, mischief was mischief. Whatever were they up to…

Wait a minute, she thought. This bed didn't have a spare pillow.

The hissing sounded again. This time Lizzie was able to identify it.

Jason pressed the button on the top of a can of shaving cream while Daniel used his palm to sculpt the emerging lump of lather into the top of the "pillow."

"Okay, okay. That's enough," Daniel whispered.

Jason lowered the can and grinned at his brother. "This is way better than the 'stinguisher."

Daniel wiped his hands on the front of his pyjamas and grinned back. "Yeah. That other stuff was too runny. This is gonna last."

Amid another round of snickers, they tiptoed through the doorway to the sitting room. The bedroom door swung almost closed behind them, leaving a crack that would be just wide enough for two children to peer through.

Lizzie hid her smile. This was a new one. If these two ever got the chance to compare notes with Jolene's boys...well, she didn't even want to consider the kind of pranks she'd be waking up to then. She yawned widely and stretched her arms over her head, bringing her elbow within a hairbreadth of the shaving cream pillow before she rubbed her eyes and sat up. She yawned again, then sighed and let herself fall back down, twisting to her side just before she would have flopped into the shaving cream.

From the corner of her eye, Lizzie noticed the bedroom door wobble. Enjoying herself, she tossed and turned for a few minutes, sitting up, lying down, always coming close but never touching the twins' handiwork. To end the performance, she made a big show of stretching and yawning, then rolled out of bed and headed toward the bathroom. Moving quickly, she pulled the bathroom door shut from the outside, flattened herself against the wall and inched over to stand beside the bedroom door.

She didn't have long to wait. Half a minute later, the door swung open and the twins tiptoed inside.

"She missed it," Jason said glumly.

"Maybe we could try tomorrow," Daniel said.

"The can's empty."

"Rats."

Lizzie chuckled and stepped up behind them. "Good morning, boys."

They spun around, their eyes wide with shock. "Hey! Miz Hamill."

"How'd you do that?"

"Do what?" she asked.

Daniel's gaze flicked guiltily to the bed. "You were in the bathroom."

"Mmm, I guess I was. It's a wonderful day, isn't it?"

she said. "This is really nice of you two to come to wish me good morning."

They exchanged a look.

"You must have known how lonesome I'd be on my first day in a strange house," she added, "so I think it's great you wanted to make me feel welcome."

Jason put the can of shaving cream behind his back. "We don't need a sitter," he mumbled. "Dad said we didn't."

"Yeah. Dad said he'd make pancakes," Daniel added. "We don't need a sitter."

They were looking at her warily, as if she were threatening to take away their favorite toy. Which might not be that far off. Obviously, they would rather have their father's attention than a baby-sitter's or a housekeeper's. And she couldn't blame them for that—children needed to feel secure about their parents' love. Otherwise, they tended to try anything to get it.

She'd been several years older than the twins when she'd lost her own parents, and she'd tried hard to win the Pedleys' love by striving to be helpful. Perhaps Alex's children felt the same need for reassurance, but went about getting it in a different way. Maybe they had discovered that the surest way to get their father's attention was to misbehave.

Lizzie felt her heart expand with a wave of warmth. No matter what she thought of Alex, she couldn't help feeling something for these children. They looked so achingly sweet, the way they were lifting their chins with that mixture of hope and wary defiance. Darn, she was such a sucker for kids. Smiling reassuringly, she squatted down to bring her face level with Jason and Daniel's. "I'd rather be your friend than your baby-sitter. Would that be okay?"

Daniel kicked his toe against the carpet. Jason lifted his narrow shoulders in a shrug. "I guess."

"And since I'm not your sitter, how about if you call me Auntie Liz instead of Miss Hamill?"

"You're not our aunt," Daniel said. "We don't have an aunt."

"Great, then it looks as if you need one." She glanced around the room. "How about a game of tag?"

"Here?" Jason asked.

"Sure. Shaving cream tag," she said. "I wonder where we can find some."

"What?"

She grinned and straightened up. Striding past them, she thrust her hand into the "pillow" and scooped up a mound of foam, then hefted it consideringly on her palm. "Well, look at this. I wonder how that got here."

The boys made a dash for the bedroom door, but she beat them to it, cutting off their escape as she whirled to face them. They squealed and changed direction but she lunged after them, tagging Daniel on the shoulder. Giggling, he wiped some of the foam off with his fingers and leapt for Jason. They traded gooey handfuls twice, then both went after Lizzie. The chase led them around the bed and over it, and within minutes shaving cream was splattered everywhere. Out of breath, Lizzie retreated to the other side of the room, bracing her hands on her knees as she bent over with laughter.

"Jason! Daniel! What are you doing in here?"

White, lime-scented foam dripping from their faces, the twins turned toward the door. "Hi Dad! Wanna play tag?" Jason asked, scrambling off the bed.

Lizzie glanced up to see Alex standing in the bedroom doorway. His clothes were cleaner than the last time she'd seen him, and his cheeks were smooth from a fresh

shave—the twins must have waited until he was finished
before they'd appropriated his shaving cream. He was sur-
veying the shambles of the room with such an expression
of horror that she only laughed harder. She waved her arm
at the scattered drifts of white foam. "Merry Christmas,"
she managed to gasp.

He twisted to look at her. The moment his gaze met
hers, her laughter died. He wasn't smiling. His expression
had that air of intense concentration she'd seen before, as
if all his energy were being directed toward her....

Suddenly, she realized what a mess she must be. She
was still in the oversize T-shirt she wore to bed. She hadn't
even taken the time to wash her face or comb her hair this
morning. And she had almost as much shaving cream
smeared over her as the twins.

Self-consciously, she wiped her hands on her shirt and
tugged at the hem. It was long enough to practically reach
her knees, and she'd always considered it quite modest,
but with the way Alex was looking at her, she felt...
exposed.

No wonder he was staring. She was in worse shape than
he'd been in when she'd arrived here last night. This
wasn't exactly the best way to convince her partner that
she could handle their business. Combing her hair back
from her face with her fingers, she reached for her robe.

Alex knew he was staring, but for the life of him, he
couldn't look away. Lizzie's hair was a glorious mass of
curls, cascading over her shoulders almost to the middle
of her back. He'd had no idea her hair was so long. She'd
always confined it in a tight bun before, but now he saw
it was wild and sensuous and so damn inviting his fingers
were twitching with the desire to bury his hands in its
softness. His pulse accelerated as his gaze strayed downward. Beneath the folds of that green T-shirt she was wear-

ing her unbound breasts swayed with her movements, making more than his fingers twitch. And then, God help him, his gaze dropped to her legs.

His mouth went dry as he took in the sight of all that bare skin. Long, firm, beautifully shaped. Naked. Because she had just gotten out of bed, there was a good chance that she wasn't wearing anything at all under that T-shirt. And if he walked over there and put his hand on her thigh and slid his fingers upward... He suppressed a groan of protest as she pulled on her robe and tied the belt firmly at her waist.

"Hey, Dad!"

He looked down with a start.

"You're it!" Daniel cried, slapping his hand. With a chortle of laughter, he raced out of the room, Jason right on his heels.

Alex rubbed the sticky white foam from the back of his hand, then lifted his fingers to his nose and sniffed.

"It's shaving cream," Lizzie said.

He'd known what it was by the scent. It was his scent, and it was all over this room. All over Lizzie's bed. And all over her. For some crazy reason, he liked that. It was as if he were staking his claim to all of them.

"I, uh, I'll help clean this up," she went on. "I encouraged them."

He wished she would encourage him. Then again, he didn't need much encouragement. If she so much as crooked her finger at him, he'd be all over her as thoroughly as that shaving cream.

He raked his fingers through his hair roughly, then shoved his hands safely into his pockets. "I apologize for the intrusion. This apartment is meant to be private. You might want to consider keeping your door locked in the future."

"I didn't mind," she said immediately. "They're sweet kids. I enjoyed it."

Yes, he knew she had enjoyed it. He'd been drawn here by the sound of her laughter. She had a beautiful laugh. It was honest and uninhibited, and it had mingled so naturally with the carefree giggles of his sons, it had struck a chord of yearning somewhere deep inside him. It was almost as if she belonged here—

What was the matter with him? She didn't belong here any more than she belonged in his company. He wanted her gone. This growing attraction he was feeling was simply a normal physical reaction, nothing more. And he could control it. He could. He had to.

She fumbled the lapels of her robe closed as she moved toward him. "They didn't mean any harm. It was just innocent fun," she said, grasping the edge of the door.

There was nothing innocent about the fun he wanted to have, he thought, focusing on her lips. And despite his valiant attempt at control, Alex couldn't make himself move away. "You've got shaving cream on your chin," he said, pulling his hand from his pocket to wipe off the foam with his fingertips.

"Oh." She swallowed. "I'd better get cleaned up before I go to the office."

"There's no hurry."

"I have a meeting at ten with Stephanie Brimwell."

"The Under Wraps campaign?" he asked.

"Yes, the women's…um lingerie. I reviewed the file last night. It's doing well."

"I heard that you salvaged the Starcourt account. I apologize for jumping to the wrong conclusion yesterday."

She raised her gaze to his, her lips parting. His apology seemed to startle her. Okay, he'd been unfair to assume the worst, but she'd done that herself when she'd found his calendar in his briefcase the other day. It still bothered him that she believed he was trying to cheat. He'd only been attempting to do what was best for their company.

But he didn't want to think about the office, or his clients or his campaigns. Right now, he was having difficulty thinking at all. He tilted his head and leaned closer. "You missed some," he murmured, pulling his other hand from his pocket. He brushed the back of his fingers along her cheek where there was a fleck of foam. He smiled as her skin warmed beneath his touch.

"Uh, thanks."

"And there's some more here," he said, moving his thumb to the corner of her mouth. He stroked the place where a dimple always appeared when she smiled, and his gaze went to her lips. Her tempting, ready-to-break-into-a-smile lips. He stepped over the threshold and slid his thumb along her lower lip to the place where he wanted his mouth to be.

Her breath caught. "Alex?"

Why couldn't she lose her balance this time? he thought longingly. There were bits of foam all over the floor, so why couldn't she stumble into his arms the way she'd done before? Then he'd have an excuse to catch her, and pull her close, and feel her hands on his chest and watch the way her eyes sparkled as she tipped back her head to look at him in that earthy, sensual way....

Aw, hell. If she wasn't going to come to him, then he might as well take matters into his own hands. Sliding his fingers into her hair, he lowered his head and kissed her.

At first she didn't move. She stood frozen in place, one hand still gripping the door, the other holding her robe together. Alex brushed his mouth along hers in a coaxing caress, gently exploring the fullness of her lower lip, the delicate bow of the upper, memorizing the shape and texture that had fascinated him for days. She tasted of warmth and early-morning tenderness, direct and honest and even better than he could have imagined.

He increased the pressure gradually, curling his fingers around the back of her head to hold her steady as he slid his other hand around her waist. Despite the difference in their heights, she seemed the perfect match for his size, her body swaying into his as if she were made for him. He drew her closer, feeling her robe brush his pants as her bare toes nudged his shoes. And he thought about how wonderful it would be to greet every morning with a kiss.

With a muffled moan deep in her throat, Lizzie let go of both the door and her robe and grasped his shoulders. Alex smiled against her lips as he felt her breasts mold to his chest. This was better than he could have imagined, too. She was all feminine curves and softness, sweet and giving, just the way a woman should be. He ran his tongue along her lips, his pulse racing as he caught the hint of lime. Tasting his scent on her gave him a tremor of primitive, possessive satisfaction. And he thought about greeting every morning with far more than a kiss...and possessing her with more than his lips...

Wrapping his arms around her, he pushed his tongue into her mouth. Her fingers dug into his shoulders as she tipped back her head and parted her lips, accepting him, welcoming him. She returned the kiss with an exploration of her own that sent his heartbeat off the scale. Passion swept through him, hard and demanding. He tightened his arms and lifted her off the floor.

"Hey Dad!"

Jason's voice reached him dimly, sounding as if it came from a great distance. Alex tried to ignore it and took a step toward the bed.

Lizzie made another noise in her throat, but this one

didn't sound like one of desire. She brought her hands to his chest, arching backward to break the kiss.

Alex lifted his head and blinked, trying to bring her face back into focus.

"Dad," Daniel called. "Aren't you playing?"

Squirming in his embrace, Lizzie gave him a hard thump on his chest. "Alex, put me down," she whispered quickly.

The pounding of children's footsteps across the sitting room floor snapped Alex the rest of the way back to reality. Instantly, he released his hold on Lizzie and moved away.

The twins burst through the bedroom doorway. "You're supposed to be it!" Jason said, skidding into Alex's knees.

"Yeah," Daniel added. "You have to chase us. Don't you know the rules?"

Alex rubbed his face and took a few deep breaths. Rules? He'd just broken pretty well every one he knew. Good God, what had he been thinking?

He glanced at Lizzie. Her lips were red and swollen from their kiss, her cheeks glowed with a spreading blush and her breasts rose and fell with breaths that were as rapid as his. And she looked so damn inviting that he wanted to do it again. He was already swaying toward her when Jason squeezed between them to run to the bed.

"Hey, there's some left!" Jason exclaimed, scraping up one last handful of shaving cream from the pillow.

Daniel skipped over to join him, then smacked a handful of the foam into his brother's chest. "Now *you're* it!"

In a flurry of bare feet and foamy pyjamas, the boys pounded back across the room and left as quickly as they had arrived.

Alex knew he should be grateful for the interruption. And once his heartbeat returned to normal and his body settled down, he probably would be grateful. But that one taste of Lizzie hadn't been anywhere near enough to satisfy him. It only made him want more.

The smart thing to do would be to apologize to her and swear this mistake wouldn't be repeated. Instead, he heard himself say something else entirely. "Where were we?" he murmured, reaching for her again.

Lizzie adroitly sidestepped out of his grasp, then smoothed her robe and combed her fingers through her hair. "Alex, no. I have to get to the office."

His gaze went to the gap that had opened in her robe when she'd lifted her arm. "It won't matter if you're late," he murmured. "The company can get along without you for another few hours."

"No, I…" She moved her hand to her mouth, pressing hard against her swollen lips. "Oh, my God. Now I get it."

"What?"

"That's what the kiss was all about."

"What?"

"You want me to miss the meeting with Stephanie Brimwell, don't you? You want me to flub the Under Wraps campaign."

He shook his head. "What are you talking about?"

She stared at him, her chin trembling. "This is part of your campaign, isn't it Alex? You're still trying to…to dazzle me, to encourage me just like Jeremy said. You want to distract me into neglecting the company."

His logical mind seemed to have shut down the instant he had touched her, so it took a few moments for what she was saying to filter through to his brain. When it did, he felt as if he'd just been punched in the gut. "Lizzie, you can't think—"

"Don't bother to deny it," she said, holding up her

palm. "I know you're determined to do anything to win, but I hadn't guessed you would stoop this low."

"Now wait just a minute—" he began.

"Forget it. I'm not that gullible. I can tell when a man is only pretending. I'm not going to make that mistake again."

Again? What was she talking about? "I kissed you because I felt like it. That's all. This has nothing to do with our professional relationship."

Her eyes narrowed. "Then why did you tell Jeremy that a personal relationship between the two of us was out of the question?"

Had he said that? Of course he had. Because it was true. He didn't want to get close to any woman. Especially Lizzie. "It was just a kiss. That's all."

"You're right. That's all it was. Nothing more. And it won't be repeated. Excuse me," she said, giving him a shove backward. "I don't want to be late."

The unexpected strength of her push took him off guard, sending him backward across the threshold. Before he could react, the door swung shut in his face.

"Lizzie?" he called.

There was the click of a lock sliding into place.

"Lizzie!" He hit the door with his fist.

From within her room, another door slammed. Half a minute later there was the sound of running water.

Alex raised his fist to hit the door again, then stopped and stared at his hand. What was he doing? He was about to pound on her door. This wasn't like him. He didn't act impulsively. He didn't give in to his temper or any other kind of passion. What was it about that woman that made him lose control?

Leaning his forehead against the wood panel, he took a few deep breaths to force his heartbeat back to normal, then muttered a string of oaths. It had only been a kiss, not a ploy or a distraction or whatever it was she accused him of. Why was she so determined to believe the worst of him? She thought he wanted her shares, not her.

But she was right. That's what he *should* want. So maybe it was a good thing that she had reminded him.

Hell, this was going to be a long month.

Chapter Seven

This was going to be a long month, Lizzie thought, crossing off another day on the calendar. One week down and three more to go. She smothered a yawn, then leaned her elbows on her desk and rubbed her eyes. So far, she'd been keeping her head above water, but every day had been filled to overflowing. She'd been so busy, she'd barely had time to order in meals and more often than not she ended up falling asleep at her desk.

Of course, maybe that wasn't so bad, since by eating at the office, she could avoid seeing Alex. And the catnaps she managed to grab here helped compensate for the restless nights she spent under Alex's roof. Because whenever she crawled into bed, she was plagued by ridiculous dreams of princes with lime-scented love potions and adorable, giggling twin cherubs.

And whenever she was awake, she was haunted by memories of a kiss that had rocked her to her toes.

Idiot. That's what she was. Why hadn't she figured out what Alex was doing sooner? How could she have been so gullible as to believe that he had been overcome by passion? Hah. Considering the smeared, disheveled mess she'd been that morning, a man would have had to be blind or desperate to have wanted to kiss her. So a rich, sophisticated man like Alex who had an ex-wife named Tiffany obviously would have been motivated by something other than desire. Sheesh. If it wasn't so pathetic, she would laugh.

At least the penny had dropped before she'd let things go any further. That was one consolation. She would be on her guard if he tried it again. So far he hadn't. For the past week, during those brief occasions when she'd been unable to avoid him, it had been strictly business between them. But if he ever got that look in his eye again, that burning, intense concentration that made her palms sweat and her toes curl, she wouldn't let herself be fooled. She wouldn't mistake it for anything genuine.

Because thanks to Bobby Johnson, she had learned the hard way that she couldn't trust her judgment when it came to men.

Why hadn't she seen the similarity between Alex and Bobby sooner? Probably because she'd been too...dazzled to realize that the situations were almost the same. With Bobby, Lizzie had let her fantasies and wishful thinking cloud her reasoning. She had wanted love and a family of her own, and she'd believed that Bobby had wanted that, too, but he'd only been after her stepfather's farm. Once he'd discovered that Warren Pedley was determined to run the farming operation himself despite the accident that had left him confined to a wheelchair, Bobby had suddenly remembered his undying passion for Candy Mae down at the Dairy Queen. He'd even had the nerve to ask Lizzie to return his ring.

Of course, Lizzie had been a good sport about the whole thing and had given back the engagement ring. Ever practical, she had turned the house on Myrtle Street—where once she'd hoped to raise her own family—into a day care center. She'd even wished Bobby and Candy Mae well and had worn her good navy suit to their wedding. And last fall she had smiled and claimed it didn't bother her when she had accepted two of their children into her day care. That's because she was good old Lizzie, never making waves, always trying to be nice and helpful so that people would like her.

Well, good old Lizzie wasn't going to make the same mistake twice. Bobby had taught her that much, at least.

On the other hand, she might not have been such a good sport about giving up Bobby if he had kissed like Alex.

Lizzie sighed, dropping her head into her hands. Oh, Lordy, could Alex kiss. It had been a week, but the memory hadn't faded in the least. He didn't need any love potion to have a woman make a fool of herself over him. All he had to do was fit his mouth to hers in that gentle way, and woo her with those teasing tastes, and then sweep her away with that bold thrust of his tongue and she would not only bet the farm, she might be persuaded to give it away.

"This is starting to look just like old times."

At the cheerful voice, Lizzie snapped her head up.

Mandy Brown walked into the office, dumped an armload of poster boards on the couch, then propped her hands on her hips and looked around. "It's just the way Roland used to decorate."

Lizzie shook her head, trying to dispel the lingering memory of Alex's kiss. He'd done it to distract her, and despite her efforts, he had succeeded. Well, she wasn't going to let him win. "You mean the office?"

"Sure. When he was still working here, sometimes the furniture was stacked so high with other stuff that we ended up having meetings on the floor." She walked over to the desk and pushed aside a pile of envelopes so that she could perch on the edge. Her initial guardedness with

Lizzie had disappeared after the rescue of the Starcourt account that first day. Not only was Mandy proving to be a valuable ally in the office, Lizzie was growing quite fond of her. They might become good friends...assuming, of course, that Lizzie was still going to be here at the end of the month.

Mandy cocked her head to study her. "You look a lot like him, you know."

"You mean Roland?"

"Same hair color and eyes. The resemblance is uncanny."

"I never met him."

"That's not surprising," Mandy said. "Roland never told anyone here that he had a niece. Actually, he never talked about his family at all."

"He and my father didn't get along."

Mandy laughed and shook her head. "That was Roland. People either loved him or hated him, no in between. You've probably already noticed it with the rest of the staff."

That was true, Lizzie thought. Since she'd started working here, she'd noticed that the people who had been hired by her uncle, like Mandy, Addison and Pamela, had accepted her presence far more easily than those who had been hired by Alex. "I'm guessing that Rita fits into the second category," she said wryly, thinking about how the antagonism of Alex's secretary was becoming increasingly obvious to everyone.

"Rita?" Mandy repeated. "No, she didn't hate Roland. The poor woman worshipped him."

That jarred her. "What?"

"From the day she started working here," she said. "We all knew it was hopeless."

Lizzie hadn't thought of that. Could Rita's hostility stem from the resentment of a woman scorned?

"Roland used to joke about how he was immune to love because his heart had been broken years ago," Mandy continued. "But I always thought it wasn't entirely a joke."

"Do you know what happened?" Lizzie asked.

"Not me. I used to wonder if he was still carrying a torch for someone, but he kept his private life out of the office."

Lizzie leaned back in her chair, adding this latest bit of information to the picture she was beginning to form of her uncle. Over the course of the week, she had learned more about the man Roland had been, but her curiosity was far from being satisfied. His creativity and his knack for dealing with difficult clients were legendary. He'd been flamboyant, yet private; shrewd, yet generous. An intriguing, contradictory man whom she wished she could have known.

All those lonely years, after she'd lost her parents and had been trying so hard to fit in with the Pedleys, she'd had an uncle. If Roland's quarrel had been with her father, then why hadn't he made the effort to contact her after her father had died? If only...

She pulled herself back from those useless thoughts. There was that phrase again. If only.

Mandy waved her arm toward the boards she'd brought with her. "Want to see the preliminary mock-ups for the Under Wraps presentation?"

"You're finished already?" Lizzie asked, pushing away from her desk. "That was fast."

"It's after eight," Mandy pointed out. "Everyone else has already left."

"Oh." She glanced at her watch. "I'm sorry. I hadn't realized how late it was."

"My hubby will keep the wine chilled and the home fires burning for a while," she said, slipping off the desk to join Lizzie in front of the couch. She took the topmost poster off the pile and held it out in front of her. "I wanted to get your approval on these before I go home, or I'll worry about it all weekend."

Lizzie blinked when she saw the sketch of the woman, clad in nothing but a pink teddy, who was lounging against the hood of a fire truck. "It's, um, certainly colorful."

"That's what they wanted," Mandy said, flipping to the next one. "But I'd better tell you that the modelling agency wasn't all that crazy about posing models in underwear around heavy equipment. They wouldn't schedule it until the end of next week."

"Stephanie Brimwell wanted visual impact for these ads," Lizzie said.

"There's that, all right. But will it sell underwear?"

"Lingerie," Lizzie murmured, thinking about the scandalous concoctions of lace and satin that Stephanie had sent over this morning as samples. "White cotton is underwear. Under Wraps makes lingerie." She looked through the posters in silence, then drew her bottom lip between her teeth.

"You hate it," Mandy said, lowering the last poster.

"I wouldn't put it that strongly. I'm just not sure about the value of those trucks."

Mandy tossed the boards back to the couch and sighed. "I guess it's time to worry."

"Not necessarily," Lizzie said, picking up a poster. "There's still time to change the concept before the presentation. The idea of contrasting the women in the lingerie with all that machinery is basically good. It's very dramatic and eye-catching, but I think it's missing something."

"Like what?"

She hesitated. "Well, machines are just so impersonal."

Mandy snorted. "Not if there's some big hunky construction worker at the controls."

Lizzie lifted her eyebrows. "That's a possibility."

Snatching the poster back, Mandy took another look. "That's what's missing. If we're going for the whole fantasy thing, why not throw in some macho guy?"

"And if we did that, maybe we could get rid of the fire truck idea. He'd be enough of a contrast."

"I like it," Mandy said. "Instead of doing the male fantasy of big equipment, let's go with a female fantasy of big...er, romance."

"Romance?" Lizzie asked.

"We need a man."

"We could call him the Under Wraps Man," Lizzie said.

"That's it!" Mandy said, pointing to the poster. "The lingerie models could vary, but if we had only one male model for background, he could be like a trademark. A signature."

Lizzie nodded. "Good idea."

"Good idea? It's sensational. He could be the biggest thing since Fabio."

"But we'd want someone who is basically unknown to the public, a man who would be unique to Under Wraps Lingerie," Lizzie said.

"Right. Someone with a face like a choirboy and a body like the devil himself. Someone who would inspire fantasies."

Naturally, the first person that came to Lizzie's mind was Alex. His face was too decisively masculine to be described as a choirboy's, and she hadn't yet seen enough of his body to know for sure there, but he definitely could inspire fantasies.

For what was probably the hundredth time today, she forced his image from her mind and tried to concentrate. "The trouble is, we'd have to find this model by Wednesday if we want to meet our schedule."

"That doesn't leave much time," Mandy said. "I doubt whether the agency we use has anyone like that hanging around, or they would already be working." She shrugged. "At least the trucks are booked."

Lizzie pursed her lips in thought. "We might try Zack."

"Who?"

"My youngest stepbrother," Lizzie explained.

"Er, the computer expert?" she asked doubtfully.

"He's very photogenic, and he's trying to put himself through college so I know he'd appreciate the work." At Mandy's skeptical expression, Lizzie went back to her desk and pulled her purse out of a drawer. She dug through it for a minute before coming up with a small folder. "I probably have his high school graduation picture in here," she said, flipping through the photos of her family. "Ah, here it is."

Mandy peered over her shoulder, then let out a low whistle. "How many more of *them* do you have back on the farm?"

Lizzie warmed with maternal pride. Even to unbiased eyes, Zack was an exceptionally good-looking young man. "He has the Pedley smile."

"With shoulders like that, who's going to look at his teeth?" Mandy muttered.

"I'll run the idea past Stephanie before we go ahead with it, but I'm positive she'll approve."

"If she has eyesight and a pulse, she's bound to approve." Mandy gathered the posters and headed for the door. "Looks like you saved the day again, Lizzie. I'll work up some new layouts over the weekend. See you on Monday."

Lizzie waved goodbye and put the folder of photos back in her purse. She'd talk to Zack tomorrow, but she was sure he'd jump at the chance to earn some extra money. After all those summers doing heavy chores around the farm, he'd probably get a real kick out of getting paid for nothing more than standing around showing off his muscles. And she doubted whether anyone else in the family would object—Pedleys were far too practical to pass up an opportunity for honest work.

It was another unexpected bonus of her position here. Benjamin had been overjoyed about the deal with Starcourt Computers that she'd sent his way. Not only was the order for samples going to increase his business, Pedley Cheese would reap the benefits of the public attention the ad campaign would generate. Her family would have been too stubborn to accept money from her, but this was an even better way to share the benefits of her inheritance. One by one, she was managing to help her relatives, and more opportunities were bound to come up as long as she worked here.

As long as she worked here...

That was the catch, wasn't it? The performance of Whitmore and Hamill during the past week, while respectable, wasn't yet showing the kind of result she would need to win the bet. She had a lot more to learn, and only three more weeks left to learn it in. Had she thought this month was long?

Sighing, she picked up the report from accounting and sank down behind her desk. She had just finished the first page when the telephone started to ring. Keeping her finger on a column of figures to mark her place, she reached for the phone absently and mumbled a hello.

For a moment there was nothing but silence from the other end. Deciding it was a wrong number, Lizzie was about to hang up when she heard a rush of whispering.

She glanced at the phone. According to the display, the call was from the Whitmore house. She pressed the receiver more tightly to her ear. "Hello? Is anyone there?"

"Auntie Liz?"

"Jason?" she asked.

"Yeah."

She smiled. The twins had gotten over their original mistrust of her as soon as they had realized she wasn't going to come between them and their father. Although she had succeeded in avoiding Alex most days, she hadn't had the heart to discourage her budding relationship with his boys. Now what were they up to? "How's it going?" she asked.

"Okay." There was some more whispering before he spoke again. "Daniel wants to ask you something."

"Sure. What does he want to know?"

"Can you swim?"

She paused. "Yes, I can swim."

"She can swim," he repeated. There was another hurried conference. "Okay. Bye."

"Jason, wait!" Lizzie said. "What's going on?"

The only answer was the hum of the dial tone.

Shaking her head, she forced herself to wait a few seconds before she dialed Alex's number. She let it ring eight times, then tried again. This time she counted twelve rings before she hung up the phone.

What on earth was happening there? Had someone fallen into the pool? Did they need help? Her stomach knotting, she snatched up the receiver again and hit the first two digits of 9-1-1 before she paused long enough to think.

If it had been an emergency, Jason and Daniel would know to call 9-1-1 themselves—they might be a pair of imps most of the time, but they were smart imps. And if they had wanted her help, they would have asked her, and Jason had sounded relatively calm on the phone.

So what new mischief could they be into that would make them ask whether she could swim?

ALEX PULLED OFF his socks, then bent down to roll up the cuffs of his chinos. Grabbing the crowbar, he moved through the suds toward the middle of the room. Water sloshed around his ankles as he used his toes to feel around the floor for the drain, but all he managed to locate was another of the twins' miniature cars. Wincing, he lifted his foot and pulled the metal bodywork out of his heel.

He should have followed his first impulse and gone shopping when he'd discovered that the boys had run out of clean clothes. Technically, it wouldn't have been cheating. Children were always growing out of things like shirts and socks and underwear, and it would be a good idea to have plenty of extras on hand. A month's supply of extras wouldn't have been that unreasonable, would it?

But he'd wanted to be fair. He'd wanted to prove to Lizzie that he would abide by his word. He'd assumed that doing laundry was another one of those easy, no-brainer tasks that any competent adult could master. He had run a successful business for almost thirteen years. How tough could it be to run a washing machine?

He tossed the toy car across the room, then resumed his search for the drain.

It wasn't as if he were completely unfamiliar with the process involved with doing laundry. Sure, his mother had taken care of that when he'd been growing up, and Tiffany had seen to it when they'd gotten married before they'd been able to afford a housekeeper, but it wasn't that big a mystery. It would have gone more smoothly if he'd found those directions on the lid of the machine *before* he'd started it up, and if he'd realized that he'd bought the concentrated kind of detergent, but still, his mistakes hadn't merited a disaster of this scale, had they?

His toes connected with a metal grate. With a satisfied grunt, Alex leaned over to push his arm into the suds. Yes, this felt like the drain cover. Guiding the tip of the crowbar to the edge of the metal grate by feel, he tried to pry the cover up. It moved no more than a quarter of an inch before his hands slipped on the wet bar and he went down in a spattering explosion of white suds.

"I hope you can swim."

Alex pushed himself onto his knees. He hadn't really heard that voice, had he? She'd been making a habit out of staying at the office until after ten o'clock. She'd done her best to avoid him for the past week, so why would she decide to seek him out now? Then again, why not? That's just the way his luck seemed to be running today. Gritting his teeth, he looked over his shoulder.

Lizzie was standing in the doorway of the laundry room, her arms crossed, her shoes dangling from one hand as she stirred up a froth of bubbles with her stocking-clad foot. Her lips twitched, but she pressed them together to stifle her laugh.

"Go ahead," he muttered.

"Mmm?"

He flicked at the suds in front of him. "Go ahead and gloat. But don't think I'm giving up. This is just a temporary setback."

A tremor went through her shoulders. She clenched her jaw and nodded. "Mmm."

"The drain is backed up. It could have happened to anyone," he said, repositioning the crowbar. He gave it a vicious push and the drain cover popped off. His momentum sent him backward and he sat down heavily, setting off another sudsy ripple across the floor.

"Mmm. Alex?"

"What?" he growled.

She looked at him for a minute, her eyes sparkling, then suddenly her restraint shattered and her laughter broke free. She gestured toward the suds with her shoes. "It might be easier," she gasped, "if you take your clothes off before you try to wash them."

Despite the fact that he was sitting hip deep in a puddle of cold water, Alex's pride was stinging far more than his backside. And he had to admit that he looked ridiculous. He grinned. "Thanks for the housekeeping tip."

"Think nothing of it," she said, between peals of laughter. "That's what partners are for."

Extending his arm, he felt around beneath the suds until he located the drain hole. Instead of the empty space he had expected, his fingers encountered a curve of textured rubber. Using the crowbar again, he pried the object out of the hole. On a surge of bubbles, a red-and-blue striped ball popped to the surface in front of him.

Immediately there was a loud sucking noise and the water began to move. Alex scooped up the ball, then pushed to his feet as a whirlpool formed over the cleared drain.

Lizzie's laughter subsided to intermittent chuckles. "I'm sorry, Alex," she said. "I wasn't laughing at you, I was laughing at the situation."

He hadn't minded. It was wonderful to hear her laugh again. He hadn't realized how much he'd missed it. And he hadn't realized how much he'd missed seeing her. If an overflowed washing machine and a plugged drain was what it took to dispel the tension they'd lived with all week, then maybe it was worth it. "I guess I should be grateful you didn't think to bring a camera," he said.

"I'm just relieved to see it's nothing serious," she said. "When Jason called me at the office, I imagined all kinds of awful possibilities."

"I didn't know Jason had phoned you. When?"

"About twenty minutes ago. I called back but there was no answer. Now I see why."

"I thought the twins were in bed."

"They are. I checked on them as soon as I got here." At his raised eyebrow, she continued. "I'm not trying to interfere with your duties. I was concerned, that's all."

"I wouldn't mind a little interference," he said, slicking his hand down his pants to get rid of the suds that still clung to him. "Or housekeeping tips. Did you know that eggs explode in a microwave?"

Her lips twitched. "When did you find that out?"

"Just before my mishap with the laundry." The plastic jug of detergent that he'd emptied floated past, drawn into the current of the receding water. It bobbed in the suds as it spun around the drain. "There's a lot more to a house-keeper's job than I had thought."

"A housekeeper probably would have called a plumber when the water started to rise."

"I did. They said it would have been at least four hours before someone could get out here so I decided to fix the drain myself." He splashed over to pick up the mop that he'd left beside the wall. "Besides, I didn't want you to think I'd tried to cheat."

She was silent for a while as he began to clear away the suds. "I can see you haven't cheated, Alex."

He paused. That was the first positive thing she'd said about his trustworthiness in a week. It wasn't much, but it was a start. "I was wrong."

"What?"

"When I assumed that taking over the housekeeping duties would be easy. I didn't know what I was in for."

"No, I didn't think you did," she said. "But for someone who was raised with servants, you've adjusted pretty well to trying to manage for yourself."

Yet another positive statement, he thought, although it was based on a wrong assumption. He studied her for a minute, deciding whether or not he should correct her. Tiffany had always been embarrassed by his roots—she'd liked to pretend that he'd been born as privileged as she had. And he'd worked his butt off while he'd made her picture of him come true. Did he want to risk seeing Lizzie's face take on the same expression of repulsion as Tiffany's used to whenever he referred to his past?

Yet why not tell her the truth? There was already too much distrust between them. "Lizzie, I wasn't raised with servants."

"What?"

"I grew up in a basement apartment on the lower east side. My father drove a bus until his heart gave out one day while he was behind the wheel. My mother took in sewing to pay the rent." He shifted his grip on the mop and started to push the remaining suds toward the drain. "We didn't have servants. I learned how to clean floors twenty years ago at a fruit market."

She was silent for a while. Then her feet splashed across the floor as she moved toward him. "Where's your mother now?" she asked.

"I moved her out of that apartment the year I finished

college. Three years ago I bought her a condo in Sun City. The Arizona climate is good for her rheumatism.''

''She must be very proud of you.''

At her quiet comment, he straightened up, folding his hands over the top of the mop handle. ''She taught me the importance of being a good provider. My sons aren't going to go through what I did.''

''No, they certainly won't,'' she said. She reached out to place her fingertips lightly on his arm. ''You told me once that they're the reason for everything you do. I can understand that now.''

Her touch was barely there, but he felt its warmth spread over his damp skin. Without thinking, he covered her hand with his.

And instantly, the tension that Alex had thought they had managed to dispel was back with a vengeance.

No, it wasn't the same tension. It wasn't the wary caution of two adversaries. This had nothing to do with Lizzie's mistrust or their business or their bet. Awareness hummed in the air between them as he felt Lizzie's gaze move across his face like a caress.

He wanted to feel her fingers on more than his arm, he thought, his pulse accelerating. And just like every day this week, he remembered how good, how *right* it had felt to greet the morning with a kiss. How would it feel to end the day with one? What would she do if he lowered his head and claimed her lips with his? If he lifted his hands to ease the pins from her hair and let it tumble around her shoulders, would she make one of those soft moans in her throat? And if he stroked his wet hands down her back and pulled her into his arms, would she sigh as she felt her body fit against his?

But the last time he'd given in to his impulses, she had

accused him of pretending. She'd slammed the door in his face.

And that had been just as well, right? He couldn't risk letting his libido ruin this tentative truce, because he didn't want to go through another week of strained, suspicious silences. And he couldn't risk the future of his company on a momentary impulse—he wanted her shares, not her.

Why did he have so much trouble keeping that straight?

The drain gurgled loudly. Clenching his jaw, Alex let go of Lizzie's hand and turned back to the mop.

Lizzie swallowed hard and took a step back, spattering a mound of suds. Despite the slick floor, she moved away from Alex as fast as she dared.

He'd had that look in his eye again, that gleam of intensity, as if all his energy were being directed toward her, as if he had wanted to kiss her again. But she knew better now, didn't she? He hadn't meant anything by that other kiss. It had only been a ploy to dazzle and delay her, to make her lose her concentration.

But there was no meeting that he could make her late for today. And tomorrow was Saturday. And she'd made a mistake by assuming he'd been born to wealth, so perhaps she'd been mistaken about the other thing, too....

What if she *had* been wrong? If she couldn't trust her judgment when it came to men, didn't that go both ways? What if she was so determined not to repeat her mistake with Bobby that she was seeing a toad where there really was a prince?

In desperation, she tried to summon up some of the righteous indignation she'd used to distance herself from Alex before, but instead, she felt a spark of admiration. She searched for her anger, but all she found was a surge of tenderness.

How could she be angry at a man who was in bare feet

with his pants rolled up? How could she continue to hold herself aloof from a man who was able to laugh at himself while he waded across a flooded laundry room with a mop?

And how the heck was she supposed to stop herself from sloshing back through the suds and throwing her arms around him?

Oh, Lordy, she'd better start swimming, because she was in deep trouble now.

Chapter Eight

The Whitmore kitchen had been designed with the same eye for magazine perfection as the rest of the house. There were top-of-the-line stainless steel appliances and a wooden butcher block work island with copper-bottomed cookware hanging from hooks above it. The cushioned bench and maple table where Lizzie sat were built into the curved nook of the bay window where an array of potted plants were artistically arranged to catch the morning sun. She was sure that under ordinary circumstances, the room would have made Martha Stewart proud. But obviously, Alex had never met Martha.

He'd probably done his best, she thought. Evidence of his attempts to restore the room to its original condition was everywhere, but so was the evidence of his repeated failures. And his spaghetti suppers, she thought, glancing at the dried smears of dull red that marred the front of one cupboard. Pasta seemed to be the only thing Alex had managed successfully so far. Actually, he also had mastered cold cereal—fortunately for the twins, he hadn't yet found a way to burn corn flakes.

Lizzie took a swallow of coffee and barely restrained herself from grimacing as she set the cup back down— Alex still hadn't figured out the right proportions to use in the coffeemaker, but he'd been making an effort to learn. At least the brew no longer made her eyeballs wobble. And if she wanted to get through the day, she could use the caffeine, whatever form it came in.

She seemed doomed to sleepless nights. Either she was staying awake thinking about a kiss that shouldn't have happened...or she was tossing and turning wishing it had.

Nibbling on the corner of a piece of toast, she picked up the report from accounting and frowned at the figures.

"Do you need some help?" Alex asked, clearing the rest of the dishes off the table.

"That's not in our agreement," she mumbled around the toast.

"Technically, neither are the housekeeping tips you've been giving me."

"Tips?"

"Like not washing my clothes while I'm still wearing them," he said. "That advice is bound to prove valuable next time I take on that particular task."

Her lips quirked as she glanced up at him. His shirt and pants were wrinkled but clean—she didn't want to think about the damage he might do with an iron. He hadn't found the time to shave yet. Odd, but she was starting to like the look of that black stubble. It was somehow endearing, like the wrinkles in his clothes, like more of those intimate little things that a couple shared...

A couple? *Oh no, you don't,* she told herself. No fantasizing about their situation. Business, nothing more.

"And if you're so set on following the agreement," he continued, "you should have let me fix your breakfast."

"Thanks, but I can burn my own toast."

He chuckled, then rinsed off the twins' cereal bowls and put them in the dishwasher. "Now that the laundry is done,

I have some spare time this morning. If you'd like, I could explain those financial statements to you.''

She arched one eyebrow. ''It's very generous of you to offer, Alex, but I think I'll manage. The accounting system Whitmore and Hamill uses isn't that different from Pedley Cheese.''

''Your stepbrother's company?''

''Uh-huh. I set it up for him.''

''You set up the accounting system?''

''I took some correspondence courses after high school. They come in handy when I have to do the taxes.''

He poured himself a cup of coffee, then crossed his ankles and leaned back against the counter. ''It's very admirable of you to do the day care center taxes yourself.''

''Uh-huh. Along with everyone else's in the family. It's getting more complicated now that Ben's expanded Pedley Cheese, and Tim never remembers to save the receipts from his sign-painting business, but I've always enjoyed working with numbers. I look at it as sort of a hobby.''

Alex gulped his coffee, then shuddered and turned around to pour the remainder of his cup down the sink. ''Accounting and doing tax returns are some hobbies. I see why you don't need me to explain the finances.''

''Thanks, anyway.''

''Any other interesting hobbies? Like astrophysics?''

She grinned. ''No, just chess.''

He shook his head. ''I'm beginning to suspect that you have a habit of deliberately downplaying your abilities.''

''Do I?''

''You know you do. You're just like Roland, putting on the fresh-from-the-country innocence where in reality you've got the smarts of a barn cat.''

''I wouldn't have thought that you'd have a lot of experience with barn cats on the lower east side.''

"No, we had a vicious bunch of strays that lived off the rats and the garbage. They were a far tougher breed than their country cousins."

"Oh, really? Country mice aren't exactly wusses."

"That may be true, but our cats are smarter."

"Our cats are bigger."

He lowered his voice. "We grow things pretty big around here, too."

Her cheeks heating, she returned her gaze to the paper in her hand. Had he been flirting with her? No. Impossible. It was that voice of his that made his comment seem suggestive. "Maybe there is something you could clear up about this entry, Alex," she said, pointing to a line in the middle of the page.

He pushed away from the counter and walked over to stand behind her so that he could look over her shoulder. "Which one?" he asked.

She felt his warmth even though he didn't touch her. She breathed in his scent greedily for a moment before she tapped her fingertip to the paper. Business, she reminded herself yet again. "These lease payments. They're not for the office equipment place we deal with, they seem to be for a car dealer."

"That's because they're for my cars," he said, bracing his hand on the table as he leaned closer.

"Your cars? You mean the Mercedes sedan and that cute little green thing?"

"Only you would refer to a BMW MZ3 as a cute little green thing."

"Well, it is. And according to this, both cars belong to Whitmore and Hamill."

"Technically, the Mercedes and the Beemer belong to the company, but that's simply for tax purposes. They're meant for my personal use."

"So technically, the company owns those cars."

"Yes, but—"

"Do you know how much it costs to travel from here to the office by taxi every day?"

"No, I've never needed to."

"Exactly. It seems to me that I could save a lot of money if I used a company car to get around instead of taxis or that limousine service you used when I first got here."

He paused. "You want Whitmore and Hamill to buy you a car?"

"Heck, no. That kind of expense would eat up any profit I managed to make."

"Then you want to lease one?"

She tapped at the paper again. "According to this, I'm already leasing two of them."

"Lizzie, those are my cars."

"You can only drive one at a time. Seems to me it's a waste of company resources to leave one unused like that." She turned her head and smiled. "So, which one do you want to keep?"

Because of the way he was leaning over her shoulder, their faces were so close together, she could feel his breath on her cheek. Her gaze locked with his. And for a rebellious moment, her imagination took over. What would it be like to lean closer, to close the remaining distance between them, to press her lips to his? What would the shadow of his morning beard feel like against her cheek? Would he taste as good as before, or had she built up that memory into an impossible ideal? Or would he taste better?

"What do I want?" he murmured. "Is that what you asked?"

She cleared her throat. "Yes. Which car?"

He lifted his hand and tucked a stray lock of hair behind her ear, his fingertips lingering on the delicate skin at the side of her neck. "Car?"

Oh, Lordy, she thought, feeling her pulse speed up as the familiar tingles zipped across her nerves. How did he do that? "It's only fair that you make the choice. Your needs are different than mine."

His gaze fell to her lips. "Are they? I would have thought we both experience the same kind of needs."

"You probably would need a bigger, um, a larger one."

"Size is an important factor, but as they say, it's not everything. It's all in the skill of the driver."

She swallowed hard, her palms suddenly damp. "Um, right."

"Ideally, the right size should be combined with the right power. You'd want maneuverability that would get you in and out of tight places with ease." He traced the shell of her ear with his thumb. "And you'd want the kind of reliability that gets you to your destination every time. You'd want…staying power."

Had she thought that she needed coffee to get her blood moving this morning? Much more of this kind of stimulation and she'd be awake for a month. "Alex, we were talking about your cars."

"Were we?"

She took a steadying breath. "Since you'll be driving the boys, I'll take the Beemer."

"You'll take the…" Suddenly, he dropped his hand and straightened up. "The Beemer?"

"Don't worry, I know how to handle a stick shift."

"No."

"Sure I do. I've been driving since I was fourteen. I can handle anything from my stepfather's combine to Zack's Harley."

He took a quick step back. There was no mistaking his expression or the tone of his voice now. He looked horrified. "But—"

"You'd really be better off with the sedan," she said reasonably. "That little sports car is a two-seater, so you'd never be able to go anywhere with Jason and Daniel along."

"Lizzie, no one drives my car except me."

"*Our* car, Alex. Whitmore and Hamill owns it, so the way I see it—"

"No," he said, pacing across the room. "No way."

"We *are* partners."

He spun around when he reached the counter, crossing his arms over his chest as he looked at her. "Right. We're partners. Thanks for reminding me."

"I'll take good care of it," she said, trying to reassure him. "I'll even be sure to fill the gas tank with high-test every time, okay?"

"How generous of you."

"Well, I did notice that Whitmore and Hamill also has two gas company credit cards. You wouldn't object if I used one, would you?"

He watched her in silence for a while, a muscle working in his jaw as he appeared to be grinding his teeth. "You're probably lethal at chess."

Lizzie smiled, sensing he was ready to admit defeat. "Not compared to Dimitri."

"Dimitri?"

"He's the foreman at Pedley Cheese. He was a Grand Master in Russia before he moved to Wisconsin."

"Let me guess. He taught you everything you know, right?"

She lifted her shoulders. "We had to do something to pass the time after I finished setting up the accounts.

There's only so much a person can find to say about children and cheese.''

"I'm sorry I ever made that comment.''

"So you don't object if I use the cute little green thing?'' she asked.

"Do I have a choice?''

"I don't think so. You could always check with Jeremy, but from what I've seen of the original partnership agreement you signed with my uncle, everything is still fifty-fifty.''

Exhaling hard, he rubbed his face. "Damn, why did I ever let Roland talk me into that,'' he muttered.

"Actually, I've been wondering the same thing.''

"What?''

"How did you become Roland's partner, Alex? From what I've learned during the past week, you two had completely different styles of management.''

"That's true. We did.''

"If you were so different, why did you team up?''

"You'd have had to know Roland. He could be very persuasive.'' He gave her a long look. "You must have inherited that trait through the Hamill genes, along with the red hair.''

"My father didn't have red hair,'' she said, laying the papers facedown and squaring up the corners. "And he never talked about his brother, so I'm only starting to get to know my uncle now. I think you're probably the one who would have known him the best.''

He hesitated, then finally walked back to the table and slid into the seat across from her. "I'm not sure if anyone really knew Roland. For all of his flamboyance, he was basically a private person.''

"Then how did you meet?''

"We met fourteen years ago at a bank that had just

refused to give me a loan. I was trying to get the financing to start up a promotions company, and I'd been turned down by one bank after another. Roland liked my ideas, so he decided to take a chance and invest his own money.''

''Do you mean my uncle gave you the money that allowed you to form Whitmore and Hamill?''

''Partly. It was because of his backing that we eventually were able to talk the bank into reconsidering the loan. Or I should say *he* was able to talk us into a loan.''

She propped her elbows on the table and dropped her chin on her hands. ''Until yesterday, I wouldn't have believed it would have happened that way. I'd have guessed that you would have provided the money and my uncle would have provided the ideas.''

''Just goes to prove that you shouldn't jump to conclusions without knowing all the facts.''

He was right, of course. She'd been jumping to all kinds of conclusions when it came to Alex. But she wasn't quite ready to let go of all of them yet. ''You were telling me about my uncle,'' she said.

''Roland was shrewd when it came to business,'' Alex continued. ''He made his initial investment back within five years, but once the company was established and profitable, he started to lose interest. It had been the risk that had attracted him. He was a gambler at heart. Sometimes the chances he took paid off big, sometimes they didn't.''

''And you don't like taking chances,'' she stated.

''No. I remember too well what it was like to do without. I prefer to maintain a steady, conservative approach to the business. Things run much more smoothly that way.''

''Considering all that, I'm surprised you agreed to our wager.''

He just looked at her. "It isn't gambling when you bet on a sure thing. I'm not going to lose."

She returned his look. Instead of feeling annoyed by his confidence, she felt…stimulated. "Back on the farm, we have a saying about that."

"Something about counting chickens?"

She smiled. "You got it."

"Hey Dad!"

At the sound of his son's voice, Alex's expression changed. It didn't soften exactly, Lizzie thought. His features were too rugged for that. Yet there was always something special in his face when he looked at his children. It was the same emotion he'd revealed the night the twins had put the car in the rose garden. He loved his children fiercely, and he was determined to give them a better start in life than he'd had.

Once again, she thought about what he'd revealed yesterday about his childhood. The fact that he'd been poor shouldn't have caused that big a change in her attitude toward him, but it did. It must have taken an incredible amount of drive to achieve the success he had now. It was only natural that he'd be willing to go to any lengths to hang on to what he'd struggled so hard to win so he could provide a good life for his sons.

But it wasn't as if she wanted to take it all away from them. She just wanted a chance to keep what her uncle had given her.

Alex should be able to understand that, she thought. Now that she knew his life hadn't gone smoothly, either, she realized they had something in common. He wasn't as far out of her league as she had once believed. So maybe it wasn't all that unreasonable to hope their partnership might extend beyond the end of the month….

Oh no, you don't, she told herself firmly, yanking back on the reins of her runaway imagination.

"Dad, catch!" Daniel called, barreling into the room. He lobbed a baseball toward his father, but his aim wasn't as good as his speed. The ball rifled toward the bay window, on a collision course with a hanging clay pot that trailed a wilted philodendron.

Alex made a grab for the ball, but it was too far out of his reach. Automatically, Lizzie leaned backward and flung out her arm, snatching the ball out of the air before it could do any damage.

"Hi, Auntie Liz," Jason said, skidding through the doorway behind his brother. "Neat catch!"

"I'm hungry," Daniel declared, dropping his baseball glove as he climbed onto the counter. Swinging open a cupboard door, he stood up and stretched on his toes to reach the top shelf.

Alex was out of his chair and had crossed the room in nothing flat. "Careful," he said, holding out his hands to make sure Daniel didn't topple backward.

"Where are the cookies?" he asked.

"What cookies?"

"This is where Mrs. Gray used to keep them." Daniel dropped to his knees, then slithered back down to the floor. "How come we don't have any more?"

"We'll buy some at the store later." Alex glanced at Lizzie. "As long as that's not against the rules?"

She waved magnanimously. "Even housekeepers buy ready-made sometimes."

"Hey, Auntie Liz," Daniel said, scooping up his baseball glove. "Throw me the ball."

She balanced it on the inside of her elbow, then quickly straightened her arm to pop the ball into the air toward him.

Daniel laughed and dived for it, grinning as he came up with the ball in his glove. "I'm gonna catch a home run."

"Me, too," Jason said. "Dad, can we take our gloves to the game?"

"Sure," Alex said. "But we'll be sitting too close to home plate to catch a home run. You can catch the foul balls."

"All right!" Daniel said, punching the ball into his glove. It dropped to the floor and he scrambled after it.

"Can Auntie Liz come with us?" Jason asked.

"Yeah, can she, Dad?"

Alex turned toward her. He hesitated. "Would you like to join us, Lizzie?"

Would she? Maybe a little too much. "Sorry, I have some files I need to look over."

Jason shoved his hands into his pockets. "That's what Dad always says."

A hint of something that looked like guilt flickered across Alex's face. "I don't always say that," he said. "I'm not busy today."

"Yeah. He's on v'cation," Daniel said, tossing the ball and dropping it again.

Jason looked at his father. "Please, Dad? She's fun."

"It's up to Miss Hamill," Alex said.

The boys turned their gazes back to her. "Please?"

She chewed her lip for a while. Oh, Lord. How was she supposed to say no to two little angels like that? "This isn't part of our agreement, Alex."

"In actual fact, it is."

She lifted her eyebrows. "How do you figure that?"

"If you'd had time to finish studying that report, you'd see that Whitmore and Hamill has season tickets on the first baseline at Yankee Stadium. It's part of the entertain-

ment budget, but when we don't need them for clients, I
let the employees make use of them.''

''Ah, you wouldn't want to waste company resources.''

''Exactly. To use the same reasoning you did with my
cars, two of the four tickets are actually yours.''

How could she refuse when he put it like that? She
really would rather go to a ball game than spend the day
working. Maybe it wouldn't hurt her to take the afternoon
off. It didn't mean this changed anything about the bet or
her resolve to keep away from Alex. The invitation had
been from the twins, not him.

She returned her gaze to Jason. ''Thank you. I'd love
to come.''

''Great,'' Jason said, moving closer. ''Wanna see what
I found today, Auntie Liz?'' he asked her, pulling his hand
from his pocket.

She could tell by the glint in his eyes that he was up to
mischief again. Steeling herself for the worst, she held out
her hand. ''Okay, what did you find?''

Grinning, Jason brought his hand forward and dropped
something cold and slimy into the middle of her palm. She
drew in her breath, staring at what had to be the biggest,
ugliest slug she had ever seen.

The twins giggled, obviously waiting for a reaction.

Not wanting to disappoint them, Lizzie lifted the slug
to her nose. ''Mmm,'' she said, taking a long sniff. ''It's
tempting, but I've already had breakfast.''

''Ew!'' Jason said. ''That's gross.''

''Gross!'' Daniel echoed.

She held it out to Jason. ''Maybe you'd like to give it
to your Dad.''

Not missing a beat, Alex came over to take it from her
hand. ''No thanks, I already ate, too. We'll save it for later,
unless Daniel wants it. He mentioned he was hungry.''

"Ew!" the boys chorused, breaking into laughter.

Alex smiled at her. It was a warm, intimate smile, the kind one parent gave to another when they shared a private moment of amusement over their children. And it hit Lizzie with the impact of a runaway train.

Or maybe a runaway imagination.

She snatched her hand back and wiped it on her thigh.

She was a sucker for kids, that was all. And Alex had a pair of wonderful kids. So it was understandable that some of the affection she was beginning to feel for his children would start to spill over on to him, right?

Um, sure.

THE YANKEES LOST to the Blue Jays, but it was a wonderful afternoon, anyway. Jason and Daniel didn't seem to care that they hadn't caught any foul balls. They cheered wildly at everything, jumping up to stand on their seats every time the crowd rose to its feet. They showed almost as much enthusiasm for the hot dogs and popcorn that Alex bought them. Despite the way they stuffed themselves, they pleaded to go to McDonald's on the way home.

Alex checked with Lizzie first, but with the twins looking at her so hopefully, she couldn't very well insist that Alex struggle through another homemade spaghetti dinner. He'd already proven that he was taking his housekeeping duties seriously, despite his lack of skill, so she declared the occasion warranted the fast food and that it wouldn't be cheating this one time.

She was on her way back to the table with some extra paper napkins when she paused to look at Alex and his sons. If someone had told her two weeks ago that she'd be watching the impeccably groomed and charming Alexander Whitmore sitting in a noisy restaurant on a Saturday afternoon—and actually looking as if he were enjoying himself—she wouldn't have believed it. But he seemed as at ease among the crumpled hamburger wrappings and paper cups as he had among the crystal and china of that fancy place he'd taken her to on her first night in New York.

Was it only her perception of him that was changing, or was he really becoming more relaxed? He tipped down the brim of his baseball cap as he leaned back against the padded vinyl bench. It didn't take long before Daniel adjusted the brim of his cap so that it was the same as his father's. As soon as he saw what his brother had done, Jason followed suit. Within seconds, all three Whitmore males were lounging in their seats with their arms crossed and their baseball caps jauntily tilted at identical angles.

Lizzie couldn't prevent her lips from lifting into a sappy smile. Alex had bought them all ball caps before the game, and the twins hadn't taken them off since. It was clear to her that those two adored their father as much as he adored them. Whatever problems her management of the business might eventually cause him, there was an unexpected benefit from his enforced vacation. Alex might never be able to cook a decent meal, but his relationship with his children was growing stronger with each day. Maybe it was a good thing that the bet had forced him to spend all this time with them.

"Are they twins?"

At the voice, Lizzie looked around. An elderly woman was standing beside her, a loaded tray in her hands. Lizzie stepped back quickly, belatedly realizing she was blocking the way. "Yes, they're twins."

"They look just like their father," the woman said, smiling as she tipped her head toward Alex. "And they look like quite the handful."

"They're absolute angels," she said fondly.

"All children are angels to their mothers." The woman squeezed past Lizzie. "I'm sure your husband hopes the next one will be a girl with your red hair," she added over her shoulder.

Lizzie shook her head. "He's not...I mean, we're not..." she began, but didn't get a chance to finish her protest before the woman moved away. It was an understandable mistake, she thought, walking slowly back to the table. To a casual observer, they would appear like a family.

The thought should have disturbed her. But it didn't.

And the fact that it *didn't* disturb her was the most disturbing thing of all.

Chapter Nine

"Good morning, Mr. Whitmore."

"Hello, Pamela."

"And who are these handsome young men?"

Jason grinned and grabbed a felt marker from the top of the reception desk while Daniel picked up a stray elastic.

"These are my sons," Alex said,

"Are you enjoying your vacation?" Pamela asked.

Alex retrieved the marker before Jason got the cap off but he wasn't fast enough to stop Daniel from shooting the elastic across the hall. "It's been interesting," he replied, catching their hands before they could reach for Pamela's telephone. "How have things been here?"

She smiled. "Interesting is a good way to describe it. It's wonderful to have a Hamill working here again."

Alex would have pursued the conversation, but Daniel started to sneeze. The moment Alex released his hand to take a tissue from his pocket, both boys slipped away and raced down the hall. "Excuse me," he muttered, striding after them.

Mandy Brown stepped out of the layout studio directly into the twins' path. They barely had time to blink before the collision. Computer printouts and poster boards went flying in every direction.

"Oops," Jason said, backing up.

"Sorry," Daniel mumbled.

"Gotta go."

"Yeah, gotta go."

"Not before you help Ms. Brown," Alex said.

"Aw, Dad."

"Make it a race," he suggested. "See who can pick up the most things first."

The twins accepted the challenge good-naturedly and retrieved what they'd knocked down in short order. As soon as they handed everything back to Mandy, they were off, picking up speed as they neared the end of the corridor.

Alex broke into a run. "I'm sorry about that," he said over his shoulder.

"No problem," Mandy called, grinning. "They're just what this place needs."

Just then the door to the office beside his opened and Lizzie appeared. As soon as the twins spotted her, they veered into the open doorway and stopped in front of her. "Hi, Auntie Liz!"

"Well, hello you two," she said immediately, squatting down to bring her face level with theirs. "What are you doing here?"

"Dad brought us."

"We're going shopping. Wanna come?"

"Not this time," she said gently. "Would you like to see my office? The chair spins."

"Hey, neat!" Daniel said, rushing past her.

Jason paused to glance over his shoulder. "I'm gonna play here, okay, Dad?"

He nodded, pleased that Jason had thought to ask. "Just clean up whatever you spill," he said.

Lizzie straightened up as he approached. "Hello, Alex. This is a surprise."

He'd had it all reasoned out logically in his mind before he'd come here. Instead of relying on Rita's report to find out what was happening today, he was going to observe firsthand what kind of impact Lizzie's management was having on their company. He was going to check the progress on the current projects and question each of the employees personally. He was going to reassure himself that there would be a company left to come back to at the end of the month.

Showing up first thing in the morning was logically thought out, too. It was an efficient use of his time, since he needed to do some shopping for groceries, now that he'd depleted everything in the freezer and didn't think he could look at another strand of spaghetti for the rest of his life. He also needed to find a decent coffeemaker, one that didn't make fresh ground coffee taste like fresh ground. And the traffic wouldn't be as heavy if he finished his business and returned home in early afternoon. And the twins usually got cranky by dinnertime.

Besides, he was supposed to have full access to the company, the same way Lizzie had full access to his house. After the pleasant weekend they'd had, he didn't want to lose the ground he'd gained and let her avoid him for another week. They were living under the same roof. They were business partners. Why shouldn't they see each other?

Yes, there were plenty of logical reasons to explain this visit. But the minute he saw Lizzie, he knew there was one that outweighed the rest.

It simply felt good to see her.

He smiled. "Hello, Lizzie."

She blushed.

Alex's smile grew. He liked the way she still had that innocent, wholesome look about her, even though he now knew that she concealed a barnload of intelligence beneath her good-old-girl exterior. "How did the cute little green thing handle this morning?"

"Fine."

"I noticed that you took my parking spot."

"It went with the car," she returned.

"And you wouldn't want it to go to waste, of course."

"Of course." She crossed her arms. "And while you were at the parking spot, I suppose you checked the car over for damage?"

He should have known she would guess he would do that. In fact, he'd walked around his BMW three times, but he hadn't found any sign of abuse. Not that he'd be able to detect stripped gears or worn brakes from a visual inspection. Yet despite the way he still didn't like the idea of letting her use his car, he had to admit he felt a grudging admiration for the way she had finessed him into it. "Now, would I do that?"

One corner of her mouth lifted. "Does manure flow downhill?"

He chuckled. "That's one way to put it."

"I'll see about arranging for another spot for you, if you're going to make a habit out of visiting. Did you have to walk far?"

"The exercise was good for the boys. It let them work off some of their energy."

She glanced over to her desk. Jason and Daniel were squeezed side by side into her chair and were spinning it around by pushing against the side of her desk with their feet. "If you could channel that energy, you'd light up the city for a month."

"Probably." He looked around. Rita had told him that Lizzie had taken over Roland's office, so he'd been prepared for some of this. Yet he hadn't anticipated the degree to which she would have left her mark here.

Files, reports and stray bits of paper were everywhere and a new computer had been set up on a table in one corner. Some of the framed awards that had hung in his office were now on her walls. He focused more carefully. No, not merely some of them, exactly half of them. "I see you've made yourself at home here."

"I figured since no one was occupying my uncle's office, anyway, it would be practical to make use of it," she said, moving inside.

He started to follow her when he noticed the nameplate on the door. "You had a sign made for yourself."

"It was Addison's idea. It looks classy, doesn't it?"

Where there had once been a thin plate with Roland's name, there now was a shiny new one. The letters of Lizzie's name were engraved in brass, just like the sign on his own office. It did look classy. But it also looked...permanent.

His smile wavered. "I thought you didn't want to waste company resources. You'll just need to take it down at the end of the month."

Her chin came up. "It won't be a waste, Alex."

"That's true, you'll be able to take it with you when you leave. It might look nice on the day care center door."

"Thanks for the suggestion," she returned. "But it would get confusing for the clients, since I plan to run the company from here when I take over at the end of the month."

He arched an eyebrow. "Now who's counting their chickens?"

"I never cared much for poultry. They're too noisy."

"Excuse me, Lizzie?" Mandy said, pausing in the doorway. "I have those revised layouts for the Under Wraps account. Did you want to take a look at them now?"

"Sure, just put them on…" Lizzie hesitated as the twins stopped spinning the chair and started rocking it. She glanced at the couch, which was buried beneath stacks of files, then held out her hands. "I'll take them, Mandy."

"What's this?" Alex asked after Mandy had left. "Is there a problem?"

"No, we just needed to make a few changes before the presentation," she said, flipping through the posters quickly before she leaned them against the wall.

"Stephanie Brimwell has very definite ideas about what she wants," he said, concerned. "We had that campaign laid out weeks ago. It might be best to check with her first before you change direction."

"I already did. She loves it."

"Oh."

"Alex, don't worry. I have a very good reason to keep this company in good shape."

"That's true. If you keep us from losing too much, your shares will be worth more when you sell them to me at the end of the month."

"Mmm. I was thinking more along the lines of having earned the money to be able to afford the cost of your one percent when you sell it to me."

Alex grinned, enjoying the banter. She wasn't giving an inch.

Wheels squeaked as the boys grew bored with spinning the chair and instead started taking turns pushing each other across the room. It wouldn't have been a problem if the floor had been bare, but on the second pass, Daniel pushed Jason and the chair into a haphazard stack of boxes.

"Uh-oh," Daniel said as the boxes fell over.

"What's this stuff?" Jason asked, climbing off the chair. The lid had fallen off the top box and a scrap of red fabric had spilled onto the floor. He picked it up and regarded it with interest.

Lizzie moved over quickly to ease it from his hand. "These are just some samples. I'll put them away."

"I told the boys that they need to clean up what they spill," Alex said, moving closer.

"No, it's okay," she said, reaching for the box. "I'll take care of it."

Daniel picked up a black strip of cloth and stretched it between his hands. "Hey, neat. A slingshot."

Lizzie made a strange noise and held out her hand. "That's not a slingshot, Daniel."

"Sure it is," he said, whirling away. He stretched it out and let it fly.

Alex snatched it out of the air and took a closer look. No, it wasn't a slingshot, it was a...garter belt. His gaze snapped to Lizzie. He wouldn't have thought that she was the type to wear this kind of garment. Then again, he'd already had any number of his preconceived ideas about her blown wide-open. She was wearing that sober blue suit again today, but he could readily picture her wearing something sensual and feminine underneath.

He lifted one eyebrow. "Interesting choice of office wear, Lizzie."

Her expression seemed to waver between humor and embarrassment. She glanced at the way the boys were peering into the box that she held.

"Cool," Jason said. "Look at the feathers."

"And sparkles. Maybe we could put it on our bikes."

"Yeah, like flags."

Lizzie's humor won out—her dimples deepened instead of her blush. "These aren't mine, Alex," she said. "This is a box of samples that Stephanie sent over from the new Under Wraps line."

He looked back to the lacy bit of lingerie in his hand. Of course. The Under Wraps line. He dangled the garter belt from his fingers and extended it toward her. "What were you planning on doing with this?"

"Oh, I don't know. Daniel might be right. It could make a pretty good slingshot."

His fingers brushed hers as she took the belt from his hand. He leaned closer and lowered his voice. "I'd be happy to show you another use for it, if you're interested, Lizzie."

She drew in her breath.

"Seeing as how we're partners," he added. "It's only fair if I give you some…tips." Unable to stop himself, he reached between them and took something slinky out of the box. It was a jade-green silk camisole, with fabric so fine it practically flowed between his fingers. "Now this little item has interesting possibilities."

"Alex, for heaven's sake."

He held it by the straps so that it draped across the front of Lizzie's suit jacket. "You could start a whole new fashion trend."

"Alex…"

It was all too easy to imagine Lizzie wearing silk. Under that shapeless jacket, he knew she was all womanly curves. She'd been tempting enough to kiss when she'd been wearing a T-shirt and robe, and when she'd been up to her ankles in soapy water. What would it be like to see her in something like this?

His gaze met hers. And in her eyes he saw a flash of awareness that was as quick and mindless as his own. He curled his fingers around her shoulders in a slow caress. "The color suits you."

"It would be a pain in the neck to wash."

"You would look stunning in silk, Lizzie."

She moistened her lips. "I prefer cotton."

"I prefer nothing at all."

Her gaze dropped to his chest, her cheeks flushing anew, as if her thoughts were as explicit as his. "Uh…"

His heartbeat accelerated. Tightening his grip, he drew her closer.

The phone on Lizzie's desk buzzed loudly.

"Uh, excuse me," Lizzie said, stepping back quickly. She grabbed the camisole from Alex and tucked it into the box of lingerie, then hurried to the desk. Clearing her throat, she hit the speaker button. "Yes, Pamela?"

Alex glanced belatedly at the open doorway and then at his sons, who were busy spinning the chair again. He rubbed his face in chagrin and tried to calm his pulse. Not exactly the best time or place for this…whatever *this* was.

Pamela's voice came through the speaker. "There's a, um, man here to see you, Miss Hamill."

"Who is it, Pamela?"

A brief hesitation. "He won't give me his name. He said he wanted to surprise you."

Lizzie frowned. Alex did, too. Seconds later, they both heard Pamela's protest. "Sir, if you could just wait here—"

"Hey, Lizzie!" a deep voice called from the corridor. "Which one of these cubbyholes are they hiding you in?"

Lizzie spun around, her expression one of pleased surprise as she moved toward the door.

A young blond man appeared in the doorway before she

reached it. The moment he spotted Lizzie he held out his arms. "Lizzie!"

With a wide smile, she launched herself into his embrace. "Zack! I wasn't expecting you until Wednesday."

Grinning, he wrapped his arms around her and lifted her off the floor. "One look at the chore list and it seemed like a good idea to come early."

She gave him a smacking kiss on the cheek. "Somehow I knew you'd accept my offer."

"Are you kidding?" The man laughed and set her back on her feet. "How could I possibly say no? You did mention underwear, didn't you?"

Laughing, she swatted his shoulder. "You're shameless. Too bad you've grown too big to spank."

At the sight of Lizzie laughing in another man's arms, something shifted inside Alex. He was struck by a wave of emotion, a combination of anger and alarm, that surged through him without warning.

He should have realized that a woman as attractive and intelligent as Lizzie wouldn't have gone unnoticed back in Packenham Whatever. This man was obviously someone she knew well, someone she was close to, someone who looked as if he were just her type, as fresh from the farm as she was.

Tightening his jaw, Alex sized up Lizzie's visitor. The man was young, with a lopsided, boyish smile that was probably used to good advantage on the local farmers' daughters. But there was nothing boyish about his chiseled features or his piercing blue eyes. Or the breadth of his shoulders, or the size of the biceps that were revealed by his tight white T-shirt. Despite his youth, he was a regular Adonis in blue jeans.

Logically, it shouldn't matter how many blond Adonises

Lizzie was friendly with back home. Alex's relationship with her was basically a business one.

But logic wasn't uppermost in Alex's mind at the moment. This sudden, primitive urge he had to lunge across the office and wrench Lizzie out of her grinning prettyboy's arms wasn't merely because he was concerned about his business partner being mauled in the office in broad daylight. It was pure male possessiveness.

Unable to stop himself, Alex strode to Lizzie's side. "Hello," he said, thrusting his hand in the man's direction so that he would be forced to release his hold on Lizzie. "I'm Alexander Whitmore, Lizzie's partner."

The Adonis smiled widely and took Alex's hand. "Pleased to meet you. I'm Zachary Pedley, but everyone calls me Zack."

"Pedley?" Alex repeated.

"My brother," Lizzie said, standing on her toes to brush a lock of hair back from Zack's forehead in a gesture that was unmistakably maternal. "He's the baby of the family."

Her brother, Alex thought. One of her stepfather's children that she'd helped to raise. Not a boyfriend. Not a lover. A brother. The urge to do something primitive and physical to this blond man gradually started to recede.

"I'm sure looking forward to this job," Zack continued. "It beats another summer of sinking fence posts."

"Job?" Alex asked.

"I thought that Zack might help us out with the Under Wraps campaign," Lizzie explained. "Naturally, Stephanie will have the final approval."

The Greek god named Zack hooked his thumbs into the belt loops of his jeans and winked. "No sweat, Sis. I stopped by her office on the way over here and already got her stamp of approval. So you're looking at the new Under Wraps Man.''

There was a flutter of movement in the corridor. Alex glanced past Zack's impressive shoulders and noticed most of the female employees of Whitmore and Hamill, from Pamela to Rita, had found some reason to gather nearby where they could get a look at Lizzie's brother.

Lizzie chuckled as she took Zack's arm to draw him farther into her office. ''Sorry, ladies,'' she said, swinging the door shut. She rolled her eyes at her stepbrother. ''I can't take you anywhere, can I?''

Alex stayed where he was, still trying to settle his heartbeat back to normal. That seemed to be happening more and more often lately whenever he was around Lizzie. He couldn't remember the last time a woman had affected his emotions like this, if ever. It was too bad they couldn't have met under other circumstances. If they didn't have this crazy bet between them...

That was the point where he usually cut off his train of thought. But this time, he took it farther.

He wanted Lizzie's shares, and he wasn't going to let anything stop him from getting control of his company.

But he also wanted Lizzie.

So, why wasn't it possible to have both?

Slowly, he turned to face her. Whatever had shifted inside him when he'd seen her in Zack's arms seemed to have jarred his reasoning into another perspective.

Dammit, why *shouldn't* it be possible to have both? What was really stopping him? His priorities would always be his children and his business, but that didn't mean he had to ignore everything else. And this physical attraction between Lizzie and him was getting too strong to ignore. He wasn't interested in a permanent relationship with any woman—Tiffany had helped him lose his illusions about love and marriage years ago—yet there was no risk of permanence with Lizzie since she'd be leaving by the end of the month.

So, what did he have to lose?

She'd once told him that she was a big believer in doing what came naturally. Well, maybe it was time for him to quit fighting it and take her advice. Why not make the most of the time they had left? If he let nature take its course...

"Oh, heck, I almost forgot," Zack said suddenly, reaching into the back pocket of his jeans. He drew out a folded envelope and handed it to Lizzie. "This came for you on Friday."

Lizzie took the envelope and turned it over. "It's from Clarke, Parker and Stein."

"Yeah, Jolene was picking up your mail and she said it looked important, so I thought I'd bring it with me."

"They're the law firm who handled my uncle Roland's will," she said, slipping her index finger under the flap to tear open the envelope. "They wouldn't know I'm still in New York. I wonder... Will you look at this? There's another envelope inside."

Alex moved closer. Why would Roland's attorneys be sending something to Lizzie now? He'd thought the will was all settled. Unless there was a problem...

He could see that the second envelope was smaller, and it bore Lizzie's name in a handwritten scribble that looked very familiar. As a matter of fact, he recognized it—he'd seen it practically every day for the past thirteen years. "That's Roland's handwriting," Alex said, surprised.

Lizzie's eyebrows angled together as she looked up at him. "But it's addressed to me. How—" She focused once more on the envelope. "Why would my uncle have written me a letter?"

"Well?" Zack said. "Aren't you going to open it?"

Her hands unsteady, Lizzie broke the seal and lifted out a single piece of paper. It was covered with Roland's distinctive scrawl. She scanned it quickly, then went over it again more carefully, her face paling. For a minute she stood unmoving, then she backed up and sat down abruptly on the edge of her desk. "No."

"What is it?" Alex asked, concerned.

She shook her head violently. "No, this can't be."

Alex brushed past Zack and took Lizzie's hand in his. Her fingers were like ice. "Lizzie, what's wrong?"

"My uncle Roland." She swallowed hard and lifted her gaze to his, her eyes suddenly moist. "He wasn't my uncle."

"Of course he was your uncle," Alex said. He didn't stop to consider how much easier things would be for him if the will proved invalid. All he cared about was comforting Lizzie. He rubbed her fingers to warm them. "Anyone can see the family resemblance."

"According to this, he wasn't my uncle," she said, holding out the letter.

"But—"

"He was my father."

Chapter Ten

My Dearest Lizzie:

A lifetime ago, I promised your mother that I would never try to contact you as long as I lived. I've kept that promise. That's why I've instructed my lawyers to give you this letter after I'm dead.

How can I explain the mistakes of my youth? I loved your mother with all my heart, but I was too restless and eager for the excitement of the big city. I had planned to make my fortune and return to Packenham Junction with a big limousine and a snazzy diamond ring so I could give your mother everything she deserved. I would like to believe that I wouldn't have left if I'd known I had created a child. But I was so young then, and I was too full of my own ambition to understand that I already had what mattered the most.

My brother was an honorable man, and I know he was a good father to you and a caring husband to your mother. They both believed it would be best for you if you didn't know the truth. I hope you've been happy, Lizzie.

And I hope when you find love, you never let it go.

Your loving father,
Roland Hamill

Lizzie grabbed a tissue from the box on her lap and pressed it to her eyes. She was surprised she had any tears left—they seemed to have been flowing from the moment she'd first read this letter.

"Oh, Uncle Roland," she whispered. Her chin trembled. No, not her uncle, he'd been her father. How was she supposed to think of him now? He would never take the place in her heart of the man she'd always called dad, yet he could no longer be the distant, intriguing unknown relative. All these years he'd kept the secret of her paternity, trying to be true in his own way to the woman he'd loved. It was so sad, so poignant. She blotted her tears, then tucked the letter back into its envelope and put it on the coffee table.

How could a single piece of paper have such a powerful impact? she wondered, slumping back on the couch. She'd gone through the day in a fog, wanting to deny the words in Roland's letter, wanting to crumple it up and throw it away and pretend she'd never read it. But it was too late. She couldn't deny the truth when it had been staring her in the face every morning.

She didn't look anything like the man she'd always thought of as her father. Was that why there were no pictures of Roland in the family albums? Was it due to more than bad feelings? Had her parents been worried that she would eventually notice the resemblance?

She couldn't blame them for wanting to keep the secret. Perhaps they would have told her eventually, if they'd lived long enough. Perhaps not. While an out-of-wedlock baby wouldn't be considered a major scandal these days in most places, Packenham Junction wasn't most places. It was a small, tight-knit community, held together by old-fashioned values. And thirty years ago, those values had

been even stronger. It was perfectly understandable that
Jacob Hamill would have stepped in to save Lizzie's
mother from the stigma of unwed motherhood and to up-
hold the honor of his family's name. As Roland had said,
he'd been an honorable man.

Lizzie drew up her knees and curled into the corner of
the couch. There was so much to think about. Whatever
had been the reasons for their marriage, her parents had
always seemed to have gotten along well together. Even
if they hadn't married out of love to begin with, they'd
been...comfortable with each other. And although her
memories of her mother had been dimmed with time,
Lizzie had always thought of her as basically a happy
woman.

Still, there had been times, especially on Lizzie's birth-
day, when her mother would get a faraway look in her
eyes and her expression would turn melancholy. Had she
been thinking about Roland? Had she been remembering
the love they'd shared...and lost? And what about Roland?
He'd told Mandy that he was immune to love because his
heart had been broken. Had he really carried a torch for
her mother all these years, preferring to live alone so that
he could be faithful to his one true love?

Hot tears spilled over her cheeks anew. Sniffing hard,
Lizzie wiped her tears on her sleeve. If only she'd known
sooner. If only...

There was a soft knock on the sitting room door. A
minute later, it was pushed open and Alex stood in the
doorway. ''How are you doing?'' he asked quietly.

His concerned tone only made the tears come faster.
Lizzie snuffled, then hid her face against her knees. She'd
retreated to the housekeeper's suite as soon as she'd arrived at Alex's tonight, figuring she'd be able to mope in

private. Ever since her first morning in this house, Alex had been careful not to enter her rooms while she was here. Why did he have to choose tonight to change his routine? "Go away, Alex."

"You missed dinner," he said. The couch dipped as he sat beside her. "I wouldn't want you to say I wasn't living up to our agreement."

"How's that?" she mumbled.

"Since you didn't eat at the office, it's my responsibility to feed you."

"I'm not hungry."

"It wasn't spaghetti," he said reassuringly.

"What was it?"

"The jury's still out on that, but it started out as chicken. Now I know you said you never cared much for poultry because they're too noisy, but I assure you it hardly squawked at all. As long as I chewed fast."

She hiccuped.

"Of course, I could always go outside and dig up Jason's slug again, if you'd rather try that. It might beat my cooking."

Groaning, she lifted her head. "That's awful. Now I see where the twins get their sense of humor."

"Uh-huh." He pulled a fresh tissue from the box and held it out. "Here."

"Thanks," she mumbled.

"Don't mention it," he said, tucking a lock of hair behind her ear. "That's what partners are for."

His kindness, along with his sweetly touching attempt to make her smile, brought on another spurt of tears. She drew in an unsteady breath. "It's kind of dumb to be so upset by a letter. All of this stuff happened thirty years ago. It shouldn't make any difference to me now."

"You're just finding out about it now, so it doesn't matter how long ago it happened. It was a shock. It's understandable that you'd be upset." He waited while she dabbed her eyes and blew her nose. "If you want to talk about it, I'm here to listen."

"I just can't seem to grasp the fact that Roland was my father."

"I should have seen it before this," Alex said, dropping his hand to her shoulder. "It's not only the physical resemblance. You're very similar to him in personality."

"A lot of people have been telling me that lately."

"It's true. The more time you spend at the company, the more obvious the resemblance gets."

"I don't like thinking about 'if only's,' but I wish I'd known about him while he was still alive. Why hadn't he tried to come back after my father had died, before my mother married Warren? And then afterward, when I was trying so hard to make myself a part of the Pedley family, why didn't he ever tell me?"

"He'd made a promise to your mother."

"But it was so pointless."

"It must have mattered to him." He gave her a wry smile. "I've heard that Hamills take the concept of honesty and sticking to their word very seriously."

She nodded. "It's the way I grew up. All those old-fashioned values are a way of life back home."

"So, what are you going to do now?"

"What do you mean?"

"Now that you know that Roland was your father, is it going to make any difference to your life?"

"I feel as if it should. I mean, my whole picture of who I am has just changed."

"You're still the same person inside, Lizzie. Or do you

believe it would have been better never to know the truth?''

She hesitated, thinking it over for a while. ''It might have been easier not to know, but I'm glad that I do. And it doesn't make any difference to my feelings for my parents, especially my dad. Or the man I always thought of as my father.''

''He was your father in every sense that mattered, Lizzie. Fatherhood is more than merely providing the genes.''

''You're right. He was there for me all through my early childhood, and I never doubted his love for me, whatever his feelings were for his brother.'' She blinked at another wave of tears. ''I loved my parents, and this doesn't change that. If anything, it makes me feel even closer to them now that I've found out they were…well…''

''Human?'' Alex suggested.

With his usual knack for insight, he had zeroed in on the core of the matter. Yes, her parents had made mistakes and they hadn't been perfect, but they'd still given her love and a stable home as long as they'd lived. Knowing the truth about Roland didn't mean she would lose all that. In fact, her life had just been enriched, because even though she hadn't known it at the time, her real father had loved her, too.

Was that why she had felt such a sense of connection when she'd first touched her fingers to the sign that bore his name? Was that why Roland had resisted Alex's attempts to buy him out over the years? Had he wanted to be able to pass on his half of the company to his own child in the same way Alex wanted to preserve the company for his children?

''There's a lot for me to think about,'' she said finally, echoing what she'd realized earlier.

"Yes, I imagine there is," Alex said. "It's going to take some time for you to get adjusted to this."

"Zack will have spread the news to the rest of the family by now." She frowned. "By the way, where is he?"

"The first photo shoot for Under Wraps doesn't start for two days, so he said he was going to visit some cousin in New Jersey."

"Oh, right. That would be Bernie. From the Tuttle side of the family." She straightened up, swinging her feet to the floor. "I'd better call to make sure Zack got there okay."

"He's fine," Alex said, curling his arm around her shoulders. "Instead of worrying about everyone else, why don't you let someone worry about you?"

Afterward, Lizzie would wonder why she accepted his offer of comfort so readily. She would wonder why she hadn't made any protest as he'd drawn her closer and settled her snugly against his side. Maybe it was because she seemed to fit so perfectly into the angles of his body, and because he felt so invitingly warm and solid, and because being close to him seemed so natural. And it was understandable that the shock of discovering that she wasn't who she'd always thought she was made her need the reassurance of physical contact...

And maybe she'd been wanting to do this for days, and was happy to take advantage of any excuse. "This isn't part of our agreement, Alex."

"Sure it is, Lizzie."

"How do you figure that?"

"You're in my house. It's my duty as housekeeper to see to your comfort, isn't it?"

"Well..."

"Furthermore, as half of Whitmore and Hamill, I have an obligation to make sure you're not too upset to function adequately at the office. Otherwise, the company might suffer unduly while it's under your management.''

''Well, when you put it that way…''

''Good. I'm glad you agree.'' He hooked his foot behind her calf and lifted her leg onto the coffee table, then stretched out to prop his feet alongside hers.

She should have pulled away then—they were getting way too cozy. Relaxing with him on the couch like this after a long, stressful day was like another one of those little, intimate things that a couple did. But somehow, Lizzie couldn't summon up the willpower to resist. She sighed, tipping her head back to lean against his shoulder. ''Are the boys in bed?''

''As far as I know.''

She smiled. ''That's what you always say.''

''With those two, one can never be certain.''

''They're great children.''

''Thank you. Coming from an expert like yourself, that's quite a compliment. You've been very nice to them.''

''I told you already. I'm partial to kids.''

''Part of those old-fashioned values you grew up with?''

''I suppose so.''

He was silent for a while before he spoke again. ''I would have thought that a woman like you would be married with a whole houseful of her own children by now.''

''I came close once, but it was just as well it didn't work out. I'm perfectly happy as I am,'' she said automatically. ''I have plenty of nieces and nephews to keep me busy.''

''You came close?'' he repeated. ''Do you mean you were engaged?''

She paused, deciding whether to tell him anything more. What the heck, why not? This seemed to be the day for revealing everything there was to know about her. And Alex's shoulder felt so comfortable. "His name was Bobby Johnson," she said. "We went to high school together, but we didn't start seeing each other until after my stepfather's accident when I was running the Pedley farm. Bobby broke our engagement when Warren made it clear that he intended to take over the management of the farm himself."

"You make it sound as if your fiancé was only interested in the farm."

"That's right. Bobby was only faking his interest in me so that he could get his hands on the Pedley property. I know by New York standards it wouldn't be anything much, but back in Packenham Junction, all that acreage along with the dairy herd is a pretty substantial business concern."

"I'm sorry, Lizzie. That must have been painful."

"It was years ago. As I said, it was just as well we didn't get married."

There was another silence. Finally, Alex shook his head and muttered a short oath. "No wonder you didn't want to trust me."

"I thought it would be a good idea to have Jeremy put that clause about cheating into our agreement at the time—"

"I'm not talking about our bet, Lizzie. I'm talking about when I kissed you."

"Oh."

He shifted closer, pressing her more firmly to his side. "Are you involved with anyone now? Any boyfriends waiting for you back home?"

"No." She licked her lips. The warmth of his embrace had changed somehow. This was no longer exactly...comfortable. "Why do you want to know?"

"Three reasons. First, considering the fact that we're business partners, and you've been living with me for almost two weeks, I thought we might as well get to know each other better."

"I haven't been living with you," she said quickly. "Well okay, I've been staying in your house, but we're not living together, uh, *that* way."

"All right. We're not living together." He wound one of her stray curls around his finger and rubbed it against her cheek.

For a moment, she closed her eyes, enjoying the gentle caress. Warning bells were probably ringing somewhere in her head, but she wasn't listening. "What was the second reason?"

"Reason?"

"You said there were three reasons you wanted to know, uh, about—"

"About your love life?"

"Uh, right."

"The second reason," he said, trailing the edge of his thumb along her jaw. "Seeing Zack arrive at the office like he did today made me wonder whether some other farm boy might show up and take you away from your duties there."

"No, I already told you, there's nobody waiting for me back home."

"And that's good. We have to think of what's best for the company. For as long as you're there, of course."

"Of course," she murmured, leaning into his touch. "And the third reason?"

He tipped up her chin, tilting her face toward his. "I need to be sure you're not already involved with anyone else before I kiss you again."

The gleam in his eyes should have warned her even

before her brain finally registered what he'd said. "Alex…"

"Yes, Lizzie?"

"This isn't a good idea."

"On the contrary," he said, leaning forward. "I've thought it all through quite logically."

"But—"

She didn't get to finish her objection, even if she could have come up with one. His mouth settled softly over hers, and the only sound she made was a sigh of contentment.

It felt wonderful. Better than the first time, better than she had remembered. And it felt so natural it was like coming home. So instead of pushing him away, she slipped her hand around the back of his neck and urged him closer.

He obliged without hesitation, angling his head so that their lips fitted together. She closed her eyes, deliberately shutting out the rest of the world, concentrating only on this moment and the incredible sensations Alex's kiss was awakening.

He eased his hands into her hair, loosening the pins that held what was left of her French twist together, smiling against her lips when her curls tumbled free. He spread her hair across her shoulders, letting it slide slowly through his fingers before he wrapped his arms around her back and pulled her more solidly into his embrace.

This was better than the first time, too, Lizzie thought hazily, snuggling closer. Her breasts rubbed across his chest, sending sharp tingles of awareness through her hardening nipples. She wriggled her shoulders, enjoying the friction created by their clothing even as she was imagining how good it would feel to have no barrier between them.

As if he could sense her thoughts, Alex tugged loose the hem of her blouse and slipped his hand inside, splaying his fingers over the side of her ribs. His thumb stroked her midriff, slowly moving upward until he touched the underside of her breast.

The contact was electrifying. Lizzie's eyes flew open and she lifted her head.

Alex's gaze burned into hers. "I'm not trying to distract you, Lizzie. And I'm not pretending."

She took a shaky breath. "What?"

"This kiss. It's only a kiss." He rubbed his knuckle along the curve of her breast. "I want to get that straight before we go any further."

The breath she'd just managed to draw in whooshed out again. Further? How was she supposed to form a coherent thought when he tempted her with something like that? Her mind instantly filled with teasing fantasies of Alex's tall, lean body all naked and gleaming....

"It's not a ploy to interfere with our bet," he continued. "I hope you trust me enough by now to believe that."

Did she? Probably. Maybe she *had* been wrong to assume he was like Bobby. Because he sure as heck didn't kiss like Bobby. Maybe her judgment was all skewed again because her emotions were in turmoil over that letter, but she'd worry about that later. She moved her hands to his chest, working to loosen the top button of his shirt.

"Lizzie," he said, his voice vibrating beneath her fingers. "Lizzie, I—"

"Alex, will you please shut up and kiss me again?"

He smiled. Twisting his wrist, he unhooked the clasp of her bra, then boldly covered her breast with his palm. And as she gasped with pleasure, he pressed his mouth to hers and eased his tongue past her parted lips.

Oh, this felt too good to question, Lizzie decided, shifting her torso to give Alex better access. He took full advantage of the change in position, using his fingertips and his palm in a tender exploration that made her breath hitch. Oh, there was a lot to be said for a man without calluses, she thought dreamily.

One by one, she undid the rest of his shirt buttons, then parted the fabric and spread her fingers over his bare chest. Soft, springy curls teased her fingertips. Beneath her palm she felt his heartbeat, strong and steady, pounding in time to her own racing pulse. Eagerly, she learned his contours and textures as thoroughly as he was learning hers.

With a low sound in his throat that sounded like a growl, Alex turned her around and urged her down until she was lying on the couch. He came down on top of her, his hands quickly opening the front of her blouse before he finally broke off the kiss to press his lips to the hollow at the base of her throat. His hair brushed her chin as he traced a path downward, his hands cupping her breasts. "You're even more beautiful than I'd imagined," he murmured against her skin.

The feel of his breath on the valley between her breasts made her tremble. She curled her fingers into his shoulders, enjoying the sleek resilience of the muscles that corded beneath his skin. "So are you."

He squeezed gently. "So, you thought about this, too, Lizzie?"

"Every day," she said unsteadily. "Alex, I…oh. Alex, what are you doing?"

He didn't reply for the simple reason that his mouth was already full. Circling his fingers around her breast, he closed his lips over her nipple and drew her into his mouth.

Pleasure, pure and mindless, zipped through her body without warning. It was fast, way too fast. Groaning, she arched her back off the cushions. Oh, goodness. She hadn't dreamed about *this*. If she had, she might not have wanted to wake up. Sinking her fingers into his hair, she yanked his head up. "Alex!"

He smiled, his eyes half-closed. "Yes, Lizzie?"

"Stop. We can't..." She swallowed. "We shouldn't."

He dropped another kiss to her breast, flicking his tongue teasingly across the tip. "You asked me to kiss you," he murmured unrepentantly.

Trembling, she tightened her grip on his hair and wriggled out from underneath him until she had retreated to the corner of the couch. "I know, but not like that. Not...there."

"Then maybe you should give me a list of how and where you would like me to kiss you," he said, bracing his hands on either side of her. "Seeing as how I intend to do it again."

"Alex..."

He tilted his head, pressing his mouth lightly to hers. "What about this?" he asked against her lips.

"Mmm."

"That's okay?"

"Mmm..."

He slipped his tongue inside with a bold, possessive sweep, kissing her senseless. Long minutes later, he lifted his head, his nostrils flaring with his rapid breaths. "And that?"

She should tell him to stop, but the words wouldn't come. "Uh..."

"And this?" he whispered, dipping to the side to take her earlobe between his teeth.

When had this started to go out of control? she wondered. When had it turned from a friendly kiss to a...a...well, whatever it was, it went far beyond friendly. "Alex," she gasped. "This isn't a good idea."

He sucked gently, releasing her ear only to trail a series

of lazy, nipping kisses down the side of her neck. He pressed his nose to the angle of her shoulder, inhaling deeply, then finally pulled back to meet her gaze. "Could we put those kisses on the list?"

"We shouldn't kiss at all," she said desperately.

"Why not? Do you still believe I'm only pretending to be attracted to you?"

Where were those convenient suspicions when she needed them? She knew she shouldn't trust her judgment when it came to men, but right now, she wanted to trust her instincts instead of her brain. If Alex was only pretending, then she wouldn't want to see him when he was seriously trying to make love. No, on second thought, she did want that. Actually, at this moment she couldn't think of anything else she wanted more. "We can't get involved."

"As I said, I've thought it all through logically, and I can't think of any good reasons why we shouldn't. You're single and unattached. So am I."

"But...but what about our bet?"

He lifted one hand to her cheek, lightly stroking her skin with his knuckles. "What's going on here right now between the two of us has absolutely nothing to do with our business relationship, Lizzie. As I said, it was only a kiss."

"*Only* a kiss?"

"Maybe more than one."

"I'm surprised we didn't burn a hole in the couch."

His lips, still gleaming with moisture, stretched into a very pleased, very masculine smile. "I'm glad you liked it."

She fumbled her bra closed, then clutched the edges of her blouse together. "That's not the point. You said you didn't want a...personal relationship with me."

He sat back, making no move to refasten his buttons. "I was wrong. I'd like to get very personal."

Oh, God, why was she arguing? she wondered, her gaze dropping to the wide expanse of bare skin revealed by his gaping shirt. This was what she'd dreamed of, wasn't it? A partnership that included more than just their business?

Yes, that's what she'd hoped for right from the start, and despite her best efforts to stamp it out, the hope was still there. It had been growing with each sweet, tender, funny thing Alex had done, with all those trivial, day-to-day intimate things they'd shared. Yes, she still hoped they could be a real couple, and share a life and a home and a family and love...

"I'm not trying to pressure you, Lizzie," he added. "It would be a no-strings relationship."

She took a few steadying breaths. "No strings," she repeated.

"That's right. No commitment, no complications, just two adults enjoying each other's company."

So much for dreams of home, family and love, she thought. He didn't want love, he wanted...sex. Lizzie pressed farther into the couch cushions. "Is that the city term for it?" she asked, refusing to acknowledge the twinge of hurt from his words. She was doing it again. Letting her imagination build simple kisses into something more, something deeper. Physical attraction, that's all it was for him.

"City term?"

"You call it enjoying each other's company. Back where I come from, we'd call it a roll in the hay."

"A bed is far more comfortable," he said, trailing his fingers down her arm. "But I'm willing to experiment."

God help her, so was she. Any woman would be, with a man as persuasive and as devastatingly attractive as

Alex. Jerking away from his touch, she scrambled off the couch. "That's not the way I was raised, Alex. Maybe I'm old-fashioned, but I'm not looking for a quick affair."

"Well, I wouldn't say quick," he murmured. "I like to take my time."

"Alex..."

He stayed where he was for a moment, lounging against the couch with his glorious chest bare and a seductive half smile on his lips. Then he rose to his feet and followed her, his big body moving with the deceptive grace of a predator. "I'm sorry, Lizzie. This has been an emotional day for you, and I don't mean to take advantage of that. We'll talk about this later."

How could he be so noble at the same time he was trying to get her into bed? Only Alex would do that. He was a regular...prin—

No, no more fantasies. Holding her blouse closed with one hand, she gestured toward the door with the other. "Good night, Alex."

Without hesitation, he pulled her against him and kissed her thoroughly enough to singe her hair and curl her toes. Then he stepped back and smiled. "Good night, partner."

Chapter Eleven

Alex was on his way downstairs after tucking the boys into bed when he heard the Beemer pull to a stop in front of the house. Smiling in anticipation, he strode through the foyer and opened the front door. "Hello, Lizzie," he said, watching her swing her legs out of the low-slung car. Her skirt pulled above her knees as she leaned over to retrieve her briefcase, and Alex's smile widened. There were some unexpected benefits to letting her borrow his car. "How was your day?"

She pulled her arm back to slam the car door, then caught herself and eased it closed. Tucking her briefcase under her arm, she stalked into the house. "Just don't gloat, that's all I ask."

"All right." He took her briefcase from her hand and set it on the hall table, then slipped his arm around her back and pulled her against him for a kiss. The taste of her mouth was so good, he braced his legs and bent her backward until she had to clutch his shoulders for support. Before she could collect her wits to make a protest, he straightened up and released her.

She rubbed her forehead. "Alex, you have to stop doing that."

"Why? It's on the list."

"You and your list," she muttered. "I don't remember agreeing to that particular—" she waved her hand "—whatever you call it."

"I thought you wouldn't object as long as I kissed you on the mouth. Unless you want to change the terms? I'd be more than willing to discuss an amendment with respect to body parts."

Her lips quivered as she held back a smile. "Alex…"

"We could have Jeremy draw it up in legalese if you like," he said, draping his arm over her shoulders to steer her toward the living room. "With as many *whereas*es and *notwithstanding*s as you want. I could call him up right now and ask him to come out to the house."

"Don't you dare."

"Ah, so you don't care if it's put into writing? Does this mean you're starting to trust me?"

She made a face and ducked out from beneath his arm. "Alex, I already told you I'm not interested in a roll in the hay. Or on any other piece of furniture."

"You're not?"

Pressing her lips together, she moved away. The color in her cheeks and the gleam in her eyes were telling him something completely different from her words. "Where are the boys?" she asked.

"They're asleep." He paused. "As far as I know," he added with a smile.

She rubbed her forehead again, then went over to sit in what he was starting to think of as her chair. Despite her continued denial that they were living together *that* way, they were beginning to function like a couple, from the way he met her at the door with a kiss to the way she would collapse into that chair and make pithy comments about the goings-on at their company. Even though she was continuing to hold him off, he was enjoying their relationship nonetheless.

It had been the right decision to bring this attraction between them out into the open, he decided. He couldn't remember the last time he'd felt this strongly drawn to a woman. It was the anticipation, the chase, the challenge. And just like with their business relationship, he was finding his pursuit of Lizzie far more…stimulating than he'd expected.

"Would you like some wine?" he asked, offering her a glass from the bottle he'd chilled earlier. "Our dinner will only take about twenty minutes."

She hesitated, eyeing the wine for a moment before she took the glass. "Thanks for the wine, but I'll skip dinner."

"I'm fixing steak."

She lifted her eyebrows.

"Don't look so skeptical. The boys ate theirs."

"They did?"

His lips curved. "All right, I admit I had to cut it into tiny pieces and drown it with ketchup, but they ate it."

"It's not your cooking, Alex. I'm just not hungry."

"Rough day at the office?"

She took a quick sip of her wine. "About as rough as the road up Hanson's Bluff after a rain."

"I take it that means yes." He sat on the arm of her chair and placed his hand on her shoulder. "You're stiff as a board. What happened?"

"I met with Byron Chalmers."

He was silent for a moment. Then he shifted so he could move his hands to the back of her neck, rubbing lightly against the knot of tension there. "Chalmers Industries has been one of our biggest accounts for the past five years, but it's true that Byron can be a difficult client."

"He's worse than John Fletcher. We turned around the Starcourt account, but I'm not sure about Chalmers."

"What's the problem?"

"You haven't heard?"

He eased off her jacket and tossed it onto the antique settee, then pressed his thumbs along the top of her spine in a light massage. "I did speak with Rita this afternoon, but that was before your meeting. Is the Chalmers account in trouble?"

"Probably. But that's good news for you, isn't it?"

"I want to win, Lizzie," he said, not stopping the motion of his hands. "And I will, but I don't want to see the company flounder in the meantime. Has Chalmers changed his mind again about sponsoring the tennis tournament?"

"Again?"

"He has second thoughts every year."

She sighed, tipping her head forward as Alex worked his way across her shoulder blades. "The man looks like an oak stump and has the bullheadedness to match. I tried to explain to him how sponsoring a charity event doesn't mean he won't get any monetary return. The publicity he'll get from the television coverage is worth more than any percentage of gate receipts. His company logo on the fence is going to show up in at least three camera angles." She rolled her head from side to side. "Oh, that feels good."

He leaned close enough to put his lips next to her ear. "It'll feel better if you take off your blouse and lie down," he murmured.

"Alex…"

"We could use the couch over there. Don't those cushions look inviting?"

"Alex!"

"Just trying to be helpful." He rubbed his nose along the side of her neck, inhaling with pleasure. She had a unique scent that was a mixture of soap and perfume and...Lizzie. But her shoulders were still knotted with tension. He straightened up, giving her a gentle squeeze. "Don't worry about Byron Chalmers. He always likes to create a crisis so he's sure he's getting his money's worth from us. He's done the same thing before."

"How did you handle it?"

"I gave him his money's worth. I let him create all the crises he wanted, scheduled emergency meetings, answered all his calls until he decided to go with our original strategy."

"You mean you humored him."

"Exactly. All he wants is attention." He kneaded his fingertips across the top of her shoulders. "Relax, Lizzie. You're on your way to developing a tension headache."

"You sound as if you've had experience with them."

"Oh, yeah. The little men with big hammers used to be regular visitors."

"Used to be?"

He paused, considering it. "I haven't had a headache for a while now. Maybe it's all this leisure time I've been having on my vacation."

"Leisure time?"

"Between the smoke alarms and the floods."

"Uh-huh. You mean while you're lying on the couch with your feet up eating chocolates and watching the soaps, just like all the other housekeepers in the world."

Chuckling, he resumed his massage. "Sorry, I haven't gotten around to perfecting that particular skill yet. Maybe I'll have to take a vacation from my vacation."

"Speaking of vacations, I understand now why you haven't taken one in years. There's a lot more to your duties at Whitmore and Hamill than I'd thought at first."

"Yes, there is. But you're not doing too bad."

She shook her head. "I underestimated your job. I thought that with my knowledge of accounting and the experience I had managing the farm and the day care it wouldn't be that difficult."

"We both did some serious underestimating when we started out, Lizzie."

"Sure, but the terms of our bet don't depend on how well you manage a housekeeper's job, only that you don't cheat. You can laugh at your disasters, but mine will be measured in black and white at the end of the month."

He rested his hands at the curve of her neck. "Are you saying you want to concede the bet?"

She set down her wine and twisted around to face him. "Not on your life, partner."

He shouldn't have been pleased, but he was. He'd known that Lizzie wouldn't give up. And she would probably be as challenging and stimulating a lover as she was an adversary. He smiled.

"The month isn't over yet," she continued, obviously mistaking the reason for his smile.

"That's right, it isn't."

"I still plan to get what I want."

"So do I," he said, leaning closer. "And speaking of our partnership..." He planted a quick kiss on the tip of her nose. "How about a swim before dinner?"

"What? It's dark."

"I'll put on the lights. Nothing gets rid of a day's tension better than a refreshing dip in the pool." He fingered the collar of her blouse. "No, actually, I can think of at least one better way to get rid of tension."

"Alex," she said warningly.

Before she could argue further, he rose to his feet. He knew she was softening toward him. Now it was just a

matter of finding the right time. "I'll go check on the boys
and be right out."

LIZZIE PAUSED at the edge of the terrace, chewing her lip
as she fingered the belt of her robe. This wasn't a good
idea. Nope, not a good idea at all. It was difficult enough
to resist Alex when he was fully clothed. Did she really
think she'd be able to keep her wits when he was practically naked with his skin all slicked with moisture and his
muscles flexing and...

A swim would do her good, she told herself firmly. She
needed to relax. It had been a rotten day, she was all tied
up in knots and some exercise might help her sleep better
tonight.

Right. Sure. She could justify it however she wanted,
but she'd been wanting to see Alex naked and moist practically from the moment they'd met. Unless she took him
up on his offer of a roll in the hay, this might be the only
chance she'd get to have a good look at his body. Oh, she
was shameless, wasn't she? Pressing a hand over her
thumping heart, she opened the gate in the safety fence
and padded across the tiles that led to the pool.

The water glowed turquoise, lit from below by the lights
along the sides. Not a single ripple disturbed its surface.
Obviously, despite the extra time she'd taken nerving herself up to wear this bikini, she had still managed to arrive
here ahead of Alex. She glanced around, debating whether
it would be better to wait for him in one of the lounge
chairs. She imagined what it would be like to lie there and
watch him walk toward her, and see that intense look come
into his eyes, and feel his hands on her body as he untied
the belt of her robe and came down on top of her and...

Blowing out her breath in a shaky sigh, she turned away
from the chairs and walked to the edge of the pool. On

second thought, it might be better to wait for him in the water. No point letting herself get overheated. Dropping her robe to the tiles, she lifted her arms and dived in.

After thirty minutes of swimming laps, Lizzie decided that Alex had been right about one thing. This was a good way to get rid of the tension she'd brought from the office with her. She rolled over and floated on her back for a while, enjoying the healthy warmth the swim had brought to her limbs. It really had been a bad day. The worst one so far. Tomorrow she'd have to remember Alex's advice about humoring Byron Chalmers. She could hold on to her patience a little longer if she knew there was an end in sight.

She fluttered one hand, propelling herself in a lazy circle. It was odd, but she hadn't even questioned Alex's motives when he'd given her that advice earlier tonight. It would be to his advantage if he deliberately steered her in the wrong direction, but somehow, she trusted him. It was more than odd, it was downright strange. Whoever heard of helping the person who wanted to take control of your company?

Then again, Alex still believed he was going to win their bet. That was so typical of him, all part of his confident male attitude. It went along with his determined nature, that inner strength that had helped him achieve the success he had despite his humble beginnings. How could she be offended by his confidence when it was one of the things she found so attractive about him?

Of course, there were plenty of other things about him that she found attractive, not least of which was the way he kissed her. She smiled as she thought about Alex's list of acceptable kisses. She'd never suspected that her partner had such a playful side to his nature.

Speaking of kisses, shouldn't he have been here by

now? She treaded water, turning in a circle to look around but she was still alone. Her brow furrowed. Had he changed his mind about joining her? She doubted it. The more she got to know him, the more she realized that he was a man of his word. He was a far cry from the dishonest, manipulative schemer she'd first accused him of being. As a matter of fact, at times he could be almost *too* honest.

He'd been completely frank with her about this affair that he wanted. She didn't think she'd ever been pursued with such single-minded determination. It was flattering. And increasingly hard to resist. She was tempted, really tempted, to take what he was offering. But she wasn't that kind of woman, was she? Maybe it was those old-fashioned values that she was raised with. Or maybe it was her pesky imagination, that stubborn part of her that still wanted all those fairy-tale dreams of love and, well, marriage.

Alex didn't want love from her. And he had made it perfectly clear to her that he didn't want to marry again—his experience with Tiffany seemed to have soured him on the entire institution. It was such a shame that he was determined not to take another chance with love, but he had this thing about maintaining control, in both his personal and his business life.

She ducked underwater and swam to the shallow end, then pulled herself out of the pool. Okay, that was enough mooning around over a man she was doing her best to keep away from. Alex must have changed his mind after all. He'd said he'd be right down after he checked on the boys....

Her hand tightened on her robe as she turned to face the house. Was something wrong? Was that why Alex hadn't joined her? Flinging the robe around her shoulders, she retraced her path past the gate and through the terrace door.

Taking the steps two at a time, she bounded up the curving staircase to the second floor. She headed for the light that spilled through the open door to the left. But the moment she reached the doorway, she slid to a stop.

The beds that had been built into the custom-designed oak fantasy of shelves and curtained alcoves along the opposite wall of the large room were empty. So were the child-size chairs and table in front of the overflowing toy box. But the room wasn't empty. Three occupants sat in the hand-carved rocking chair beside the window.

With one twin balanced on each knee, Alex was leaning back in the chair, a book discarded on the floor beside him. Mellow light from the lamp on the table touched one side of his face with gold, highlighting his masculine cheekbones and square jaw and creating a tender little shadow in the cleft in his chin. His thick, black hair fell boyishly over his forehead, gleaming with the same soft sheen as that of his sons. And like Jason and Daniel, he appeared to be fast asleep.

Lizzie pushed back her wet hair and slumped against the door frame. So this was what had kept him busy, she thought, a silly grin working its way across her face. While she'd been looking forward to seeing his body all sleek and glistening in a swimsuit, he'd been up here still fully dressed and reading a bedtime story to his children.

Dammit, how could she help falling in love with a man like that?

Her smile froze. Falling in love? Had she really been dumb enough to go and do a fool thing like that?

Jason made a soft, sleepy noise and snuggled against his father's shoulder. Alex jerked his head, his eyes snapping open. His arms tightened reflexively around his sons for a moment before he looked up and met Lizzie's gaze.

God, yes. That's exactly what she'd done. This was

more than lust or a physical attraction for his body. This was love. For the entire man.

"Hi," he whispered. "Jason was restless so I read them both a story. I must have dozed off."

She nodded numbly, crossing her arms in a vain attempt to hold the feelings inside. Love. This wasn't what Alex wanted from her; it wasn't what he'd asked for.

He rocked forward, glancing from one twin to the other, then back at Lizzie. "I hate to wake them up. Would you mind giving me a hand getting them into bed?"

She swallowed hard, not moving. "I'm all wet," she whispered.

"That's okay. Use the blanket," he replied, tipping his head toward the nearest bed.

The smart thing to do would be to turn around and walk away. If she went to him now, the way she was feeling, she was liable to do something really stupid. Yet the picture he made, with the soft light playing across his chiseled features and his dark hair falling loosely across his forehead…and his children cradled protectively in his taut, muscular arms…oh, Lord, how could any woman resist? A tremor went through her body. One wavering step at a time, she crossed the room.

Lizzie picked up the small quilt from the foot of Daniel's bed and leaned over to take the sleeping boy from Alex's lap. The back of her hand brushed Alex's thigh, and she heard him suck in his breath. But she wouldn't look at him, instead concentrating on transferring Daniel as gently as possible to his bed. He barely stirred as she pulled the sheet up to his shoulders and stroked her hand gently over his hair.

The wooden runners creaked on the floor as Alex got out of the rocking chair. He carried Jason to the other bed, then leaned over to give him a light kiss on the forehead.

At the unconsciously tender gesture, Lizzie felt her heart turn over. Why was it that of all the kisses Alex had tried to woo her with over the past week, something so sweet and completely innocent would have such an impact on her senses?

Yes, he was the most incredibly attractive man she'd ever known, but it was more than his looks that drew her. He had so much love inside him, such pure emotion. Yet, except for the affection he lavished on his sons, he kept his feelings tightly locked away.

What would it be like to share it, to have that deep emotion directed toward her? Her pulse started to throb, her breathing grew shallow, and she took a halting step toward him.

Alex took the damp quilt from her and dropped it on the chair, then switched off the lamp, leaving the room in the glow of the small night-light between the beds. Without a word, he took Lizzie's hand and led her out of the room. When they reached the hallway, he turned to face her, his lips lifting into a smile. "Thanks for the help."

"You're welcome," she said shakily. "That's what partners are for."

He lifted their joined hands to his lips. "You're trembling. Are you cold?"

Should she tell him the truth? Should she say that she was trembling from the love that just kept on expanding inside her, racing through her nerves like a chain of heat lightning? "Yes," she said. "That must be it. I'm cold."

"Then maybe we should get you out of those wet things."

This was her cue to leave. But she couldn't. "Yes," she murmured, finally meeting his gaze. "Maybe we should."

He stared at her, his gaze sharpening. His grip on her

hand tightened. "Are you sure, Lizzie?" he asked, his voice rumbling with quiet intensity.

She was only getting in deeper. She wasn't sure of anything, except for the fact that she loved him, and that if he didn't stop being noble and kiss her in the next second...

It must have been her body language, because she didn't need to say a word. Before she could tell him what was in her heart, Alex cupped her face in his hands and sealed his mouth to hers.

The kiss was different from the countless ones they'd shared over the past week. Lizzie could feel it in the way his fingers slid firmly into her hair to hold her head steady, and in the way his tall frame hardened with purpose. He was no longer merely flirting. He was kissing her as if he didn't intend to stop.

Lizzie lifted her arms to clasp her hands behind his neck, swaying toward him. Her robe fell from her shoulders, landing on the floor at her feet, leaving her naked except for the scraps of wet fabric that clung to her skin. Water dripped from her hair, tracing a path down her back and another shiver tickled along her spine. But this one wasn't from cold, either.

With a throaty groan, Alex slipped one arm around her waist, pulling her tight to the front of his body. Her head fell back as her breasts molded to his chest and, suddenly, she was enveloped in heat.

"Lizzie," he whispered, pressing his lips to the side of her neck. That was all he said, just her name. But it was enough to make her knees weak. She clung to him, feeling reckless and shy and captive and free and—

Her breath caught as Alex slipped his arm behind her thighs and lifted her off the floor. She hung on to his neck, pressing herself into his embrace as he strode toward his bedroom. He carried her inside, then kicked the door shut with his heel.

"This time," he said, his gaze steady on hers. "We won't be interrupted."

The sensations that were building inside her made her voice unsteady. "No."

His jaw hardened. "What?"

"No, we won't be interrupted," she said, smoothing her fingertips along his jaw.

He turned his head, capturing her index finger between his teeth in a gentle bite. Then he shifted his grip on her legs to let her slide slowly to her feet. His gaze dropped. And his eyes widened. "Oh, Lizzie," he whispered.

She started to cross her arms but he caught her wrists to keep her from covering herself. Her robe had concealed what she was wearing earlier, and when he'd started to kiss her he hadn't taken the time to look, but now he was. "I didn't have a swimsuit of my own," she began.

"Where—" He swallowed, skimming his hands down her hips. "Where did you get this?"

"Stephanie. It was in that box of samples from Under Wraps and I figured it would do for a…oh…" Her words dissolved into a sigh as he leaned over to continue his caress down the length of her legs. "Alex, what are you doing?"

"Helping you out of your wet things." He turned her around, then slid his fingers to the knot in the middle of her back that held the sides of the bikini top together. He tugged it open, then pushed her hair aside and made quick work of the remaining strings at the back of her neck. Peeling the triangles of fabric away, he stepped up behind her and slipped his arms around her to cup her breasts in his palms.

"Oh," she gasped, dropping her head back against his

shoulder. The touch of his warm, strong fingers against her damp flesh was better than anything she could have imagined. "Oh, Alex."

"You're beautiful," he murmured, pressing his lips to her ear. He rubbed his thumbs over the hard buds of her nipples until she quivered with delight. "Absolutely beautiful."

She wanted to tell him then. She wanted to let him know that this was much more than simply sex. But then he moved one hand downward and pulled loose the knots on either side of her waist. The rest of the tiny bikini dropped to her feet. Alex's fingertips grazed the curls at the apex of her legs, and the only sound Lizzie could make was a moan.

She didn't know how they finally got to the bed. Alex got rid of his clothes on the way there and fell to the mattress with her wrapped in his arms. For long, sweet moments out of time they indulged themselves in all the touches they'd denied before, all the kisses they hadn't been able to finish, all the longing they'd kept under control. And just when the pleasure built to the point where it verged on pain, Alex lifted his head and rolled Lizzie onto her back.

Through a haze of desire, Lizzie focused on his face as he knelt above her. Had she thought she'd seen emotion there before? Had she believed she'd seen desire? The passion that glowed in his eyes nearly sent her over the edge. Without hesitation, she pulled him down on top of her. She smiled as she felt his hands slip beneath her hips and he positioned himself between her thighs.

Hot, heavy and pulsing with life, he joined his body to hers.

And Lizzie's smile became a gasp of pure wonder.

There were no words of love spoken between them, only

words of need. There were no promises, no commitment, no mention of a future. And that was all right, Lizzie told herself. He'd warned her, hadn't he? She was in love and she was shameless, and she'd take whatever he was willing to give.

Chapter Twelve

"Tell me, Lizzie. Is that overgrown package of raging testosterone behaving himself?"

At Jolene's question, Lizzie dropped the receiver on the desk in shock, then fumbled to bring it back to her ear. "What?" she squeaked.

"When he called me this morning, he sounded as if he were having the time of his life. I'm trying to decide whether or not to be worried."

"He called you? Why?"

"Well, he is my brother," Jolene said, a smile in her voice.

"Your..." Lizzie bit her lip. Of course. Jolene was talking about Zack, not Alex. She couldn't possibly know about Alex. Considering the controlled, businesslike image he liked to project to the world, very few people would know about Alex. Or what they had done last night. "Jolene, Zack's old enough to take care of himself."

"I suppose so. It's those city girls I'm worried about," Jolene said wryly. "The females around here know enough to shield their eyes when they look at him."

Lizzie laughed. "He's working with professional models. I'm sure they're accustomed to young men who look like that."

"Still, it's hard to believe Zack's getting paid good money just to stand around in his old jeans."

"The photographer loved the worn denim look. He said it looked genuine country."

"Country?"

"Haven't you heard? Country is in."

"Well, that's reassuring," Jolene said with a chuckle. "By the way, Dad's getting a real kick out of the stories Zack's been telling about those New York types."

"That sounds like Warren, all right." Lizzie pushed aside a stack of files and propped her elbow on the desk, shifting the receiver to her other hand. "How's he doing?"

"Fine. He asked me to thank you for the boxes of books you sent him. He's pretty well gone through everything in the Packenham library. And Tim and I both want to thank you for sending that billboard business our way."

"All I did was tell Tim about the possibility of doing those signs. It was his talent that won him the contract."

"Speaking of contracts," Jolene continued, "thanks to the publicity from those Starcourt computers, Benjamin has more business than Pedley Cheese can handle. He hired a second shift."

"That's great."

"And Zack mentioned that there's a possibility of continuing his modeling job after he starts college in the fall."

"Uh-huh," Lizzie said. "Stephanie promised she'd make sure to work out a schedule that wouldn't interfere with his studies."

"Well, Lizzie, it looks like you've done it again."

"Done what?"

"You've managed to help everyone in the family," Jolene said. "You're still taking care of us."

"I'm happy to share my good fortune."

There was a brief silence. "Okay, what about you?"

"Mmm?"

"How are you doing? I know it must be a big adjust-ment."

For a second she thought that Jolene was talking about the change in her relationship with Alex. But then reason kicked in and she realized what her stepsister meant. "It gets easier as time passes," she said. "My memories of my parents will never change, and I'll always think of Jacob Hamill as my father, but I'm glad that I finally know the truth about Roland."

"Somehow I knew you'd think that way. You're always so sensible."

Was she? Maybe not lately. "Knowing about Roland has made me look at what I'm doing differently."

"You mean your inheritance?"

"Exactly. It's no mystery now why he wanted to give me everything he had. This company is his legacy."

"And speaking of that, how's the bet going?"

She glanced at her calendar. "It's still too close to call. I'll have a better idea when I get the preliminary report from accounting in a few days."

"I have no doubt that you'll win," Jolene said staunchly.

"Thanks."

"But why didn't you tell me about your partner?"

"I thought I did."

"Hardly. You gave me the impression your partner was an old man."

"Did I?"

"Yes, you did. I couldn't believe my ears when Zack told me the real story."

Lizzie twisted the phone cord around her fingers. "There's no story."

"Hah. I heard your Mr. Whitmore practically broke our

baby brother's hand before he found out Zack's last name was Pedley.''

"He did?"

"Sounds like the behavior of a jealous man to me," Jolene said.

Lizzie was surprised by the quick burst of pleasure that went through her. Had Alex been jealous? Did that mean his feelings for her might be deeper than he wanted to believe?

"And according to Zack," Jolene continued, "this partner of yours looks at you like a fox eyeing a henhouse. Just how close is this partnership?"

She hesitated. "I'm not sure, Jolene."

There was a long exhalation from the other end of the line. "Maybe I should be asking you how close you *want* your partnership to be."

"That's something I've been trying to figure out for almost a month," Lizzie said.

"Good God, Lizzie," Jolene said. "Do you mean to tell me that you've got...feelings for this man?"

"Yes, I think I do."

"But you're trying to take over his company."

"It's my company, too. My father wanted me to have it."

"And you deserve it, but I'm talking about what your partner must think. The terms of your bet don't leave much room for feelings."

"Winning this bet is the only way to keep what's mine," Lizzie said.

"And what happens when the month is over? What are you going to do then? I thought only one of you could win."

"Well..."

"Has that Mr. Whitmore changed his mind? Has he agreed to share the company?"

"Well, not exactly. He still wants to buy me out."

"He sounds like one real stubborn son of a—"

"Alex worked hard to achieve the success he has, Jolene," she said immediately. "He's a very fair and intelligent man, but he truly believes he needs to have complete control over the company in order to ensure its stability."

"How can you defend him when he wants to get rid of you?"

How? Because she'd gone and done a fool thing like falling in love. She rubbed her temples. She was starting another tension headache. Or maybe the tightness in her head was from lack of sleep. Alex had kept her up most of the night making love... No, it hadn't been love, not for him.

"Lizzie, are you all right?"

"Yes, I'm fine, Jolene," she said. "Sorry, I have to go."

"Lizzie—"

"I'll call you later," she said, putting the phone down. She dropped her head into her hands.

Now what? It had seemed so clear last night. Giving in to her feelings about Alex had seemed to be the most natural thing in the world at the time. Her heart had given her no choice. But reality had returned with the daylight. The end of the month was a week away. She might be in love with Alex, but he hadn't changed his mind about their relationship. He assumed he was going to win their bet, and that once he paid her for her shares, she would leave. Exactly as he wanted. A quick, no-strings, no complications affair.

She needed more time, that's all. If she had another month or two, maybe she'd be able to help Alex past the aversion to commitment that his marriage to Tiffany had left him with. In time, maybe she could convince him to take a second chance with love.

But if she lost the bet, she wouldn't have more time with Alex. She would have to sell him her shares and leave. Oh, Lord, she couldn't even contemplate losing, not now that so much more than merely the company was riding on the need to stay.

The phone on her desk buzzed. Jerking her head up, Lizzie hit the speaker button.

"Excuse me, Miss Hamill."

Lizzie swallowed a sigh at Rita's terse tone. The secretary's attitude toward her had thawed only minimally when the news about Lizzie's true parentage had filtered through the office. If Rita really had been in love with Roland, then one would expect her to be pleasant to Roland's natural daughter. On the other hand, perhaps rather than seeing Roland in Lizzie, Rita saw Lizzie's mother. Or maybe having failed to win the man she loved had made Rita too bitter to change. Whatever. Lizzie couldn't afford the time to worry about Rita. She had enough problems looming in her own life. "Yes, Rita?" she replied.

"Mr. Chalmers is waiting for you in the conference room."

"What?" She straightened up. "Byron Chalmers?"

"Yes. He asked to speak with the team that is handling his account."

"When did he get here?" Lizzie asked, digging through the files on her desk. She grabbed the notes that Rita had typed up yesterday. "Who's with him?"

"Miss Brown and Mr. Smith. They've been waiting for thirty minutes."

"Half an hour? Why didn't you tell me?" she asked, getting to her feet.

"You were occupied with a personal phone call, Miss Hamill," Rita said primly. "I didn't feel it was my place to interrupt."

Of all the clients to keep waiting, it would have to be someone as touchy as Chalmers. Gritting her teeth, Lizzie headed for the conference room.

"I'M NOT HUNGRY," Jason said, pushing his plate away.

Alex lifted his eyebrows as he looked at the untouched food. "I thought you liked hot dogs. Maybe you'd like an apple," he suggested. "Or how about a banana?"

"Not hungry," Jason repeated, slouching farther down in his chair.

Alex shook his head. The boys had probably filled up on cookies again. "Well, if you get hungry later, let me know."

"I'll eat it," Daniel said, reaching across the table. He grabbed the hot dog and munched down on one end. "These are good," he mumbled. "They don't crunch this time."

"No, they don't," Alex agreed. After three weeks, he'd finally mastered the art of cooking wieners. Not bad. His culinary skills were definitely expanding. And this morning he'd managed to do two loads of laundry without any mishap. Things were looking up, he thought as he lifted his mug to his lips. Even his coffee tasted better than usual. Maybe the new coffeemaker was finally breaking in. Then again, it would take a lot more than bad coffee to bring him down to earth today.

Considering the way he'd spent last night, was it any wonder that he couldn't get the satisfied smile off his face?

Making love to Lizzie had been everything he'd anticipated, and more. She'd been…perfect. Her responses had been honest and without inhibition, her passion a match for his. As a matter of fact, he couldn't remember ever enjoying sex so much in his entire life.

Propping his elbows on the table, Alex felt his lips lift into yet another smug grin. Lizzie had enjoyed it, too. She hadn't needed to tell him that in words—her soft moans and those throaty little cries she gave when she'd trembled in his arms had been testimony enough. And the way she'd wrapped those long, marvelous legs around his waist and...

Taking another swallow of coffee, Alex shifted restlessly on his chair. After last night, he would have thought his appetite for Lizzie would be sated, or at the very least dulled. Instead, he was already hungry for more of her. He glanced at the clock on the wall. She probably wouldn't be leaving the office for at least another seven hours. He hoped he could talk her into taking another swim. This time, he'd make sure to join her. He looked forward to helping her out of that minuscule excuse of a swimsuit...

"Dad!" Daniel tugged at his sleeve.

Alex cleared his throat and turned toward his son. "Yes?"

"When's Auntie Liz coming home?"

"I'm not sure. Probably late."

"I want to show her something."

So do I, Alex thought, shifting uncomfortably. "What do you want to show her?"

"The bird's nest we found. She'd like that."

"Yes, she would."

"She's cool," Daniel added. "She liked my snake."

"What snake?" Alex asked warily.

"The one Grandma gave us."

Alex chuckled. The twins had loved the rubber rattle-snake his mother had sent them. It had been one of the tacky souvenirs she'd picked up while she'd been on her latest tour with her seniors' group.

Tiffany had never liked the gifts his mother had sent the boys. She'd insisted that all their toys be more...suitable. Just like their housekeepers and baby-sitters. That's why she'd made it a condition of their custody agreement that Alex continue to hire the help from the agency she'd chosen. She'd been more concerned with appearances than with what their children actually wanted.

His smile faded. Once he resumed his place at Whitmore and Hamill, there were going to be some changes to his household. Somehow, he'd find a way to spend more time with his sons—he didn't want to lose the new closeness they'd established during these past weeks. And he wasn't going to underestimate the complexity of housekeeping and child care duties again.

"Dad, my stomach hurts," Jason said.

Alex rubbed his face ruefully. Speaking of complexities, how did anyone manage to get children to eat a balanced diet? Maybe he should try storing fruits and vegetables in the cookie jar. "You might feel better if you go and lie down for a while," he suggested.

Jason nodded and slid down from his chair. "Okay."

His agreement startled Alex into looking at him more closely. "Jason—"

"Owww," he moaned.

Alex knelt in front of Jason and reached out to touch his forehead. His skin was cool and clammy. Alarmed, Alex peered into his eyes. "Besides your stomach, do you hurt anywhere else?"

"Just my stomach. I...*owww!*" Grimacing, Jason clutched his stomach and doubled over. *"Dad!"*

The alarm turned instantly into a gut-clenching panic. "Take it easy, son. I'll help you."

"What's the matter with him?" Daniel asked, crowding against Alex's shoulder.

Despite the sick feeling in his own stomach, Alex tried to sound calm for the sake of his boys. "Probably just something he ate," he said, scooping Jason into his arms.

"Told ya we shouldn't've had all those cookies," Daniel said. "Hey, Jase. Your face is green."

"Let's get you to the bathroom," Alex said, striding across the kitchen. "Maybe you'll feel better after you get rid of whatever's bothering you."

Jason's solid little body shook with a sudden spasm. He parted his lips. But instead of moaning again, this time he screamed.

"AS THE REPORT SHOWS, Mr. Chalmers," Lizzie said, "the survey that our marketing department recently compiled proves that the broadcast of the tennis tournament will reach your target group."

"When was this report done?" Byron Chalmers tapped his thick finger against the glossy cover. "The market is constantly changing."

Doing her best to keep a pleasant expression on her face, Lizzie turned toward Addison. "What was the date of the survey, Mr. Smith?"

Addison flipped his pencil between his fingers, a sure sign he was becoming agitated. "The sample was taken between the twelfth and the seventeenth of the month," he said.

"How accurate is it?" Chalmers demanded.

"We employed standard survey techniques, so our results would be accurate to within four percentage points."

"Four points? You mean plus or minus two?"

"No, four either way."

"That means you could be out as much as eight in your numbers," Chalmers persisted.

"This kind of margin of error is generally accepted in the industry," Addison said, his pencil blurring. "And even if the figures are off by the full four percent, you'll still be reaching an excellent number of—"

"I want another survey done as soon as possible," Chalmers interrupted. "Now, what about the placement of those signs? I think they blend into the fence too much. We should change the background color to yellow."

"The signs are already in production, Mr. Chalmers," Mandy said. "Changing the color now would put us behind schedule. And you approved of the design two weeks ago—"

"That was before I saw the color of the fence," Chalmers said.

"We'll do a mock-up with the yellow," Mandy said. "We'll let you make the final decision then."

Lizzie's cheeks were starting to ache from the smile she was forcing for the sake of her client. At least it was diverting her attention from the ache in her head. Shuffling the papers in front of her, more to keep her hands safely occupied than to actually accomplish anything, she listened while Mandy took over the defense of the advertisings that Byron Chalmers had already approved.

Just as Chalmers interrupted Mandy with yet another whining complaint, a movement at the door of the conference room caught Lizzie's eye. Rita entered the room and walked directly to where Lizzie sat at the head of the table.

"Excuse me, Miss Hamill," Rita said quietly. "There's a call for you on line one."

Lizzie clenched her jaw. Rita hadn't seen fit to interrupt a personal call in order to tell her that an important client was waiting, but now she was interrupting a meeting with

an important client in order to tell her she had a call.
·''Take a message, please.''

Rita smoothed her hands over her pastel-colored suit. ''I thought you might want to take it here.''

''Who is it?'' Lizzie asked.

''Mr. Whitmore.''

Chalmers scowled and crossed his arms. ''Whitmore's on the phone?'' he asked immediately, obviously having listened to the entire exchange. ''Let me talk to him. Then we'll get this straightened out.''

''Mr. Whitmore is on vacation,'' Lizzie pointed out.

''He shouldn't have left when we had unfinished business,'' Chalmers said. ''I'm accustomed to dealing with the people in charge.''

''I am in charge,'' Lizzie said through her teeth. ''Excuse me a moment, Mr. Chalmers.'' She swiveled around to reach the telephone on the credenza behind her. Talking to Alex might be just what she needed if she was going to have the strength to get through the rest of this meeting without throttling their client. She picked up the receiver and punched the blinking button. ''Hello?''

''Lizzie?''

Something in the tone of his voice alerted her. Her annoyance with Chalmers was pushed into the background by a shiver of foreboding. She cupped her hand around the mouthpiece and lowered her voice. ''Alex, what's wrong?'' she asked.

''I…'' He cleared his throat. ''I wanted to let you know I might not be there when you get home tonight.''

''Where are you?''

''I'm at the hospital.''

The shiver turned instantly to a fist around her heart. No. Not Alex. She'd lost her mother. She'd lost not one but two fathers. She couldn't lose Alex. "What happened? Are you hurt?"

"I'm fine. Jason went into surgery forty minutes ago."

"Oh, my God!"

"It's his appendix." He inhaled unsteadily. "I got him here as soon as I could, but..." He cleared his throat. "They took him in right away."

Jason? No. Not Jason, either. She couldn't lose any of them. She loved the boys as much as she loved their father. "Is Daniel okay?"

"Yes. He's with me."

"Give me the address," she said, grabbing a notepad. She scribbled down the name of the hospital and rose to her feet. "Okay, I'll be right there."

"Lizzie, you don't have to come."

"You're wrong, Alex," she said. "I do." She dropped the receiver back into place and headed for the door.

"Miss Hamill!" Chalmers said indignantly. "We still have concerns to discuss."

"I'm sorry, Mr. Chalmers," she said over her shoulder. "This is an emergency. My staff will be able to handle your questions."

"You can't brush me off to some underlings the way Whitmore did. I demand that you stay and finish—"

"Mr. Chalmers," Lizzie said, pausing by the door, her patience cracking. She'd done her best to humor this man, but like any spoiled child, his complaints only got worse the more attention he gained through them. "As far as I'm concerned, we've already covered your concerns every which way from Sunday. If you're so starved for attention, get yourself a dog."

Mandy snorted. "You tell him, Lizzie," she muttered.

Chalmers levered his stumplike body out of the chair, his face reddening. "Mr. Whitmore will hear about this."

Lizzie glanced at Rita. "I'm sure he will. Rita, you're in charge while I'm gone."

Rita looked startled. "Me?"

"I'll call later," Lizzie said, moving through the doorway. This would probably mean the end of the Chalmers account. It might even mean a drop in the company's profits. But right now she didn't care. There were certain things that were more important than business, things that didn't show up on a financial statement. She detoured only long enough to grab her purse from her office before she sprinted for the elevator. Hoping that Alex would understand why she was abusing his car, she left smoking black skid marks on the pavement as she squealed the Beemer out of the parking lot.

LIZZIE FOUND Alex on the sixth floor of the hospital, wearing a track into the carpet of the waiting room. Head down, hands clenched behind his back, he paced across the floor. On the other side of the room, Daniel was curled up in an orange vinyl upholstered chair, his Yankees cap pulled down low over his face, his expression uncharacteristically subdued. Lizzie's heart lurched painfully as she hurried toward them.

"Alex," she called.

At the sound of her voice, he whirled toward her. Deep lines of worry creased his face. "Lizzie," he said.

She stopped in front of him and grasped his hands. "How's Jason?"

"He's still in surgery," he said. His fingers were like ice where he gripped hers. "They said they'd let me know, but it's been too long."

She shook her head. "It only seems long, Alex. It's been less than twenty minutes since you called me."

"I told you that you didn't need to come, Lizzie. You can't just leave the office—"

"Sure I can."

"But—"

"Don't worry about the business, Alex. That's my job."

He glanced at Daniel, then looked anxiously toward the doors that led to the operating rooms. "They should have been done by now."

"I'm sure the doctors know what they're doing."

"They told me appendectomies are routine operations, but Jason's only five."

"Kids are amazingly resilient. They do better than adults in a lot of these situations."

"He has to be all right. He has to."

Feeling her eyes fill at the fear in Alex's voice, Lizzie cradled his hands against her cheek. "He'll be fine," she said. "I just know it."

He held himself stiffly, his jaw rigid with tension. Lizzie could see that he was struggling to maintain his control over his emotions. She could also see that he was unwilling to lean on her—this wasn't the kind of closeness he wanted. But still, he didn't pull his hands away.

"I should have seen it sooner," he said. "He was restless last night. I should have known something was wrong."

"You couldn't have known, Alex."

"He was so pale. And he was trying so hard to be brave."

"He's one stubborn, terrific little boy," Lizzie said. "And he's strong like his father, so he'll pull through this."

A shudder went through his body. "I have to believe that."

"Mr. Whitmore?"

At the voice, Alex pulled away from Lizzie and turned around. A small, bespectacled man in surgical greens was walking toward them. Alex swallowed hard. "How is he, Dr. Andrews?"

The doctor peeled off his cap and smiled. "Jason is fine, Mr. Whitmore. The operation went well. We were able to remove the appendix before it ruptured, so the risk of infection is minimal. He's in recovery right now."

"Thank God," he said. "When can I see him?"

"Give us another few minutes. We want to keep a close eye on him until he's out of the anesthetic."

Unable to speak, Alex simply nodded and shook the doctor's hand. A muscle in his cheek jumped as he watched him walk away.

Lizzie put her hand on Alex's arm. "Come and sit down," she urged.

Alex stayed where he was, the muscles of his arm rigid beneath her light touch. Another shudder went through him. Then without a word he turned toward Lizzie and wrapped her in a tight embrace.

She slid her arms around his waist and pressed her head to his chest.

Coming here had been the right thing to do. Whether Alex wanted to admit it or not, he needed her. He might not want her love, but she was going to give it to him anyway. For as long as she was able. And when the month was up—

I hope when you find love, you never let it go.

The words she'd read in Roland's letter whispered through her mind, almost as if someone had spoken them. Shaken, she lifted her head and looked around. Of course, it was only her imagination. That pesky imagination, the one that kept dreaming of being part of Alex's life.

But she already *was* part of Alex's life. At least until the end of the month. And then…

And then? Was she going to let him go? Was she simply going to give him up without a fight because of some agreement they had made? She was willing to gamble everything for her shares in his company, why wasn't she willing to gamble for his love?

Roland had lost the woman he'd loved because of his ambition. Then instead of going back to fight for her and his child, he'd promised to exile himself from their lives. He'd kept away from Lizzie's mother, even when she was free. He'd kept away from Lizzie. He'd stuck to his word no matter what.

It all seemed so pointless in the long run.

So what if Alex didn't want a commitment? So what if he expected her to follow the terms of their bet? Was honor more important than love?

Was this going to be yet another one of those points in her life that she would look back on someday and say, "if only?"

Was history going to repeat itself?

When you find love…

Closing her eyes, Lizzie tightened her hold on Alex. Since she'd read Roland's letter, she'd learned countless ways in which she resembled her father. And she'd been fascinated to discover each new similarity.

But when it came to holding on to the one she loved, she hoped there was no similarity to Roland at all.

Chapter Thirteen

Alex leaned against the door frame of the twins' bedroom, listening to the quiet breathing of his sons. It was a sound he never tired of. Over the years, on days when his responsibilities to the company had kept him at the office late and he'd arrived home after the boys were in bed, he often used to stand in the doorway like this and simply listen to them sleep.

For three nights, he hadn't been able to listen to Jason. He'd known it was for the best, and that Jason was getting excellent care at the hospital, but leaving him there each night and driving home with only Daniel had been one of the most difficult things he'd ever done. It was as if a giant hole had opened in his life. Now that Jason was safely back with him once more, Alex felt as if the world had wobbled back into its proper orbit.

"How's Jason?"

At the whispered question, Alex glanced over his shoulder to see Lizzie standing in the hall behind him.

She'd wanted to accompany him to the hospital when he'd gone to bring Jason home this afternoon, but he'd insisted on doing it himself. She'd already been taking far too much time off, and he had to think of what was good for the company.

No, his reasons for not taking her along were more complicated than that. He'd wanted Lizzie with him…and that was precisely why he'd kept her away. He didn't want to depend on her, and he didn't want to get close to her. He didn't want to set himself up for that kind of vulnerability and disappointment ever again. His relationship with Lizzie was good just as it was—she'd come willingly to his bed every night this week—and besides her shares, that's all he wanted from her.

Wasn't it?

"He's sleeping fine," he answered.

"He's an amazing little guy."

Alex returned his gaze to his son. "The first thing he wanted when he got home was a hot dog."

"Really?"

"He's hungry enough to eat even my cooking."

"Definitely a good sign." Lizzie moved beside him, her shoulder brushing his arm. "What did the doctor say about his care now that he's home?"

"You were right about the private nurse. He definitely doesn't need one. All I need to do is try to limit Jason's activity for a few days until his incision has a chance to heal properly."

"Knowing Jason, that's not going to be easy."

"No, it's not. He's almost back up to his usual energy level. If it wasn't for the tape over his stomach, I could almost believe none of this really happened."

She slipped her hand through the crook of his elbow and squeezed his arm. "It happened, Alex. But it's over and Jason's fine and he'll have a scar to brag about that will have Daniel wishing for an appendectomy of his own."

Alex smiled, feeling Lizzie's touch drain away some of

the strain that seemed to be his constant companion lately. "How did it go at the office today?"

She hesitated. "Fine."

He could tell by her tone that things hadn't gone smoothly, but he didn't press her for details. Rita would let him know soon enough—she had been quite diligent about reporting every problem that had come up. And there had been a large number of them lately, just as he'd surmised when he'd agreed to Lizzie's wager.

But right now, it wasn't his business relationship with Lizzie that was foremost in his mind. No, it wouldn't be recalcitrant clients or multiplying losses that they would be occupying their time with tonight. "Are you hungry?" he asked.

"I didn't expect you to cook me dinner, Alex, not with Jason coming home today. I already ate downtown."

"That's just as well. We're out of hot dogs."

She laughed softly as she leaned her head against his shoulder. "There's something really special about watching children sleep, isn't there?"

Yes, there was. But it was even better to be able to share the experience. He knew that Lizzie cared about his sons— she had the kind of warmth and patience that children were drawn to. She'd make a good mother someday. There were probably plenty of men back in Packenham Junction who recognized that as well. There were only three more days until the end of the month, and once she got back home...

No. He couldn't think about that aspect of their relationship, either. Better to concentrate on the pleasure they would give each other. That was what he wanted, wasn't it?

Lizzie felt a wave of renewed tension harden Alex's arm. He must still be worried about Jason. She'd done her best to be there for Alex throughout this crisis, to give him the emotional support he needed, but he hadn't really wanted that. He'd been eager enough to accept her body each night, yet she wasn't any closer to winning his heart.

And there were only three more days until the end of the month.

Alex lifted his hands to her hair and unfastened the clip that held the twist in place at the back of her head. Her hair, released from its confinement, tumbled over her shoulders and down her back. Lizzie sighed in pleasure as Alex combed his fingers carefully through the mass of curls before he lifted a handful to his lips.

Oh, how she wished it could be like this every night, to stand beside him as they watched the children sleep, to feel him take down her hair in another one of those small, intimate things that a couple shared. But she was already on borrowed time.

She sighed, trying in vain to block out the memory of the financial report that Oscar had brought to her after the rest of the staff had gone home tonight. The results of her month at the helm of Whitmore and Hamill had been printed there in stark black and white. Even though technically she had three days left, there was no way to change those numbers significantly enough to reverse the outcome.

She'd sworn Oscar to secrecy until the end of the week, and he'd assured her that no one else would see the figures until then, especially Rita. Maybe it was cowardice, maybe it was denial or desperation, but she wasn't going to tell Alex the outcome of their bet until the last possible minute.

Maybe she wouldn't be able to change the numbers in three days, but she had to believe she'd be able to change Alex's mind about her...

"Lizzie," he murmured.

She recognized that deep, slightly husky love-potion tone. It sent a tremor of response along her nerves, as it always did. She tipped back her head to look into Alex's face.

The light in the hall was dim, but it was enough to reveal the desire in his eyes. "Let's go to bed, Lizzie."

How she wished they could do this every night, too, she thought, lacing her fingers with his as they walked into his bedroom. But there were only three more nights until he learned what was in that report. And then…

Somehow, she had to pack as much of her love as she could into the time she had left. Tightening her grip on his hand, she steered him toward the bathroom. "I think you need to relax," she said.

"I'm relaxed." He nuzzled the side of her neck.

"No, it's been a long day for you. I can feel how stiff you are."

"I thought you liked to feel how stiff I am."

"Alex!"

A low, wonderfully masculine laugh rumbled from his chest. "All right, what did you have in mind?"

"Well, I've been meaning to try out that hot tub you have, but I never seem to have the chance."

"The hot tub?" he asked, following her into the bathroom.

She glanced at the large raised tub. "Do you think there's room for both of us?"

"We'll just have to experiment," he said, smiling as he pulled off his shirt.

She took off her jacket, then sat on the edge of the tub and opened the faucet. As the steam rose around her, she turned to admire Alex. "You have a beautiful chest," she said.

"So do you." He reached out to flick open the top button of her blouse. "You also have a beautiful neck," he said, leaning over to lick the base of her throat.

"Mmm."

"And a beautiful waist," he said, lowering the zipper at the back of her skirt. He eased the garment down to her hips and sank to his knees. His breath whispered warmly across her stomach. "I think I'm becoming partial to red hair, too," he murmured, nudging the edge of her panties downward.

How did he manage to do this so easily? she wondered hazily as she felt the tingles of excitement spread through her body. She reached for his belt and proceeded to undress him as leisurely as he was undressing her. By the time they both slipped into the tub, their limbs fitting together in a delicious tangle, her own needs were churning like the bubbling water.

She wanted to make this night special, to show him her love in a way that he would never forget. So she picked up his soap and slowly lathered every inch of his skin that she could reach. She smoothed her palms over his sleekly muscled arms, rubbed her fingertips in the springy mass of black curls on his chest, traced the rippling contours of his abdomen and followed the silky, wet line of hair downward, under the surface of the swirling water.

Alex groaned when she closed her hand over him. "Lizzie," he said breathlessly. "Wait."

The bubbles, the steam, the familiar scent of his soap…and the throbbing strength she held…it was… incredible. She caressed him with the pad of her thumb, feeling a rush of power as he jerked within her grasp. Smiling, she slid her feet alongside his hips. "Why?" she asked.

"Why?"

"Why wait?" She moved closer. "Unless you don't think we can manage…"

The sound he made in reply wasn't exactly a word. But

she understood him perfectly. Bracing his feet against the end of the tub, he grasped her waist and lifted her on top of him.

"Oh," she sighed, hooking her ankles behind his back. "Oh, Alex."

He flexed his hips, lifting her up again only to fit her down on him more fully. Water surged around them in an echo of their rhythm, splashing over the rim and spreading across the floor.

Lizzie grasped the edge of the tub to steady herself as the world seemed to spin around her. "Alex, that's... that's...*oh!*"

He held her close as she collapsed against him, rubbing her back as the tremors gradually faded. With one hand, he reached out to shut off the water jets, then dropped his head to give her an openmouthed kiss on her shoulder. "Now can we go to bed?" he murmured.

She pulled back her head to look into his face. At the expression in his eyes, another tremor quivered through her body. She released her grip on the tub to clasp his shoulders. "Oh, Alex. Yes."

He smiled. Somehow, he managed to lever himself up without slipping. Keeping one arm locked around Lizzie, he stepped out of the tub. "I like the way you say my name."

"You do?"

"And I like that sound you make in your throat just before you...say my name."

She held on as he carried her into the bedroom. "I love the sounds you make, too."

"You do?"

"Uh-huh. I love the feel of your skin and the taste of your mouth." She nipped his lower lip in a playful kiss as he lowered her to the bed.

"Anything else?" he asked, bracing his hands beside her shoulders as he came down on top of her, their damp bodies sliding together.

"Everything."

"You love everything?"

"I love you, Alex."

He stilled. "Lizzie…"

Had she said that out loud? From the look on his face, she must have.

Well, why not? What did she have to lose? she thought recklessly. She might as well tell him. There was no point keeping the truth to herself forever. She wasn't going to put this in a letter for him to read thirty years from now.

Taking a deep breath, Lizzie reached up to cradle Alex's face in her hands. "I love the way your eyes twinkle when you laugh," she said. "And I love the way you can be stubborn and fair at the same time. I love feeling your body next to mine when I wake up in the morning and I love your wicked sense of humor and all the little things you do each day that show me the kind of man you are." She feathered her fingertips over his mouth, then dropped her hands. "So I guess that means that I'm in love with you, Alex."

For a long, tense minute Alex didn't move. Finally, he slipped his arms around her and rolled them to their sides. He stroked her back gently, his fingers toying with the ends of her hair. "Lizzie, we're good together. Let's not complicate what we have."

All right, she'd known he hadn't wanted to hear all of that, but now that it was said, there was no going back. "Alex, love isn't complicated."

"What we have between us isn't complicated, but you're trying to make something more of it."

"Something more than sex, you mean?" She slid her

hand over his chest until she could feel his heart beating beneath her palm. "Alex, I love being with you, whether we're having sex or not. This hasn't been just some roll in the hay for me. I love you."

"I'm not denying that the sex has been good—"

She shoved him hard in the shoulder. "For God's sake, stop being so stubborn."

He caught her hand and lifted it to his lips. "I'm being realistic. I never meant to hurt you, Lizzie. That's why I tried to be frank about our relationship."

Oh, he'd been frank, all right. She was the one who hadn't been completely honest. She'd been in love with him for days. Maybe even longer. "Alex, I understand all about how you need to be in control of your life. Love and any kind of commitment to a woman don't fit into your plans. But that doesn't mean you can't change those plans."

"Lizzie, I was married once. Not wanting to repeat the mistake isn't stubbornness, it's just good sense."

"Well, fine. No one's asking you to marry Tiffany again. I'm not Tiffany."

A muscle jumped in his cheek. "I know that, Lizzie."

"Do you?"

He brushed a soft kiss over the back of her knuckles. "You bear absolutely no resemblance to my former wife," he murmured, his breath warming her fingers. "You laugh about shaving cream on your pillow and slugs for breakfast. You have legs that can make me break out in a sweat. You have a mind that's so sharp it blows me away."

"And I love you. Don't forget that."

"Lizzie…"

"What are you so afraid of?"

"I'm not—"

"Sure you are. You want to shut me out because you're

afraid to trust anyone again. I know how that is.'' She shifted closer. ''It's going to take time, but I'm willing to risk it. Alex, I don't want our relationship to end when the month does.''

His grip on her hand tightened. ''What?''

Here it was, the point of no return. Time to put her money where her heart was. Except her heart was pounding too fast, and her stomach was clenching and her palms were growing damp… The sensation was familiar. It was the same restless, stretching kind of tickle she'd been feeling the day she'd arrived in New York.

She used to consider herself to be the least adventurous person she knew. But somehow, over the past month, she'd learned that wasn't true at all. She was no longer merely Auntie Liz, good old Lizzie, everyone's favorite baby-sitter and bridesmaid. She was a full partner in her father's company, and she was in love with the man of her dreams.

And dammit, she wanted to have it *all*.

Lifting her chin, she met Alex's gaze squarely. ''Let's tear up that agreement we signed.''

Something flashed in his eyes. ''Tear it up?''

''Yes. Those terms we agreed to are all wrong. The bet doesn't have to be winner takes all.''

''And what happens to Whitmore and Hamill?''

''We can share it. We can work together and be real partners.''

He released her hand and rolled to his back.

A distance that was more than physical was threatening to open up between them. Mere minutes ago they had been trembling in each other's arms, but now they were on the verge of being adversaries again. She wrapped the sheet around her and sat up beside him. ''I know you don't want to give up control of the company, but I'm sure we'll be able to work something out.''

"I had a partner," he said. "That didn't work."

"I'm not Roland."

"No. You're not Roland. You're not Tiffany. But you want me to ignore what I learned from both of them."

"Alex, are you telling me that what we have means nothing to you?"

"What goes on between us is completely separate from Whitmore and Hamill. I tried to be honest with you from the start, Lizzie," he said. "I'm sorry if I gave you false expectations."

She clutched the sheet more securely. No, he hadn't given her any false expectations, she'd supplied them all on her own. "So you still want to buy me out."

"You've managed things far better than I had expected, but you don't know the business like I do. I've worked too hard and I've come too far to give up control now. I won't put the security of my sons at risk because of our personal relationship."

"So if you had to choose—"

"Lizzie, don't," he said hoarsely. "Don't make this worse. Let's keep our personal relationship out of the business. We have something very special between us and maybe once the bet is settled..." He fell silent.

She swallowed hard at the lump in her throat. "Then what, Alex? Another roll in the hay?"

"Lizzie." He lifted his hand and brushed her hair over her shoulder, then curled his fingers around the nape of her neck and guided her head toward his. "Let's talk about this in the morning."

She felt Alex's lips touch hers in an achingly tender caress. Despite herself, she sighed and leaned into his kiss.

Fool. She was a complete fool. She had told him she loved him yet nothing had changed. All he needed to do was kiss her and her good sense dissolved in a wave of desire. If she was on borrowed time, then she might as well make the most of what was left.

THE LIGHT that filtered through the rain-streaked windows wasn't enough to dispel the shadows that clung to the study. Alex switched on the lamp as he sat behind his desk, then slid open the top drawer and stared at the paper that lay within.

Twenty-eight days ago, when he'd slipped that paper into the drawer, things had seemed so much simpler. He'd known what he wanted. He still did. He wanted control of Whitmore and Hamill.

But he also wanted Lizzie.

She'd asked him to tear up their agreement. And God help him, he was tempted to do just that. Simply because she'd asked him.

But personal feelings had no place in business decisions. He needed to think clearly. That had been impossible last night while he'd been lying in bed with Lizzie still naked and flushed from their lovemaking. The physical attraction between them was more than strong, it was phenomenal. It would cloud anyone's reason. That's the only explanation there was for the crazy impulse he'd had to do exactly what she asked.

Alex raked his fingers roughly through his hair, then picked up the signed agreement and turned it toward the lamp. The terms of the wager were plain. The deal was a fair one. Lizzie would be a rich woman once he paid her for her shares. It was what he had planned from the start. He would gain control, she would leave, and his life would get back to normal.

No more midnight swims. Or midnight baths. No more trips to the ball game together, no more hearing Lizzie's laughter mingle with the giggles of his sons…

Jason and Daniel were going to miss her. They had become accustomed to having her around. She'd become a part of their family, as if she belonged in their home. She acted more like a mother to them than Tiffany ever had.

To Tiffany, the boys had been another one of her acquisitions in her endless status seeking. The requisite children to go with the house and the car and the successful husband. They had been just another benefit that Alex was able to provide. She'd always told him that she loved him, and at first, he'd wanted to believe it. But she'd really only loved what he could give her.

And so he'd sworn to himself that he would never let a woman get close to him again. He'd never get married. He'd never fall in love, because love wasn't something that could be controlled or verified like numbers on a balance sheet. It didn't follow reason or logic. It left a person completely vulnerable.

Lizzie said she loved him.

His first reaction to her declaration had been a sudden, fierce joy.

But then caution had returned. Along with an ugly whisper of suspicion. Whenever Tiffany had mentioned love, it was because she had wanted something.

Lizzie had said she loved him, then she'd told him she wanted to change the bet.

But Lizzie wasn't Tiffany.

Paper crinkled as his hand clenched. He focused on the agreement he and Lizzie had signed. It had seemed like a good deal at the time. Back then, she'd told him that if she lost, she'd leave. Back then, he'd wanted her to go.

But now he didn't.

Because the truth was, while he'd been thinking everything through logically, his irrepressible Lizzie had sneaked right into his life.

What are you so afraid of?

He knew the answer to that one. He was afraid of falling in love. That's the main reason he hadn't wanted to listen to her last night. He was afraid of trusting again and making another mistake. It was so much easier to divide his energy between his sons and the business, without worrying about anyone or anything else. He didn't want to gamble....

He swore under his breath. What was it about those Hamills? Lizzie had already talked him into one gamble. And now here he was, seriously considering taking another. Only this time, he wouldn't be risking his company, he'd be risking his heart.

In two more days, according to their agreement, her reason for living with him would be gone. He wanted her to stay. She wanted to stay. So why shouldn't she?

He'd told her they would talk about it in the morning. Well, it was morning. And he was going to do more than talk. He was going to show her. Grasping the top of the agreement with both hands, he was just about to tear it down the middle when the fax machine on his desk started to ring.

He paused, tilting his head to take a look at the paper that was inching out of the machine. Judging by the Whitmore and Hamill letterhead, it was probably just another update from Rita. More problems, undoubtedly.

He glanced at the agreement in his hands, then back at the fax. He hesitated. Lizzie hadn't wanted to talk about what had happened at the office yesterday. No, she'd wanted to make love in the hot tub, and then she'd told him she loved him, and then she'd asked him to forget their wager.

The whisper of suspicion he'd ignored last night returned. Lizzie wouldn't have used her declaration of love to distract him, would she?

He wasn't sure he wanted to know the answer to that question.

But he knew that he had to find out.

Clenching his jaw, he put the signed agreement, still intact, back in the desk drawer. Then he reached for the fax and started to read.

LIZZIE KNEW something was wrong the instant she saw Alex's face. He had the look of a man who had just taken a hard punch to the gut. Reflexively, she hurried across the study and caught his hands. "What is it?" she asked. "Is Jason all right?"

Alex didn't squeeze her fingers as he usually did. He didn't smile, didn't lean toward her, didn't even look her in the eye. "Thank you for your concern. Jason is fine."

She lifted up on her toes to try to catch his gaze. "Alex, what's going on?"

A muscle twitched in his cheek. "When were you going to tell me, Lizzie?"

"Tell you? What are you talking about?"

He eased his hands from hers and turned around to walk to the window. Crossing his arms, he looked out at the rain. "I received a fax from Rita ten minutes ago."

Lizzie felt her stomach drop. "Oh? She must have gone in early."

"Yes, she did," he said, still facing the window. "I wanted to make sure that her information was accurate, so I called the office to check."

She wiped her palms on her skirt. "Well, she certainly is a devoted employee, isn't she?"

"I spoke with the accounting department. Oscar happened to be in early as well."

Oh, Lord. So that was it. Oscar had promised not to release those figures for another few days. Somehow, Rita must have learned about the financial report. Lizzie took a step toward him. "Alex, give me a chance to explain...."

"In the past, I've been guilty of jumping to the wrong conclusion when I didn't have all the facts," he continued woodenly. "So I wanted to confirm Rita's information as soon as possible. Now I understand why you hadn't wanted to tell me what happened at the office yesterday."

"You had enough to worry about. You had just brought Jason home from the hospital. I thought the news could wait a few days."

"I see. So you did know about this."

"Yes, but—"

"That's why you asked me to tear up our agreement."

She hesitated. "Yes. The terms of our bet aren't fair, Alex. They don't leave any room for compromise."

"You agreed to the terms. As a matter of fact, you suggested them."

"I know, but now I want to change them. We should still be able to work as partners no matter who wins."

"You want the company."

"I want us to be partners," she said, holding out her hand as she walked toward him. "It shouldn't be a matter of winning or losing or numbers on the bottom line of a financial report. We can share—"

"And that's why you said you loved me."

His grim tone stopped her before she could reach him. "What?"

"It almost worked. I was ready to believe you."

"Alex, I do love you."

"How convenient that you realized it on the same day you found out you were going to lose our bet."

"Convenient? Do you really believe I would…" His accusation was so appalling, it knocked the breath from her lungs. Lizzie swayed, swallowing hard. Did he think she had timed her declaration in order to manipulate him? And why did he say she had lost the bet? What had Rita faxed him? "Alex, I don't know why you would think that. You're dead wrong."

He turned around. For the first time since she'd entered the room, he finally met her gaze. She almost wished that he hadn't. The fury in his eyes was frightening. "You knew full well that you had lost the Chalmers account," he said through his teeth. "You knew that before you came home last night. Everyone at the office knew."

She shook her head. "The Chalmers account? Is that the information Rita faxed you?"

"Oscar confirmed it. The account's been pulled. It wasn't enough that you walked out of a meeting with one of our major clients, you had to insult him on the way out."

"But you had called from the hospital about Jason—"

"And I told you not to come. That's what happens when you let your personal feelings get mixed up with your business. Emotions get involved and mistakes get made. Losing that account is going to put Whitmore and Hamill in the red."

"You have it all wrong."

"No, I finally have it right. You've been after my company all along."

"It's *our* company."

"Too bad I hadn't realized just how far you were willing to go to get it."

"*What?*"

Uncrossing his arms, he leaned toward her. "The sex

was good, Lizzie, but do you really think it was worth half of Whitmore and Hamill?''

It took a moment for the full import of his words to sink in. Pain that was worse than anything she'd felt before knifed through her heart and she reacted without thinking. She drew back her fist and punched him in the face.

His head snapped back from the blow. Muttering an oath, he made a grab for her wrist.

Lizzie jumped out of reach. "How dare you!"

He rubbed his jaw and watched her warily. "You can stop the act."

"You...you...*toad!* I don't know how I could have thought that I loved you!"

"I don't know how I could have wanted to believe you. I made the mistake of trusting a woman once before. I should have known better than to trust you."

"That's what this is really all about isn't it?" she said, backing away. "You're stuck in your past. You're too afraid to trust anyone to loosen that control you keep over your emotions, so you look for any excuse to deny them."

"This isn't about emotions. This is about business."

"I can see that now. I was willing to trust you. It wasn't easy, but I got over what Bobby did because I *wanted* to take another chance with love. My feelings for you were strong enough to make me do that and I had hoped—'' Her vision blurred. She wiped her eyes quickly with the back of her hand. "Alex, I hoped we could have a real partnership, the old-fashioned kind. Marriage, children, a life together..."

He wavered. For a split second, the suspicion and anger that had tightened his expression slipped away, and his gaze was filled with raw emotion...and a vulnerability that made Lizzie want to go back to him and pull him into her arms and tell him she loved him enough to accept whatever he was willing to give her....

But that was just it. She thought she had found love, but she'd only been deluding herself. There was no point trying to hang on to something that didn't exist.

"I hope your company makes you happy, Alex," she said, turning toward the door. "I think you're getting exactly what you deserve."

Chapter Fourteen

"Hey, isn't Auntie Liz gonna eat with us?" Daniel asked.

"She's at the office, stupid," Jason said, breaking off
the charred edges of his toast. He reached for the ketchup
bottle and upended it over his plate.

"No, she's not. I saw the green car, so that means she's
home." Daniel stuck out his tongue, then tipped up the
brim of his baseball cap and twisted around on his chair.
"Dad, Jason called me stupid."

Alex scowled and rubbed the swollen lump on the side
of his jaw. "Don't argue, boys," he said, retrieving the
ketchup from Jason before it overflowed onto the table.

"Jason called me stupid," Daniel repeated. "Just 'cause
he got his 'pendix out he's a big know-it-all."

"Am not. And I know Auntie Liz isn't here 'cause when
I went to show her my scar she wasn't in her room."

"Maybe she didn't want to see your dumb old scar."

"Did, too," Jason muttered, picking up his fork to poke
at his food. "She musta had important stuff to do at the
office, just like Dad always does."

"Then how come her car is still here, *stupid?*"

"That's enough! Both of you just settle down and behave yourselves," Alex snapped.

Jason's fork clattered to the table and his chin began to

wobble. Daniel pulled his cap down to shade his eyes and thrust out his bottom lip.

Alex immediately felt guilty for taking his foul mood out on his children. But they appeared to be in just as foul a mood as he was. Since Lizzie had left, the atmosphere in the house had been as bleak and depressing as the drizzle outside. He took a deep breath and forced himself to speak more calmly. "Lizzie isn't here," he said. "She went home."

Now Daniel's chin began to wobble like his brother's. "Home?" Daniel repeated. "But she lives here."

"No, she was only visiting," Alex said. "She decided to leave."

"Why?" Jason asked. "Is she mad at me? I didn't mean to be a crybaby but—"

"It has nothing to do with you," Alex said, trying to maintain his composure. He didn't want to talk about Lizzie. She was gone. She had packed her bags, called a cab and marched out the door three hours ago without a word or a backward glance. She had walked out on him and on Whitmore and Hamill and had gone home to Packenham Junction.

The month hadn't yet ended. By walking out, she had deliberately forfeited the bet before she could officially lose.

So it was over. Finished. He could start getting his life back to normal. He could hire a real housekeeper and finally eat a decent meal. He could resume his responsibilities at his company, knowing he would be in complete control from now on.

He had won.

He should be pleased. This was just what he'd planned. And it was a damn good thing that he hadn't let himself get close to that woman, or let their relationship become serious, or let himself fall in love...

But if everything was turning out so well, then why wasn't he happy?

"Dad, when's Auntie Liz coming back?"

She wouldn't be back. Not after what he had said.

Besides, now that she had lost her half of the company, there wouldn't be any reason for her to return, would there?

"Dad?"

Alex cleared his throat. "She won't be coming back."

"Why not?" Daniel asked, his voice rising.

"Can we go see her?"

Alex shook his head. "She's going to be pretty busy when she gets home."

"Why?"

"Well, she had a business to run there," he answered.

"I hate bus'ness," Daniel mumbled. "It's stupid."

Jason sniffed. "I wish Auntie Liz would come back."

"Yeah." Daniel blinked, his eyes filling with tears. "Why can't she live here all the time, Dad?"

"Because..." Alex hesitated. "There are plenty of reasons."

"Don't you like her?" Jason demanded.

"Course Dad likes her," Daniel said. "He was always kissing her and stuff."

Alex jerked. He had tried to be careful not to let the boys see him with Lizzie, but evidently he hadn't been careful enough. "Yes, I liked her," he said. "But she had to leave and that's that."

Daniel rubbed his eyes with his knuckles, then slipped out of his chair. Head down, he shuffled toward the door. Sniffing hard, Jason followed, his little shoulders drooping dejectedly. Alex exhaled harshly as he watched them go.

He'd been concerned about limiting Jason's activity today to give his incision a chance to heal, but that didn't seem to be a problem, since neither of his sons were exhibiting their usual energy.

Seeing their unhappiness increased his own tenfold. He'd known Jason and Daniel would miss Lizzie. He shouldn't have let them get so attached to her. More than that, he shouldn't have let *himself* get so attached to her. She had only been gone three hours and already her absence was like a gnawing emptiness in his home.

Cautiously, he flexed his jaw, touching his fingertips to the parting gift his partner had given him. He should have known that a woman like Lizzie wouldn't settle for a ladylike slap. She'd been furious, and she hadn't tried to hide it.

Then again, she had been just as uninhibited when it came to expressing her other passions, hadn't she?

He'd deserved the punch. He never should have implied that she had tried to trade sex for a place in Whitmore and Hamill. Even as the words had left his mouth he'd realized that his suspicions had gone too far. Lizzie hadn't been the one to pursue an affair with him, it had been the other way around. And she was far too honest to use sex to get her way. If anyone else had insulted Lizzie that badly, Alex probably wouldn't have hesitated to take a swing at them, too.

But he'd been angry at her for hiding that information about losing the Chalmers account. And then his anger had combined with his unwillingness to trust her and his fear of falling in love and—

And he'd hurt her. He'd rejected her. And now she was gone. And the company was his at last.

He felt not even the slightest flicker of triumph over finally achieving his goal. Yes, he'd have complete control of Whitmore and Hamill, but every time he saw her name, it would remind him of everything he had lost....

Wait, he hadn't lost. He had won. Right? *Right?*

If he had won, why did he feel like kicking something? Why did he feel as if a gaping hole were opening up in his life? It was similar to the feeling of loss he'd had when Jason had spent those nights in the hospital, but he'd known that Jason would be back. Lizzie wouldn't. And he couldn't even imagine a future without ever again seeing her smile or hearing her laugh or feeling her arms close warmly around him as she gave him her love...

He'd made her leave, and for what? Just because Lizzie had concealed her business failure from him? He couldn't blame her for that. She'd known she had lost the bet, yet she'd swallowed her pride and had wanted to stay with him anyway. She'd wanted to share the company.

Would that be so bad? They could find a way to work together. They had to. The alternative, never seeing her again, was unthinkable

He'd been afraid of falling in love. He'd believed that was the worst thing he could do. He'd been wrong. The worst thing was falling in love and then letting it go.

He was in love. With Lizzie. And he'd let her go.

Alex surged to his feet. Lizzie had only left the house three hours ago. There was a chance she might still be at the airport. If not, then he was going to go after her and do whatever it took to convince her to come back to him, to his sons and to their company.

The sound of chimes echoed suddenly from the front of the house. Alex spun around. Could Lizzie have changed her mind? Could she have come back? He strode through the hall and yanked open the front door eagerly.

But instead of Lizzie, he saw Jeremy Ebbet standing on

the doorstep. "Jeremy," he said. "What are you doing here?"

"Miss Hamill asked me to bring you some papers from the office," he said, brushing the rain off his overcoat as he stepped inside. He gestured to his briefcase. "I came over as soon as I could."

"From the office?" he repeated. "Do you mean she's at Whitmore and Hamill now?"

"No, she called me from the airport to ask me to bring you these documents."

"I'll have to get back to it later, Jeremy," he said. "Right now I've got to get to the airport before her flight leaves."

"She would have left three hours ago, Alex," Jeremy said. "The flight was boarding when she ended our conversation."

"Damn!" Alex muttered. "I'll just have to charter a plane."

"Uh, Alex, I think you'd better take a look at these papers first. Miss Hamill was very insistent that you get them as soon as possible."

"What are you talking about?"

"It's concerning the agreement you had me draw up."

Taking Jeremy's arm, Alex pulled him toward his study. "It's just as well you're here. Maybe you could find a loophole for me in that agreement."

Jeremy stumbled down the hall beside him in a valiant effort to keep pace. "Alex, I drew up that document very carefully, in spite of its...irregularity. There aren't any loopholes."

Alex crossed the floor to his desk and pulled the agreement out of the drawer. He tossed it down on the desk top. "There has to be something."

"I don't understand what the problem is," Jeremy said.

"Miss Hamill has officially forfeited the wager by leaving before the month was up. She accepted your offer to purchase her shares."

"I've withdrawn my offer."

"I don't understand either of you," Jeremy mumbled, loosening his tie. He set his briefcase down on Alex's desk and opened the lid. "First Miss Hamill gives away her right to the company after she'd won it, and now you don't want to purchase her half."

Alex drew in his breath. "What?"

"It's very confusing."

"No, what was that you said about Lizzie winning?"

Jeremy poked his glasses farther up his nose and withdrew a sheet of paper from his briefcase. "Oscar Radic gave this to Miss Hamill yesterday."

Alex grabbed the paper and scanned it quickly. It was the preliminary report from accounting. And according to Oscar's figures, the loss of the Chalmers account hadn't hurt Whitmore and Hamill's profits. No, losing that account had put an end to the needless work and wasted material that Chalmers' habitual complaining had been costing them. The profits hadn't gone down, they had gone up.

"Oh, my God," Alex muttered, sinking down on the edge of his desk. "Whitmore and Hamill made a profit."

"Yes, apparently the company is doing well."

The full truth burst over him all at once, and Alex felt as if he had just received another blow to the head.

Whitmore and Hamill had made a profit. Lizzie had won the bet. And she had already known that last night.

Yet she'd wanted to change the terms of their wager so that she and Alex could still be partners. *She* had wanted to share their company with *him*. Because she loved him.

What more proof did he need that her feelings for him were genuine?

And what more proof did he need that he'd just made the most monumental mistake of his entire life?

LIZZIE WIPED the last of the green finger paint off the floor and dropped the paper towel into the trash. It seemed as if all the children had smeared their fingers with butter before they'd come to the day care center today. Either that or they'd had pure chocolate for breakfast. Maybe it was a full moon, or the beginning of a flu epidemic, or maybe it was fatigue. Her fatigue. Facing a room full of children when she hadn't slept more than a few hours in the past five days tended to affect her perspective.

Something crashed in the corner. Instantly a chorus of whining protests arose. Grimacing, Lizzie turned around.

"It's okay, Lizzie. I'll take care of it," Suzy said, hurrying toward the heap of oversize plastic blocks that had been a fort this morning.

Lizzie smiled gratefully while her assistant soothed the disappointed little builders. Suzy and her daughter-in-law Darla had managed the day care center wonderfully during Lizzie's month-long absence. The business—and all the children—were thriving.

Actually, because of the second shift Benjamin had added at the cheese factory—and the resulting upswing in business at the Packenham Dairy—the whole town was prospering. Just today she'd accepted two more children into the day care. If the trend continued, she'd have to hire another worker. It was a good thing that the rooms on the ground floor of the house were large enough to accommodate more children. She'd have to look into adding another bathroom. And she'd need to purchase more finger paints and paper towels. That should keep her busy for a while, so maybe tonight she'd be able to sleep without thinking about all the things she'd lost.

To Lizzie's dismay, she felt her eyes fill with tears. It had been five days since she'd left Alex. She'd tried her best to resume her life. She'd visited her stepfather, she'd gone on a shopping trip to McBride's store with her niece and she'd helped Jolene decorate the nursery for the new baby. But no matter how much she tried to fill her days, she couldn't fill the emptiness she felt inside.

Oh, how she missed him. Despite what he'd said, she missed him. In her head she knew that her love for him was hopeless and that her dreams were nothing more than a fairy tale, but the message still hadn't gotten through to her heart.

There was a burst of giggles. "Look at the flowers, Auntie Liz."

"They're walking!"

"It's magic."

"Lemme see, lemme see!"

Lizzie wiped her eyes on a corner of her smock and looked toward the commotion. Several children were crowding around the front window, their faces pressed to the glass. "What's going on?" she asked, glancing at Suzy.

"I don't know. It looks like… Gracious! Will you look at that."

Curious, Lizzie moved toward the window and peered outside in time to see a huge bouquet of flowers walk up to the front steps. She gaped. No, the flowers weren't moving by themselves, there was a pair of tiny feet underneath them. Another bouquet followed behind the first, the top of a child's head just visible over a spray of baby's breath and carnations.

A loud knocking came from the front door.

"It's the flowers," one of the children said.

"Flowers can't knock, they don't have hands."

"But they had feet. I saw them!"

Lizzie left the children at the window and hurried to the door. She pulled it open, then gasped as the two giant bouquets staggered inside.

"Hi, Auntie Liz!" the first one said. The flowers lowered to reveal a familiar pair of mischievous brown eyes. "Did we surprise you?"

"Yeah, did we surprise you?"

She pressed her hand to her mouth, unable to believe what she was seeing. "Jason? Daniel?"

The twins put down their burdens and grinned. "There's more in the car."

"Car?" she repeated numbly, peering past them. A long limousine was parked at the curb, its gleaming white paint and tinted windows looking as out of place on Myrtle Street as a…a…coach made out of a pumpkin. "Oh, Lord love a duck," she whispered.

"It's not ducks I'm worried about, it's us toads."

At the deep voice, her heart did a sudden flip. "Alex?"

He moved into the doorway. "Hello, Lizzie."

Not a single word could form in her throat. She stared, drinking in the sight of him, trying to convince herself that he was real and not some hallucination conjured up out of her lonely dreams.

But no dream man had hair that thick and black, or eyes that seductively brown, or cheekbones that strong or a jaw that square…

"Can we go get the rest now, Dad?"

"We won't drop them."

Alex nodded to his sons, who whooped and raced back to the car. They made one trip after another, bringing more bouquets into the house until the hall and part of the front porch were filled with flowers. Then they moved over to their father and looked up at her expectantly.

Lizzie still couldn't seem to find her voice. The flowers were overwhelming enough, but now all three Whitmore men were standing in front of her, all dressed in charcoal gray suits and crisp white shirts and looking so wonderful that they took her breath away.

Oh, God. A week without them hadn't dulled the love she felt at all. Whatever her head said, her heart wasn't listening.

Alex put his hands on the twins' shoulders and cleared his throat. "Lizzie, I want to apologize for being an idiot."

"No Dad, that's not what you're supposed to say," Jason hissed.

"You want us to ask her?" Daniel whispered.

"Yeah, we'll do it." Jason grinned. "Auntie Liz—"

"Thank you, Jason," Alex said. "But I think that I should do this part myself."

"Are you going to start kissing her and stuff?" Daniel asked in a stage whisper that could have carried to the next county.

There was the sound of giggles behind her. Lizzie glanced over her shoulder and saw that the hall was filled not only with flowers but with the children from her day care.

Suzy winked at her from the doorway of the playroom. "I think your friend is right, Lizzie," she said, shooing the children out of the hall. She held out her hands to the twins. "Would you two gentlemen like to come with me? We're having a juice-and-cookies break."

"Go ahead," Alex said, giving the twins a gentle push.

They hung back for a moment, but the promise of cookies was too strong to resist. After a hug for Lizzie, they scampered after Suzy and the other children.

And after five long days, Lizzie was alone with Alex.

He smiled tentatively. "Well, you haven't slammed the door in my face yet, so I guess that's a good sign."

Oh, that smile. It was so tender and tempting and it still had the power to make her knees weak. She grasped the door frame for balance. "Why are you here, Alex?"

"The boys and I want you to come back home."

A lump rose in her throat. Home. "Why?"

"You're part of our family."

The lump grew larger. Home and family. Two of the three things she'd always yearned for. "Why, Alex?"

"Because we love you." He took her hand from the door frame and clasped it to his chest. "I love you, Lizzie. I hope that you can forgive me for being a fool. I've come to ask you to be my partner."

"Your...partner?"

"Maybe the boys might have done a better job of this than me after all," he muttered, going down on one knee on her doorstep. He slipped his hand into his coat pocket and withdrew a glittering diamond ring. "Lizzie," he said, his voice strong and sure. "I love you with all my heart, and I would be the luckiest man alive if you would do me the honor of becoming my wife."

For a split second she didn't move, savoring the moment when every dream she ever had was coming true. Then she sank to her knees in front of him and threw herself into his arms.

Alex wrapped her in a tight embrace. "Does this mean the answer's yes?"

"Yes!" she said, covering his face with kisses. "Yes, oh, yes!"

He caught her chin to hold her head steady, then gave her a kiss that would have brought her to her knees if she wasn't already there. Then he drew back and took her hand to slide the diamond ring onto her finger. "I love you, Lizzie."

"And I love you, Alex. So much."

"I want us to be partners in everything," he said. "In marriage, in life and in business."

"Business?"

Smiling, he helped her to her feet and then reached into his jacket pocket once more. This time he pulled out a long white envelope. "Lizzie, this is a partnership agreement for Whitmore and Hamill. Half of the company will always be yours, whether you choose to work there or not. Whatever you want, Lizzie, it's up to you, but I would like it if we could run the company together."

Her fingers trembling, she took the envelope. "Alex, I know how much the company means to you," she began.

"Without you, it would mean nothing. It took almost losing you for me to realize that I already had what mattered the most."

Was it only coincidence that Alex had echoed the words Roland had written to her? Lizzie wondered. Or had fate somehow given her the chance for happiness that had eluded her father?

"Whitmore and Hamill," she murmured.

Alex slipped his arms around her waist and pulled her against him. "What would you think of changing the name to Whitmore and Whitmore?"

She considered it. "How about Hamill and Whitmore?"

"Whitmore and Hamill and Sons?" he suggested.

"Mmm. How about Hamill and Whitmore and Sons and Daughters?"

"Daughters?" He laughed and lifted her off her feet. "I'll do my best, but that might take some time."

She grinned. "Want to bet?"

COMING NEXT MONTH

#829 SURPRISE! SURPRISE! by Tina Leonard
Maitland Maternity: Double Deliveries
After months of trying to conceive, Maddie Winston had finally become the proud mother of twins. But how could she tell her husband, Sam, that she'd raided his sperm bank "deposit" during their yearlong separation? Would two bundles of joy be enough to teach Maddie and Sam that love could overcome all obstacles?

#830 THE RANCHER'S MAIL-ORDER BRIDE by Mindy Neff
Bachelors of Shotgun Ridge
The grizzled matchmakers of Shotgun Ridge, Montana, had found Wyatt Malone the perfect mail-order bride…without letting the solitary rancher know. Though Wyatt may not have volunteered for the position, he was gonna be the first man to help repopulate their little town—whether he liked it or not!

#831 MY LITTLE ONE by Linda Randall Wisdom
With Child…
Her supposedly innocent blind date had turned into one night to remember! Though her charming escort, Brian Walker, had saved her from serious injury and satiated her every need, Gail was certain she'd never see him again. Until she discovered a little one was on the way….

#832 DOCTOR, DARLING by Jo Leigh
When he unknowingly broke a one-hundred-and-twenty-five-year-old law, Dr. Connor Malloy was sentenced to take Gillian Bates on a date. But Gillian was hardly the spinster he expected. How long would it be before the intelligent beauty had Connor realizing that one night with Gillian wasn't going to be nearly enough?

Visit us at www.eHarlequin.com

CNM0500